Mage's Mercy

Pyromancer's Path

Book Two

Edited by Gail Gentry

Follow me on social media to stay up-to-date on new releases, announcements, and prize giveaways!

www.cassiecoleromance.com

Books by Cassie Cole

Pyromancer's Path
Warrior's Wrath

Mage's Mercy

Tinker's Trial

Ranger's Risk

Shadow's Savior

Standalone Novels
Broken In

Drilled

Five Alarm Christmas

All In

Triple Team

Shared by her Bodyguards

Saved by the SEALs

The Proposition

Full Contact

Sealed With A Kiss

Smolder

The Naughty List

Christmas Package

Trained At The Gym

Undercover Action

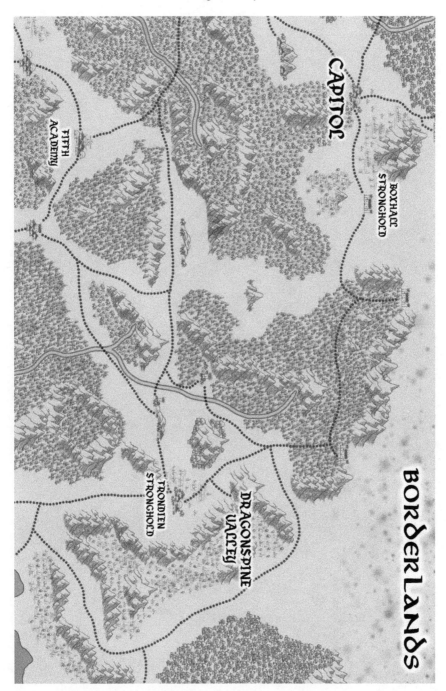

1

Alyssa

We raced through the thick forest, and the Silithik followed.

"Need to slow them!" Jax shouted somewhere to my left.

"I can't trace while at a gallop!" I replied, more out of frustration than in response to the big Warrior. Twisted in my saddle with one hand on the runetablet fastened to my belt, it was all I could do to not be thrown from the horse. Focusing on pulling sorcerous energy through the tablet, riding the waves of flame and frost that surged through my veins and threatened to consume me from the inside, was an impossibility while my ass was bouncing in the saddle.

Somehow, Arthur managed. I felt the release of runemagic to my right before seeing the glow: a blue *frostspike* forming from the tip of the Mage's outstretched hand like a crystal javelin. His hair tie had come loose, sending his silky blond hair swirling around his head in a halo of yellow as he traced. The *frostspike* launched away, pulling my eye toward the army of Silithik beetles and wasps close on our collective tail. The runemagic spell hit the ground and

7

shattered, releasing energy in a white ring that burst in all directions like a pebble dropped in a pond. Every beetle caught within the *frostspike* ring slowed and then froze in mid-slither, a line of statues interspersed between the trees. For a moment, the sight was almost beautiful.

And then the Silithik army behind trampled over them, shattering them like they were made of glass. Arthur's jaw clenched as he began to trace anew.

I tightened my fingers on the reins. If I slowed my gallop, just for a few moments, I could trace a *fireball*...

"Don't," Jax growled to my left. I whipped my head and found him staring over at me, face hidden behind the steel of his great helm. He was a tremendous sight in his armor, a god wrought in steel, and his command carried weight.

I pretended to be confused. "I don't know what you're talking about."

"If you cannot trace at this speed, then you cannot trace," he said. "If you slow, you'll be overrun."

"If we don't figure something out soon," Ryon yelled while gesturing with a dagger, "we're going to be overrun regardless!"

We'd received orders to return to the capitol, both to complete our Quintelaide bonding ceremony and to receive new orders from the Field Marshal. We were half a day from arriving when we received a *runemessage* alert that the remaining burrowing Silithik armies had surfaced outside the city. We spent the morning pushing the horses at a gallop, afraid we would not reach the city in time. Afraid the Archenon itself would crumble before the might of the Silithik Hivemind with a single blow to its heart.

And then we ran into the rear of one of the Silithik armies, still miles from the city.

I hated fleeing. Even though we had circled around the swarm and were now galloping *toward* the city so we could assist in its defense, it felt like fleeing. There were enemies behind us, and we weren't meeting them in battle.

The feeling was exacerbated by my inability to help. Runetracing required precise fingertips moving along the carved runes at the correct pace, like running one's finger along the rim of a crystal to produce a ringing sound. Anything other than perfection resulted in the runemagic fizzling away. Trace too slow, and not enough energy would accumulate, but trace too fast and it would compress on itself and disappear. And if your finger skipped over the rune, the entire thing fell away like someone had knocked the sorcerous wind out of you. From the first Academy to the fifth, runetracers were taught that it was nearly impossible to successfully trace while panicked—that calmness was the groove into which runemagic flowed.

But of course, finding calmness was impossible while being enveloped by a Silithik army. To say nothing of the bouncing in the saddle.

As if to taunt me, I felt Arthur launch another *frostspike*. The resulting burst of runemagic among the Silithik masses was even larger than before. His success only accentuated my failure.

"The wasps are getting brave!" Harry shouted on the other side of Jax. He couldn't turn all the way around in his saddle to fire his bow, and the trees blocked most of his line of sight, so he had to wait until the wasps were almost on us and steer his horse at an angle to bring them into his firing arc. He did that now, cutting diagonally toward us for a heartbeat, and releasing an arrow into the wasp that was diving at Arthur. The Ranger grabbed the reins and turned his horse just in time to avoid slapping into a low-hanging branch.

"We're not gunna make it," Ryon cursed in his deep, raspy voice. "We need to fight them now."

"Not yet," Jax commanded. "When we're out of the forest."

"I fight better in the woods," Ryon gestured with his dragon-wing knife. "Trees for cover. I could make this place a killing field."

"Perhaps you, but not us," Jax replied. He allowed a trickle of authority into his voice, which boomed from within his helm. "We will not stop until we absolutely have to."

Ryon snarled, but obeyed. I was glad I wasn't the only one who was itching to fight. To do *something*.

"We won't have a choice soon." Arthur's voice was emotionless. An academic man stating facts from a book. "I'm slowing them, but it is a bit like pulling buckets of water from a river. They flow on."

Rather than respond, Jax leaned forward in his saddle as if that could urge the armored warhorse faster by willpower alone.

The wind in my ears from the gallop drowned out most sound, but soon I could hear the chittering of the beetles behind. The Silithik sound was a steady drone, like a million cicadas closing in on me. And despite Arthur's runemagic efforts against the beetles directly behind us, there were more advancing to the left and the right. Pretty soon they would be able to cut us off.

The thought took root in my head like a stubborn weed. I tried to be positive, to focus on what I could control instead of what I could not, but that was yet another losing battle. We were going to be encircled. I might be able to get two *fireballs* away before they overwhelmed us. Before they killed us. I imagined them tearing apart our bodies with their multi-jointed arms, hacking and slashing until we became still. The intrusive thoughts were powerful. They threatened to break me down, to turn me into a puddle of fear.

"Ahh!" Jax's cry was not one of pain, but relief. The forest thinned ahead, then gave way completely to the farms that ringed the capitol. Indeed, the looming structure of the city rose above the horizon straight ahead, slate grey rectangles against an endless blue sky.

There was orange in the sky as well, I saw with surprise. Bits of flame arced away from the tall stone battlements in a dozen places, leaving trails of black smoke like the legs of a spider. The city was fighting back. It had not yet fallen.

And we were drawing another hive swarm straight to it.

My horse decided that the appearance of farmland meant he could slow down. I dug my heels into his side to urge him onward, though he continued tossing his head in anger. I couldn't blame the poor creature, but I wished I hadn't lost my other horse, Fireball, in the Borderlands while pursuing my Quint. She wouldn't have given up with Silithik this close on our heels.

"Just a few miles more," I whispered into my new horse's neck. "Then you can rest. I'll even buy you something special to eat if you get me there."

His hooves dug into the soft soil of the farm, which looked like it grew sugar potatoes or cherry peppers, though it was too early in the season to tell. Having grown up on a farm, I tried imagining what an army of Silithik would do to the crop. Most of the field would be trampled, surely. I wondered if Hivemind creatures even possessed the intelligence to know the supply damage they were causing, or if they were only focused on killing whatever was directly in front of them.

"We're not going to make it," Jax said, barely enough for me to hear. Then, louder: "Maze! Got any Tinker drinks remaining?"

"Was waiting for you to ask for it!" Maze reached into his Tinker's cloak and came away with a brass cube slightly larger than his fist. He twisted a dial on the side until steam shot out, then hastily tossed it over his shoulder.

The device changed in mid-air, two sides of the cube twisting and opening up, rods extending in parallel lines. Then the rods bent at one joint, and another, and when the cube hit the ground it landed on eight mechanical legs. The steam-powered spider raced across the ground toward the Silithik, belching buffs of white out of a pipe in the back. When it had nearly reached the pursuing army, it drove all eight of its legs into the ground and leaped into the air above the Silithik. It hung there for a long, weightless moment.

The explosion was so small I assumed it was a dud. But then I saw them in the air, a thousand tinier mechanical objects identical to the original in miniature. The smaller bombs landed among the advancing beetles and exploded, the pops coming so close together it sounded like someone tearing a length of fabric, *POP-POP-POP-POP-POP-POP,* puffs of smoke going up in a wide circle.

"Woo!" Harry shouted, pumping his bow.

But Maze's voice was strained. "No more tricks, Jax. That was my last spider mine."

Despite the carnage caused, new Silithik filled in the gaps in the advancing line within seconds. A single ax-blow against a mighty tree. There were too many of them for us to fight, and we weren't going to reach the capitol before being overrun. Two impossibilities, leaving one hard truth.

"My horse is about to collapse," Jax announced. "We must stop and make a stand."

"On what defensive terrain?" Ryon demanded. "We've nothing but plow grooves for miles. If we had stopped in the forest..."

"Perhaps I can make our own defenses," Arthur said. He made it sound like an academic exercise. "A moat of ice surrounding us for the Silithik to falter on."

"I'd prefer an actual moat," Ryon said dryly.

"If we're wishing for impossible things," I cut in, "how about we wish for a pack of gryphons to carry us to safety?"

Ryon shot a glare in my direction. "If we had a better Pyromancer tracing..."

His words cut me to my core, a reiteration of the inadequacy I already felt. I opened my mouth to say something biting, then stopped.

I sensed tracing. Up ahead.

Arthur was looking at me from his horse. His eyes were wide too.

"Wait!" I shouted to Jax. "Someone is runetracing up ahead!"

"You don't suppose it's another hive Queen, do you?" Maze moaned. "I don't want to fight another one of them, not with her entire army pressing in..."

But moments later we caught sight of the flash of a *fireball*, and then we saw the humans themselves. A Quintelaide in black-and-gold armor clustered in a tight circle, fending off two dozen beetles that were attempting to surround them. Dozens more lay dead in a ring around them.

"How about we say hello?" Jax said.

Harry's face split in a grin. "It'd be rude not to!"

I leaned low over my horse's neck as we hurried to the aid of our fellow Dragons. The Silithik army was 30, maybe 40 seconds behind us. Another Quintelaide felt like hope. Just a little bit. But even then, with two Quintelaides joined together, we had no chance against the greater Silithik army.

Stars above, a dozen Quints wouldn't be enough.

The thought flew from my head as we reached them. Jax unsheathed his sword and swung it one-handed while passing a beetle, cleanly removing a triangle of its upper thorax. He leaned across to do the same to another beetle on the other side with an equally-precise backslash. Ryon stood up in his stirrups and leaped from the horse, flipping in the air before bringing his twin daggers down into the back of an unsuspecting beetle. Blue Silithik pus flew through the air as he quickly spun to meet another beetle, removing two of its arms at the first joint, ducking from a swipe, and then thrusting upward to stab its cluster of eyes.

I pulled my horse to a halt and shot my hand to my belt. Finally stationary enough to focus, my fingertip traced the *fireball* rune with ease. Runemagic surged into my body, coursing through the veins in my arm and then chest, the pleasure and pain so intense after being denied it during our flight. I pulled enough energy into my body to form a small *fireball*, picking a target a safe distance from the other Dragons. In the blink of an eye the flame struck the beetle in the side, sizzling deep into its carapace before bursting through the other side. The beast fell to the ground with a cauterized hole the size of a fist through its body.

My next spell faded away from lack of focus. But nobody seemed to notice, and the next runespell was a success. I dispatched two more beetles the same way. When I searched for a fourth target, I found none. The Silithik lay around us in dead heaps. It had taken only seconds, but sweat beaded on my temples from concentration.

"Hope we're not intruding," Jax said.

The Warrior from the other Quint grinned, showing blood on

his teeth. One of his hands was pressed to his hip, where blood seeped from the vulnerable place between his armor. "Not that we aren't grateful, brother, but..." He nodded in the distance. "You brought a lot of friends to the occasion."

"They were uninvited," Maze said. "Silithik make terrible guests."

"Any bruisers?"

"Beetles and wasps only, best we can tell," Jax replied.

The three men and three women of their Quintelaide formed a line to meet the charging army. "How are your tracers?" the Warrior asked.

"Fresh," Ryon said dryly. "Pyro especially."

"Fresh is good," the Warrior replied, not hearing Ryon's displeasure. "Put her front and center with our Pyromancer. I'll guard any that get close. Rangers, keep the wasps from getting too friendly. The rest of you can hold the flanks. Sword be true, brother."

"Sword be true," Jax said. He dismounted and pulled his shield onto one arm. I watched him move away from me to the other side. I would have liked it better if we were closer. As things were, I felt very alone in the front. Especially with Ryon staring daggers into the back of my head.

Their Pyromancer, a chubby man with a red nest of a beard, stepped up next to my horse. "I've a flaming good *flame barrier*," he said, weariness thick in his voice. "Can trace it 20 paces out."

I nodded. "Put it in the middle and reinforce it as best you can. I'll send *fireflows* on either side of it. Funnel them into your spell."

"It's a plan," he said, switching runes from his pouch.

I did the same, moving my *flare* tablet to my runepouch and replacing it with *fireflow*. I also had *flame barrier* and *fireball* on my belt, though those wouldn't be of much use.

"Glad you're fresh," the Pyromancer said to me, blowing on his fingertips. "Might need to lean on ya, so to speak."

I tried to smile, but it came out as a grimace. "Sometimes I fail," I whispered.

He blinked at me. "Fail?"

"Sometimes the runemagic doesn't come," I said in a rush. I felt like I needed to confess to him before the battle began. "I don't know when, or why."

Within his beard, his mouth hung open. "This is the Ninety-First. Which means you're that girl..."

"I'm trying my best," I said. "I just wanted to tell you I might fail."

"Well, don't!" he snapped.

There was no time to think about it: the Silithik were nearly on us. Their Pyromancer began tracing, using his free hand to swipe in front of him like he was spreading a deck of cards in the air. He hadn't been bragging: the *flame barrier* shimmered to life, at least 20 paces wide. The amount of runemagic pouring through his body was tremendous; I could feel it, like standing next to a raging waterfall. It dwarfed anything I could do and made it difficult to think.

I turned my attention to the edges of the *flame barrier* and began tracing. The endless line of slithering Silithik were drawing close now, and the sight of them allowed all my worldly concerns to narrow. Embarrassment before another Dragon Pyromancer didn't mean anything compared to the wave of death cresting before us. I completed one trace and began a second. I held as much runemagic in my chest as I could, waiting for the perfect moment to release.

"For the Archon!" their Frost Mage cheered in a musical voice, a *frostbolt* launching from her outstretched hand.

I released my own runemagic, an exhale after holding one's breath. The *fireflow* hit the ground and rolled forward, a wave of flame so hot it was nearly invisible for the first few paces, except for a thin white mist. It poured toward the enemy and struck the first line of beetles just as they were passing the right side of the *flame barrier.* Instantly the spell ignited them with flame as if they were coated in oil. They slithered a few paces longer before collapsing to the ground, a chorus of high-pitched screeches.

Before the wave hit them, I turned my attention to the left side of the *flame barrier*, sending another spell there. The beetles there made it two paces farther, but their fate was the same. All the while beetles charged through the other Pyro's *flame barrier*, falling to the ground on our side half-disintegrated. He continued holding his palm out, tracing rapidly while sweat collected on his brow, pumping more runemagic into the *flame barrier* to keep it from failing.

The plan worked. Most of the beetles avoided the *fireflow* spells at the side and charged straight up the middle into the other Pyromancer's *flame barrier*. But the army of bugs was too wide: no matter the carnage directly in front of us, hundreds more rushed past and began attacking our sides. The other Quint's Frost Mage and Shadow, both women, protected my right flank, *frostbolts* freezing individual beetles which were swiftly shattered by the Shadow's dagger slashes. Maze held the gap between them and me, swinging his mechanical sledgehammer in a wide arc, crushing three beetles at a time.

Back and forth I traced, the ecstasy of the runemagic mingling with the adrenaline of the deadly battle. Most of my traces were successful; only one in four failed. Occasionally, a beetle escaped between the *flame barrier* and my *fireflows*, but the other Warrior dispatched them with relative ease despite limping from the wound on his hip. Wasps hovered above lazily, occasionally deciding to dive, and were filled with arrows whenever they made the attempt.

Can't keep this up forever.

A wasp fell from the sky, a pincushion of arrows, crashing among the cluster of horses behind us. One of the beasts reared up, screaming in terror, and I instinctively tried to turn to grab its reins. It struck out with its hooves, striking me in the chest and sending me flying to the ground, knocking the wind out of me. White stars floated across my vision as I stared at the cobalt sky and tried to move.

"Alyssa!" Jax yelled somewhere far away.

Maze was at my side instantly. "Up you go," the Tinker murmured, a hand curling under my back to help me up. "Got your bell rung, that's all. Anything broken?"

I shook off my dizziness and returned my hand to my runetablet. "Only my pride." Maze's grin showed white teeth, and he hobbled away on one mechanical leg to dispatch a beetle that was getting too close.

Grateful that I hadn't lost my runetablets, I continued sending *fireflows* at the Silithik streaming around the other Pyro's *flame barrier*. My brief absence from the battle had allowed them to encroach more than before, but I quickly beat them back to a manageable distance. Maze shouted something encouraging.

Two Quints working together was a force to behold, yet our task was still an impossible one. Already I felt the tingling of fatigue in my chest from too much runetracing, and each spell was a fraction less powerful. I began to fail every fourth runespell, then every third, my confidence rapidly falling apart. We were a rock in a stream of Silithik, destined to be worn away over time. But while tracing, feeling the supernatural joy of the energy heightening my senses and brightening my world, the inevitability of our doom was easy to ignore. There was only the next spell, and the next target area for my wrath. Trace, aim, release. Dead bugs. The rotten stench of burning Silithik husks.

And then, as quickly as the attack had begun, it stopped.

I released another *fireflow* to the right, igniting 20 beetles in a row, and behind them were only smoldering corpses and empty farmland. To my left, my comrades dispatched the last beetles there, then gazed around with confusion that mirrored my own.

"Was afraid of that," their Warrior rasped, pointing.

Most of the hive army had gone around us and was continuing toward the city, which loomed like a volcano spewing angry ash and fire. We'd been an inconvenience for the attacking army, not their primary target. Which meant we lived, but if the capitol fell...

For a long moment we stared at the receding dust cloud heading north.

"No rest for us just yet," Jax said. "Double up on horses. We'll be slower to the battle, but that's better than to miss it entirely."

The other Quint's Shadow and Tinker were already mounting my horse, which was still whickering and flaring its nostrils in fright. Arthur guided his horse to me and extended a hand. "May I have this dance?"

"I think that's the first joke I've ever heard you make," I said, taking his hand. I put one foot in the stirrup and swung my other leg up and over.

I could feel Arthur's frown even though he faced away from me. "Actually, I often make jokes that go unnoticed. Just yesterday I made a wonderful quip when Harry dropped his chicken drumstick in the—"

"Tell me later." I wrapped my arms around his waist. "When we're celebrating this battle over bottles of sweetwater."

As Arthur kicked his horse into a gallop, I wondered if that was a delusional hope.

2

Alyssa

The capitol rose before us, smoke billowing from half a dozen places in its great expanse of stone wall and towering battlements. Great maws of collapsed stone pocked the surface of the outer keep, a sight which froze my heart. Yet *fireballs* and various ice runespells continued shooting down from the high towers, which meant the fight still raged. I prayed we wouldn't be too late.

I pressed myself tight to Arthur, the motions of the horse rocking us back and forth. His silky hair blew into my face, but I didn't mind. It was clean and smelled like rosewater. It gave me something on which to focus other than the impending battle. The *next* battle.

With the adrenaline from the first battle fading, everything that came after began creeping to the surface. The trembling shock of nearly being overrun by the Silithik army. The burst of joy at surviving to fight again. The need to touch another human, to be close to someone, because being alone meant death, the death that had been so close only moments ago.

There was a great comfort in Arthur's touch, bodies molded together in the saddle: thigh against thigh, arm against belly, chest against back. His body reminded me of Jax's, and I allowed myself a moment to savor that feeling because it kept me from accepting that we may die in precious short minutes. I glanced at Jax riding to our left, a heroic statue in his armor. For several seconds I let myself fantasize about what he would do to me later.

Yet as great as that need was, fatigue was stronger. Exhaustion was a weight pressing down on my shoulders in the saddle. If not for the circumstances, I could have closed my eyes and fallen asleep holding onto Arthur's lithe body. He felt warm and safe.

I gave myself a deliberate shake. *I must stay awake and alert. We are about to return to battle.*

"...were one of only four Quints stationed at the capitol," the other Warrior said, voice drifting to my ears above the sound of horse hooves. "Sent out to delay the advance for as long as possible."

"Instead of fighting from the city walls?" Jax asked, incredulous.

"Two armies bore down on the capitol from two separate directions. Delaying one of them so they would not reach the city simultaneously was the only path to victory." The Warrior let out a long string of curses. "A simple order, yet we could not even succeed in that."

"It's not over, yet," their Shadow drawled in an accent I didn't recognize. "We can weep after we fail. Not before."

"I'd prefer if we did not treat death as an inevitability," Arthur whispered to himself. I patted his chest to let him know I agreed.

The distance between us and the Silithik army shrank as they reached the city walls. Soldiers along the parapets fired arrows and poured cauldrons of scalding oil down onto the attacking beetles, which slithered up the walls like tendrils of ants. Gigantic *fireballs* traced by unseen Pyromancers in the high towers arced down into the mass of Silithik, incinerating scores of them in the blink of an eye.

"Beetles on the walls means they've already crossed the moats," I said, mostly to myself.

"Indeed," Arthur replied.

Jax held up a gauntleted fist to bring the group to a walk. The chittering of the enemy was a loud chorus, a deafening, carnal buzz in the air. Jax spoke to us while scanning the writhing mass of the enemy. "We should concentrate our attack where the Silithik are strongest. Weaken them to a manageable degree."

"Where are the damned gryphons?" the other Pyro cursed. He tugged angrily on his beard. "They're supposed to be providing cover!"

"The Silithik are concentrated around the gate." Arthur pointed to the left. "See the cluster of wasps? I suspect they are trying to ferry beetles across in order to lower the bridge."

"What makes you think that?" their Shadow asked.

"It's what I would do."

"You're a human with a brain larger than a pea," Ryon said. "The bugs don't possess such tactics."

"Tell that to the tunnel they dug deep into the Archenon," Jax said with a note of finality. "Let's relieve pressure from the gates."

No one argued as we circled around toward the drawbridge, which was flanked by two round towers filled with archers. As we neared, it became clear they were struggling to keep the wasps at bay. They were thick in the air, like a flock of vultures circling a corpse, each with a beetle clutched underneath their body. Arthur's assessment looked accurate.

Jax led us into the attack wordlessly, charging into the army around the drawbridge gate. Just before reaching the rear beetles, he leaped from the horse, ducking and rolling before coming up with sword drawn, slashing into the Silithik with a roar of defiance. The other Warrior remained on Jax's horse, leading it into the fray while slashing from the saddle.

The two Shadows and Tinkers were right behind them. I watched Maze and Ryon disappear into the swarm before sliding off the back of Arthur's horse. One of my boots landed in something sticky; trails of green pus criss-crossed the ground where the beetles had traveled. The stench reached my nose and I tried not to gag.

I picked out a stretch of beetles far from my Quintmates. None of them faced in our direction: they milled around and pushed at the line of beetles in front of them, singularly focused on attacking the walls. I was exhausted from tracing *fireflows*, so I switched to my *fireball* rune. Runemagic flooded into my body, reinvigorating me like a splash of cold water. I was raw and exhausted, and my finger trembled along the carved grooves of the rune, but I managed to hold the trace long enough to build a *fireball* the size of my head. The swirling ball of white-hot flame scalded my cheeks as it shot away from me. It burned a hole clean through the first beetle, then the second, third, and fourth, each of them collapsing in a heap of cauterized shell. Somewhere around the fifth line of Silithik it finally diminished, exploding in a spray of flame and smoke, the high-pitched screech of the beetles announcing the damage.

The Silithik began turning away from the gate, but I was already launching a second *fireball*, just as large as the first. It carved another hole through the line of bugs, felling them in a long swath.

Above and behind me came the tingling surge of runemagic. Larger than a *frostbolt* or *frostspike*, the spell Arthur traced swirled high in the air above the beetles, clouds forming from a clear sky. Pregnant with precipitation, the storm finally released: hail the shape of long spikes fell among the enemy, impaling them to the ground like crystal spears. The beetles at the epicenter of the *blizzard* spell tried to flee, but had nowhere to go with the army pressing them together.

"Beautiful!" I shouted, sending another *fireball* into the fray.

More of the beetles turned toward us, chittering angrily. One charged forward, locking onto me as if it knew I was the source of the sorcery. I quickly released a *fireball* small enough that it exploded when striking the center thorax, knocking it back and consuming it in flames. Another moved toward me with serpentine speed. My next spell lit up its cluster of eyes like a blackberry before it, too, died screaming.

Maze appeared out of the mass of Silithik, swinging his sledgehammer wide. As if it were the plan all along, he positioned himself between me and the beetles, knocking aside each one that came.

"Good timing!" I yelled, though he was too far to hear.

I kept my spells small to avoid friendly fire, individual *fireballs* hissing through the air on either side of the Tinker. Arthur persisted pumping runemagic into his *blizzard*, although the frozen hail fell in spurts rather than a constant storm. He must have been growing weary, too. I sent my *fireballs* into the wall of beetles indiscriminately, only picking out individual targets when they got past Maze.

"Left flank falling!" someone from the other Quint shouted.

"Moving to assist," Arthur responded, the stream of runemagic behind me ceasing in a blink.

I felt alone without his presence, but continued tossing fire at the enemy. The weariness in my chest deepened, but did not stop me. Smoldering Silithik husks lay all around, making it difficult for both sides to advance. But advance the beetles did, slithering over the burning corpses of their brethren to reach us, each time advancing closer and closer to our position before being halted by arrows or flame.

"Alyssa!" Harry shouted, my only warning.

I whirled to my right, where a beetle towered over me. Two arrows sprouted from its third shoulder, but it didn't notice as it pulled back its arms to slash at me. I stepped back from the first attack, two claws cutting through the air horizontally where my face had just been. Another arrow appeared like a dandelion from its cluster of eyes, but it was already swinging its other two claws downward, and this time I couldn't avoid them. One claw pierced my leg like it was made of paper, through skin and flesh and bone, and I fell backwards from the dead beast with its claw still inside my thigh.

Then the pain hit me, and I screamed.

The beetle landed on top of me, the arrow in its eye cluster nearly piercing my neck. The weight of the bug smothered me, hot and foul and blocking out the light. Hot pus trickled down in several places, choking and gagging me. When I tried to move the corpse, the pain in my leg grew so bright and intense that I nearly passed out. I cried out, and it was all I could do just to clench my eyes shut and avoid biting off my tongue. I couldn't breath. The stench from the Silithik was overwhelming, and I tasted bile in the back of my throat. Worse, I knew other beetles would descend upon me any second. Ignoring the pain as best as I could, I rolled the dead husk to my left.

The corpse fell aside, its claw still lodged in my thigh, tugging me like a hooked fish. The pain was nauseating. Panting, I kicked with my boot, and the claw came free. With it came agony, and I screamed until my throat burned. It took all of my willpower not to pass out as I rolled onto my back and surveyed the battle.

No other beetles had descended on me while I was down, and it was quickly apparent why. Arthur had ridden his horse forward, putting them between me and the monsters all around. With careful precision he fired *frostbolt* after *frostbolt* at the advancing beetles, picking off the ones who advanced past Maze.

Thank the stars for my Frost Mage, I thought, gratefulness filling my heart. *At least I will live a few moments longer.*

Bells tolled in the city, deep and ominous. "They've penetrated the city walls!" Harry shouted.

Jax appeared to my left, slowly walking backwards while hacking at pursuing beetles. "It must be at the north gate. All we can do is continue our fight here and hope they can repel them there."

The words were meant to encourage, but they rang hollow in my ears. If the city was breached, then our fight here likely would not matter.

I tried to push to my feet, but the wound in my thigh wouldn't allow it. I gazed around me. Arrows and *fireballs* continued soaring from the city walls, although not as persistently. The other Quint's Shadow dashed out of the maelstrom of beetles holding a wound at her side, and then was knocked to her knees by a blow from behind. Her Quintmates broke from their formations to converge on her, leaving holes in the battle line.

My wound was bleeding, but no major artery had been cut or I would have been dead already. That gave me a flicker of courage. I rolled over, then managed to get up onto my good knee. Even that effort was enough to sharpen the pain from my wound, but at least I could reach my runetablets now. The burning in my leg helped me focus, and I traced a *fireball* just to feel the ecstasy of runemagic. The surge of power added some steel to my spine, and helped me concentrate. I sent the small *fireball* into a beetle advancing on Arthur from the right, knocking it away like a hammer blow.

"Wasps!" Harry shouted.

Six dark shapes descended from the sky. I traced a *fireball* at the right-most one, but an arrow knocked it from the sky and my spell hit open air. I started tracing a second one but the wasps were too close. Another fell from arrows. Two more reached us unimpeded, stingers stiffening to strike.

The first wasp dove toward one of the Dragons from the other Quint, but the second was flying directly into our Frost Mage. Arthur only had enough time to twist in his saddle, agonizingly slow, before the wasp crashed into him stinger-first. Horse and Frost Mage and wasp alike collapsed into the ground, each of them screaming.

"No!" Jax roared.

Before I knew what I was doing, I began crawling toward the Mage's shape, unmoving on the ground ahead. The horse cried out next to him, with the wasp fluttering its insect wings above, trying to dislodge its stinger from the animal. I clenched my teeth against the agony in my leg and dragged myself across the open ground, crawling between mounds of dead Silithik husks. Every few feet I stopped to rest a moment, using the time to trace a *fireball* at another diving wasp, fitful attempts which missed by several paces. Yet it felt better than doing nothing. A way to convince myself I could still be useful.

I'm not dead yet, damnit.

I reached Arthur's prone body long after the wasp had been filled with arrows. The horse was dead too, I saw with a pang of sadness. I positioned myself next to Arthur, sent another small *fireball* at a beetle that was getting too close, and rolled the Mage over. His eyes were closed, and his head and torso were unharmed that I could see. His leg was another story: I pulled up his black robe and found a gruesome horizontal gash in his left calf, as if a fist-sized scoop of it had been torn away. Blood pooled on the ground, and blackness spread along the skin from the wound, creeping up to the knee.

Memories from anatomy classes in the third Academy sprung to mind. Wasp stingers were coated with a paralyzing poison, one which would kill when it reached the heart. Swift runemagic healing was required, and failing that, a tourniquet to stop the poison's spread. Already the black tendrils of necrotic damage had reached Arthur's knee; I needed to tie off his leg before it advanced any further.

Another beetle chittered as it advanced: I traced as fast as I could and knocked it away when it was only two paces from me, the heat from the blast momentarily scalding my face. Another was right behind it, which I was able to kill before it got as close, but then there were two more slithering toward us.

"Flaming *die!*" I cursed, willing the tide to end. I needed to tend to Arthur. I raised my voice and shouted for help but everyone was fighting their own losing battles. Maze barely managed to knock aside two beetles before rolling away from a third, his mechanical leg scraping on the paving stones in front of the gate. No arrows flew to defend me now, a bad omen for Harry's fate. I couldn't even see Ryon or Jax. They might already be dead. In the chaos of the battle, I was too numb to feel remorse.

I was on my own, powerless to stop even Arthur from dying next to me.

I screamed in frustration as I traced, *fireballs* soaring away from my outstretched hand so fast I couldn't pick out targets, sending them all around me in reckless fury. Bells sounded in the city again, tolling its doom and ours. Even the spells and arrows arcing down from the battlements ceased. Behind me, a horse let out a terrible noise as it died. Somehow, the sounds pierced the constant drone of the beetle chittering. Like the things that mattered were coming into focus.

I couldn't think about any of that, though. All I could do was focus on my fingertip on the runetablet, scraping together enough runemagic to form another *fireball*, again and again as my strength dwindled.

Finally, the largest *fireball* I could trace was insufficient to damage a charging beetle; its snake-like lower half continued slithering toward me, ignoring the small flames licking along one of its four arms. I continued tracing another spell, even though I knew it would reach me before I completed it. The beetle loomed over me and reared back, and I imagined that I could see pleasure in its cluster of insect eyes.

Out of nowhere came a tower of steel, smashing the beetle with a shield and then stabbing with a longsword. Jax, my Warrior, stood magnificent on the battlefield, facing the walls of the city with the sun reflecting off his Dragon armor. I expected him to attack another Silithik, whichever was next to try to kill us, but all he did was raise his sword high in the air.

I heard the cheers, then. They drifted down from the city walls, the archers and runetracers above crying victory for all to hear. I rolled my eyes to the left and right. The ground was littered with corpses everywhere I looked. There were no more Silithik to kill. The endless stream had ended.

We won.

I sensed runemagic tracing, and nearly jumped out of my skin as a hand touched my wound. Ice filled my veins and numbed my leg as the other Quint's Frost Mage began healing me, the pain drifting away like a forgotten dream.

"No!" I shouted, trying to point at Arthur on the other side. Memories of Brennan, ignored while he died in the Academy attack, tormented me in their similarity. "Heal him first! A wasp stinger..."

Her smile was comforting. "Already done, dear. Stopped the spread midway up his thigh. You're the only one in danger, now." She shifted so I could see: Arthur still lay motionless, but his chest rose and fell peacefully. I couldn't see his wound, but I trusted what the Mage said.

Only when I spotted the other members of my Quint—Ryon cleaning his dragon-wing knives, Harry leaning on his bow, and Maze limping on his mechanical leg—did I close my eyes and pass out.

3

Arthur

An analytical mind was a pure mind. All Frost Magi were taught this fact in their first lesson at the first Academy.

The other four professions had the luxury of emotion. Adrenaline aided Warriors and Shadows in their physical feats, pushing them harder and faster and swifter. Pyromancers *needed* emotion, the flames springing from their hand fueled by what was in their heart. Even the calm Rangers, who must focus intently on the target for their arrow, fell into the bloodlust of battle when they threw their bow aside and met the enemy with short sword and buckler.

Yet tracing the runes in the pouch of a Frost Mage required absolute calm, a mind partitioned away from the world. Finding such calmness in one's thoughts was best accomplished by remaining cold and calculating at all times, not only when in battle. At all times, the world needed to be viewed through the lens of rational thought.

It was with such a mindset that I sat up on the battlefield and watched my leg be healed.

"I halted the spread of wasp poison before tending to your Pyromancer," said the Mage, a stocky woman with short-cropped yellow hair and more muscle than one in our profession typically possessed. She spoke plainly, imparting facts without deeper meaning. "She nearly bled out crawling across the battlefield. Now that she's healed, I can remove your poison completely."

A moan escaped my lips as she touched my ruined calf. The frigid runemagic swirled around the wound, halting the spread of the vicious poison crawling up my thigh. As I watched the black tendrils of foulness recede I felt curiosity instead of relief.

"I wonder," I said, "how long a tourniquet would have stemmed the advance of poison. Even the tightest rope cannot block the flow of blood completely. I suspect it would take no longer than five minutes for the poison to reach the heart."

She cocked her head. "I can stop the healing and apply a traditional tourniquet if you'd like to test the hypothesis."

Her comment wasn't made in jest; she was completely serious. I genuinely considered the offer for a moment. "Best not. These conditions are hardly reproducible."

"Indeed," she said. There were tears in her eyes, strangely enough. "And the information gained from such a test would not be worth the cost of delaying the healing of others."

"Oh, excellent point," I said, gazing around the battlefield in the shadow of the capitol walls. I hadn't considered the other wounded. The Mage continued healing until the skin around my calf finished stitching together, months of repair accomplished before my eyes. She removed her hand from the rune and nodded. The shimmer in her eyes confused me.

"Fare you well, Mage," she said before moving on to Ryon, who sat nearby with a diagonal gash running from his shoulder to his hip. I eyed the pink skin of my wound and pushed my robe back over my leg.

There were two primary problems with runemagic healing. The

first was that a Mage could not heal himself; only others. Theories varied as to why this was the case, and there were rumors that runemasters of old could accomplish the feat, but most such tales were dismissed outright. Suffice to say, a Mage couldn't heal himself any more than he could tickle himself. The other problem with runemagic healing was that it drained one's strength tremendously. Weeks of natural healing and energy compressed into a few short seconds. I was certainly in no condition to assist in healing the other wounded. Combined with my exhaustion from runetracing during the battle, I wanted nothing more than to lay my head back on the ground and close my eyes.

The only thing that stopped me was something the Mage had said.

I twisted around to find Alyssa laying on her back, red curls splayed around her like a halo and her eyes closed in the same deep sleep that tempted me. The black trousers of her Quint uniform bore a fist-sized hole on the left thigh, the cloth crusty and stained with dried blood.

I examined my surroundings. Dead Silithik littered the ground in every direction, especially so between me and the walls of the city. But a crimson streak ran away from Alyssa in the dirt marking how far she'd moved while wounded. She must have crawled 30 paces.

Memories of the battle returned in bits and pieces. I saw the diving wasp too late, felt the strange pinch as its stinger tore off half my calf. I was thrown from the horse. I remember thinking I was going to die, wondering whether it would be a beetle or the wasp's poison to do the job. I remember closing my eyes for the last time.

Then I'd felt the sensation of runemagic tracing. I opened my eyes to find Alyssa crouched above me, jaw clenched as she traced *fireball* after *fireball* at the advancing bugs, cursing with each one, "Die! Flaming die!" I must have passed out because I didn't remember anything after that.

I stared at the trail of blood in the dirt. Had this woman

crawled so far... to protect *me?*

More importantly, the memory triggered *another* memory, this one of a dream instead of an event. A dream I'd been having for years, as regular as the tides. *Flaming die.* How could she know...

"You look like the dullest sword in the armory," Jaxon said, heavy plate mail clinking as he approached. He held his helm under one arm, and his hair was dark with sweat. His smile touched every part of his face except his bloody eye. "Decided to flirt with poison, eh?"

"The decision was entirely not my own," I said. "If it were, I would have avoided it entirely, I assure you. Fortunately the other Quint's Mage was on hand for rapid healing." I gestured around the battlefield. "All things considered, this battle could not have gone better."

"Not all things considered," Jax said softly.

It took me an embarrassingly long time to see the body. The other Quint's Warrior and Tinker crouched over it while weeping quietly. As they shifted their feet I saw the female Shadow, the uniform and chest torn to shreds in a mess of red and black. *That is why their Mage was on the verge of tears.* Stupid of me not to deduce the reason.

"I'm sorry," I whispered, wishing they could hear me.

Footsteps announced soldiers and servants approaching from the city, carrying medical bags and stretchers. Jax turned to them and waved a hand.

"I'll carry Alyssa myself," he said, tone implying he would fight anyone who tried to argue with him. "You can take this sorcerous fool."

I realized he meant me. "Actually," I said, pushing up to one knee, "I would prefer to walk myself. Active recovery is a method of stimulating blood flow to a recently healed area..."

Suddenly the sun brightened until I could barely see anything. I wavered, and blinked. One moment I was standing, and the next I was being held upright by one of the capitol servants.

Jax roared with laughter. "Is fainting part of active recovery? That seems counterproductive."

I blinked as the servant helped lower me to the ground, where a stretcher waited. I leaned my head back on the fabric and said, "Perhaps it would be prudent to accept assistance this one time."

"A wise choice, dragon," the servant said with a grin.

Jax gently lifted Alyssa into his arms, cradling her against his armor. I could feel Jax's emotions through his bond, a swelling of care and love. For a moment I felt something close to jealousy at the sight of them. I watched him carry her toward the city, the strange tingling of emotions in my gut overruling any rational thought in my head.

Alyssa

I dreamed of being carried across the world by a one-eyed angel, floating above the bodies of fallen monsters, high above the dangers that could no longer hurt me. While I was in his arms, I felt like I was safe from *all* the horrors of the world.

I woke in a dark infirmary room. Most of the room was filled by the narrow bed in which I now rested, with a washbasin on a wooden pedestal to my left, and plain stone walls and ceiling. There were no windows, although light entered through the half-open doorway across from the bed. It was identical to the room I stayed in during my last visit to the capitol. *That was only a week ago*, I realized with a start. It seemed like a lifetime ago. So much had happened since then.

There was one difference between that room and this one: scrunched in the corner to my right was a stool, currently occupied by a snoring Warrior. Jaxon no longer wore his gleaming plate mail, although based on the filthy state of his Dragon uniform he'd only recently stripped the armor. His body was caked in dried blood and

Silithik pus where the gaps in his armor had allowed it to seep through: the neck, both elbows, and at the waist.

No matter how filthy, the sight of the man was more comforting than anything in the world. "I don't know how I managed to get any rest with you snoring like that."

Jax blinked rapidly, his one good eye locking onto me. "I snore?"

"Like a giant tearing a bed sheet in half." I smiled to take the sting out of the accusation. "You need to stop making a habit of watching over me while I sleep. No Silithik beetle is going to slit my throat in here."

I pushed up onto an elbow and hissed as pain shot up my thigh. I threw back the sheet; I still wore my uniform, which was every bit as grimy as Jax's. Halfway up my thigh was a tear in the fabric large enough to stick my fist through. I fingered the gap, wincing at the tender skin underneath. I could still feel the beetle's claw inside my flesh, twisting and tearing.

Jax had the audacity to look smug. "I'll stop watching over you when you stop getting injured in battle."

I ignored the pain and adjusted myself. Just sitting up in bed required tremendous effort, and left me wincing. "I'm merely spent from so much runetracing. In time, I'll become acclimated."

"And until then," Jax said, "I'll guard you while you recover."

I thought of another joke, but held my tongue. Despite my complaints, having someone watch over me was a wonderful luxury. I didn't want to tease him so much that he stopped, although I doubted he would.

"What of the battle?" I asked.

Jax nodded as if he'd been ready for the question. "The first Silithik army breached the north gate. That's when we heard the bells tolling in the city. The Quint guarding the gate cut the chains to the drawbridge and let it smash into the moat, but the Silithik didn't need it. Beetles poured into the moat, dying in droves, until their bodies formed a bridge across to the gate."

"Oh no..."

"By then, too much of their army had been killed. Two well-placed Pyromancers inside the city were able to hold the choke point from the remaining Silithik swarming in. Only rubble and splinters remain of the north gate and fifty paces of the wall, but the beetles didn't advance any deeper. Mild civilian casualties, but it could have been worse. So much worse."

"And the army we fought?"

Jax furrowed his brow. "When the north gate fell, apparently the remaining Silithik on the south halted their attack to join the fight at the north. While slithering all the way around the city they were easily picked off by soldiers and runetracers on the walls. I'm told it was a slaughter." He frowned in puzzlement.

I closed my eyes. "I'm not sure whether to be relieved, or disappointed we didn't kill the entire army by ourselves."

Jax's chest rumbled with soft laughter. "Perhaps next time." His expression changed to concern. "How do you fare? It has been nine hours since the battle."

I took a moment to consider myself. The ache in my gut was worse than the one in my thigh. "I'm famished. Fetching me something to eat would help more than sitting in a chair watching me sleep, if a Warrior was so inclined."

Jax's knees cracked as he stood. "If I do that, I run the risk of spoiling you too much." But he leaned over, brushed aside a lock of my unkempt hair, and kissed my forehead. "I suppose I'll take the risk just this once."

My forehead tingled where his lips had been. "I probably taste like Silithik guts and soot."

"You taste wonderful," Jax announced, then smiled. "Well. Perhaps you taste *somewhat* like Silithik guts and soot. But that taste is sweet, too."

His massive hand lingered on mine a moment longer, warm and safe. Then he strode from the room, his wide shoulders barely fitting through the door.

I slid down into bed with a sigh. My relationship with Jaxon was complicated, to say the least. We were Dragon Quintmates, although not yet bonded together. We'd slept together only the one time in the Academy, after the battle against the Silithik Queen deep underground. We'd had no other opportunities since traveling back to the capitol—Jax had set the horses to a hard pace, and the time we didn't spend in the saddle was spent catching a few hours of sleep where we could.

But feeling his touch, and simply being *near* him, made my stomach alternately tighten in a knot and swirl like a storm. When he was within sight it was difficult to keep my eyes off him, the way his muscles bulged against his uniform like they were trying to break free. Even now, mere seconds after he'd left, I couldn't wait for him to return.

Well, perhaps part of that was because he was returning with *food.* But still.

I'd never felt this way before. Not when I was a young girl at my village, catching glimpses of boys swimming nude in the river. My fling with Brennan at the fifth Academy was the most vulnerable I'd ever been with a man, but it had always been a temporary thing, a relationship destined to expire when we graduated. And with each passing day I was realizing the tangle of emotions that made up Brennan's memory in my head was more guilt than attraction, more sorrow than true love. Had he not been killed in the Academy attack, I doubt I would be thinking of him at all.

Yet as wonderful as this feeling was, I found myself over-analyzing every part of it. I worried about whether Jax felt the same way, or with the same passion. Of course he showed his affection when he could, but were those feelings genuine? Part of me, the part that whispered poison into my thoughts while I was trying to fall asleep, wondered if he was only using me as a replacement for the previous Pyromancer in their Quint. If I was nothing more than a stand-in for their beloved Danni.

There was a scratching sound in the hall, and then Arthur appeared in my view with a crutch under one arm. He stopped just outside my doorway, staring at something I couldn't see in the hall.

"You look the way I feel," I called.

He blinked as if only now realizing he was outside my door. That wasn't unusual; in the short time I'd known the Frost Mage, he seemed always lost in thought. Though perhaps that was the madness creeping in, rotting his soul from the inside-out. Losing a member of one's Quintelaide had that effect on the remaining members, I had recently learned. Hopefully our Dragon bonding ceremony would remove the madness.

Arthur leaned against the door frame. His blond hair was tied back in a tail, with only a few strands hanging down over his eyes. He didn't seem to notice. "I have not bathed since the battle. I was hoping to remedy that now."

I sighed and ran a hand over my legs. "That sounds *wonderful.* I feel like I'm coated in so much Silithik pus that—"

I cut off with a yelp of pain as my fingers rubbed across my wounded thigh. Although the skin and flesh had healed, the nerve endings seemed to remember the pain.

Alarmed, Arthur crutched his way into the room, rounding the bed. "No, it's fine," I waved him off. "Just the wound from battle."

"It shouldn't hurt after healing."

"Are you certain? Because every time I move, it feels like there's a piece of Silithik claw still inside my leg." I frowned. "You... you don't think there *is* a piece of Silithik claw stuck inside, do you?"

Arthur smiled politely as he leaned the crutch against the wall and sat on the edge of the bed. "Unlikely. You would be in far more pain if that were the case. It's more likely the Mage who healed you did a hasty job. Unsurprising, given the battle had only just ended. And given the circumstances of their Shadow. One can hardly be blamed for being distracted after that."

I stared down at my leg as if it were a broken toy. "Should I be worried? Will the wound fester? When I was a young girl, my uncle cut his arm open on a hunting arrow and neglected to properly clean it. Within three days it was a swollen, sickly shade of green."

Arthur shook his head. "Oh no, nothing quite so gruesome. But it will pain you for several days. I can heal it properly if you would like. But the pain will be tremendous, even more than it hurts now."

"What? Why?" I sputtered.

"Because I will need to re-break the torn muscle fibers." He reached inside his runepouch.

I leaned away from him. "Hold on a second. Help me understand the logic. Why would I trade minor pain for *tremendous* pain?"

Arthur looked confused. "Because if it is not healed properly, you may have a limp for the rest of your life. Better to heal it properly now. An easy decision, in my opinion"

"Every decision is easy when you're making it for others," I pointed out. "And you should have led with the limp, rather than the pain."

Rather than argue with me, Arthur grabbed a fistful of his robe and began pulling it up. As if he were intending to get *nude.* Before I could demand to know what he was doing, he extended his left leg into the air. Almost half of his calf was pink with new skin.

"In an abstract sense, I agree with you," he said with a smile. "However, in this situation I have recently made the exact same decision for myself: as soon as the critically wounded were cared for, I had another Mage re-heal my own leg."

"Oh," I said, feeling a blush crawl up my cheeks. I felt stupid for thinking he was going to remove his clothes. He lowered the robe to his ankles and finished clipping a runetablet onto his belt.

"Shall I?" he asked.

Still, I hesitated. "Tremendous pain?"

He smiled sadly. "I'm afraid so."

I licked my lips. My mouth had gone dry. This felt worse than preparing for a battle!

"A limp might not be so bad..." I said weakly.

"A limp would slow your movement," Arthur said in a voice that reminded me of an Academy lecturer. "Surely you can understand the severity of such a debilitation, especially after the fighting we've done in the past week. A Dragon Quintelaide is only as fast as its slowest member."

"I know," I said, resigned. "I was delaying. All right. You can heal me."

Arthur nodded as if there were no other possibility. He put one hand on his runetablet. "First I must explore the wound and recently healed tissue. This part will not hurt."

His touch was light, fingers sliding through the hole in my breeches to touch the new skin. He began tracing with his left hand, and then I gasped; it felt like ice water was being poured *inside* my thigh, coolness spreading up and down my leg. I looked up at his face and saw him watching me from behind his hawkish nose.

"There's no sensation quite like a healer's touch," he said, then nodded. The cooling touch disappeared, though he kept his palm on my leg. "I'm ready to begin the next part, whenever you are."

I tried to ignore how warm his hand felt on my leg compared to the previous icy feeling, and how I didn't want it to leave. "Can't you just keep exploring the wound like that? Is there really any need for the painful part?"

He stared at me, confused.

I sighed. "Very well. I'm ready."

The pain was instantaneous. It was so shocking that I let out a strangled cry and grabbed the bedsheets in two fists. It felt like someone was sawing open my leg one fiber at a time! The pain was blinding for a few racing heartbeats, and then it was over.

"That... wasn't... so bad," I panted.

Arthur looked over at me. "Unfortunately, that was only part of the wound. I must work in sections, breaking, and then healing. If I tore open the entire wound all at once I wouldn't be able to stop the internal bleeding."

"Oh," I said in a small voice.

His fingers touched my thigh again, and I sensed the runemagic trickle at his hip. The healing part of the process was... tingly? It was delicate and light, like a feather tickling a part of my body I couldn't scratch. Soothing and uncomfortable all at the same time.

"It feels like the hairs on the back of my head are being sewn together," I said.

"That's how you know it's working." His fingers pushed gently into my skin as he worked. "How are you handling the aftermath of the battle?"

I shrugged. "Fine, I suppose. How should I be handling it?"

"The violence of a battle can have long lasting effects on someone. The human mind is not meant to suffer so much trauma in such a short period of time." He glanced at me, then back down. "Some require special counseling to cope with such terrors."

"Some?" I asked. "What makes you think I am such a person? Because I'm a woman? Or a freshly graduated student?"

"Not necessarily," Arthur said, completely serious. "The ways in which men and women react to trauma can be unpredictable. One of the strongest Warriors I have ever known, a giant of a man in the Eighteenth Quintelaide, broke down weeping in a Borderlands skirmish three years ago. He threw down his sword and shield right there on the battlefield and melted into a quivering puddle of fear. He'd fought countless times over many years, and finally the stress broke him down."

I tried to imagine a massive Warrior like Jax quivering in fear. It was an impossibility, akin to a boar soaring through the air like a gryphon.

Arthur looked to me again, his piercing crystal blue eyes pulling an answer from me. I paused to consider his question more genuinely. I *thought* I was doing fine. I'd been a mess after the first Academy attack, but since then the other battles hadn't fazed me. Watching humans die was a gruesome and deeply troubling experience, but slaughtering Silithik by the hundreds? Emotionally, it felt no different than harvesting a crop with a scythe. Or burning an anthill with pitch oil.

"I suppose I'm handling it fine," I repeated.

I expected him to push me harder, but instead he surprised me by changing subjects. "You saved me during the battle."

"Did I?"

"Yes. You crawled across the battlefield, wounded, to protect me. I may have died without your efforts."

The blush began at my neck and invaded my cheeks like a swarm of beetles. I shook my head, hoping the strands of hair that fell across my face helped hide it.

"I think you saved me first. Charging forward after I fell."

"I followed standard battle tactics. Covering a fallen teammate while they recover." He spoke simply, but carefully avoided looking at me. And his fair skin brightened with his own blush, accentuating his high cheek bones.

"Ahh!" I yelped at the lightning pain shooting through my thigh as Arthur tore open the muscle of the wound again. "Next time warn a girl!"

I wasn't sure if he heard me. Although he stared down at my leg while healing, I got the impression he was looking at something far away. After a few seconds, I sensed the runemagic ending, and along with it the pain.

"Please tell me that's the last time."

Rather than answer me, he said, "There was a part of the battle I wished to ask you about. You shouted a curse. Do you remember?"

Another runemagic trace, and the tickling healing sensation returned. "I... Maybe? I probably cursed a lot during the battle. In case you don't remember, the Silithik nearly killed us."

"You specifically yelled out *flaming die* while keeping the beetles away from me."

I couldn't tell if it was a question, or a statement, so I shrugged. "Maybe. That sounds like something I would shout."

"Huh," Arthur said, that faraway look still in his eyes.

"Why do you ask?"

"No reason."

"Cursing doesn't offend your delicate sensibilities, does it?" I grinned. "Because I can't help what comes out of my mouth in the throes of battle. And in our short time together, I have heard Ryon say *far* worse."

He didn't take the joke for what it was. "I am not easily offended." He lessened the pressure of his fingers on my thigh, and both the feeling of being healed and the sensation of runetracing disappeared simultaneously. "There we go. Give your leg a flex."

I obeyed, pulling back my leg so I could bend the knee up and down. "It aches, but not like before."

Arthur jerked his head in a nod. "That is normal. You may be weak on that leg for a few days, but then you'll be back to normal, running for your life from the next Silithik army we are sent to fight."

"Why, Arthur," I said approvingly, "I do believe that's *two* jokes I've heard you tell today. Keep it up and you're going to lose your reputation as a stone-faced Frost Mage."

His face split with a grin. "We wouldn't want that."

In the week that I'd known him, I'd never seen Arthur smile so genuinely. It filled my own chest with a flurry of excitement. He was incredibly handsome when he smiled, cheekbones lifting and small wrinkles folding around the eyes. With his hair pulled back I could see his ears, a strange detail to notice, but there they were. He was an extremely attractive man, beautiful even, although without the self-awareness to know it. I was keenly aware of his hand lingering on my thigh, touching me and not touching me at the same time. I found myself wondering if his blond hair was as soft as it looked...

Jax burst into the doorway with a tray of food in his hands. "Are you well? I heard a scream."

"I didn't scream!" I protested, but when I glanced at Arthur for confirmation he quickly looked away. I blushed again, both out of embarrassment for making so much noise and because it felt like Jax had interrupted something private.

"I was re-healing her wound," Arthur explained. "The other Mage didn't do a proper job during battle."

"Good," Jax said. Then, to me, "Otherwise you'd have a limp. A Dragon Quintelaide is only as fast as its weakest member."

I narrowed my eyes. "So I've been told. I'd like to stay ahead of Maze in that regard."

Arthur gently patted my thigh, then abruptly realized that the gesture was too intimate for how little time we had known each other. "I'm going to go find that bath." He rose from the bed, retrieved his crutch from the wall, and hobbled toward the door, pausing to steal a chicken drumstick from the tray. Grease ran over his fingers as he bit into it. "Oh, that's good! Perhaps I will get supper first..."

He disappeared from sight, the sound of his crutch clicking down the hall just like Maze on his mechanical leg.

5

Alyssa

After Arthur was gone, Jax gently placed the tray of food over my lap. One plate was piled high with roasted chicken meat, and another held stringy beans and a tin of grainy mustard.

"Are you sure you're all right?" Jax asked. "You seem flustered."

"Just recovering from having my thigh torn apart and put back together again." I eagerly bit into a chicken wing, not caring about the grease that ran down my chin.

Jax sat on the bed where Arthur had just been, his weight shifting the mattress more than the slender Mage. "You had best get used to that now. Battlefield healing is often hurried by necessity, requiring additional healing after the fact." He grabbed his own piece of chicken, which was good because I'd feel like a pig if I ate the *entire* tray.

"She healed me after the battle was won. Not during."

"Yes, well..." Jax paused to chew and swallow. "She also lost a member of her Quint."

I paused in mid-bite. "Yeah. She did."

"It was admirable that she could perform her duties at all, given the circumstances." Jax shook his blocky head slowly. "I plan on recommending her to the Field Marshal for a commendation of valor."

I thought about the other Quintelaide. We hadn't known them long, but an hour during battle felt like the equivalent of a year of normal friendship. I couldn't imagine the sorrow they must have been experiencing.

But that reminded me of another topic I'd been avoiding.

"Can I ask you something?"

"Of course."

"It's about Danni."

Jax froze with his fork stabbing a stringy bean. I readied myself for what I hoped wouldn't be a difficult conversation.

"You told me you had a relationship with her that went deeper than the Quintelaide bond," I said, "but you never elaborated."

Jax bit into the bean pod with a crunch. His face was as blank as an unused chalkboard. "What needs elaboration?"

"I get the impression all of you had a special bond with... your previous Pyromancer," I said, avoiding using her name again. "Is that true?"

"Yes," he bit off the word. "To varying degrees."

"You were all... *romantically* involved with her?"

"Yes." He chewed on his food for so long I wasn't sure he could continue. "The Dragon bond is incredibly powerful. A constant connection to one another. It causes me to love Arthur, and Harry, and Maze, and even Ryon as powerfully as if they were my blood brothers. And," he said with a sigh, "it led all five of us to love Danni more than just a sister. She was mine, but she was also theirs. She was all of ours."

The pain in his voice was still fresh, a reminder that she had not been dead very long.

46

"To be clear, I was less romantically entwined with her as the others," he admitted. "We still took solace in each other's bodies occasionally, especially after battle. When we needed each other the most. But she was a close friend to me more than she was a lover."

I nodded along before he could elaborate further. "Do all Quints do that? Bed down together?"

"Of course not," Jax said bluntly. "Some Quints never develop romantic feelings, remaining only as close as brothers and sisters. In others, there are individual pairings, like a Tinker and Shadow becoming lovers but no one else. The Forty-Fourth, one of the most tenacious Quints in the Archenon, is comprised of six men who all go to bed together. Every Quint is unique. Dragons may not have any idea how they will end up until they are bonded."

"But you have already been bonded," I said, pushing forward with the difficult part. "I'm joining late. Taking the place of Danni. Is it expected that I... That the rest of... Will I be..."

Jax quickly took my hand and squeezed it between both of his. "Sweet girl, nothing is expected of you. Our bonding with you will replace the bonding we had with Danni. A new relationship will form between all of us, whether it involves mere friendship... or something deeper."

"How can you be so certain?" Tears threatened my eyes, blurring the edges, and I didn't know why. "Nobody has ever been re-bonded. You said it yourself. What if the bond with me isn't as strong as it was with *her?* What if the others hate me for it?"

"Because whatever happens, happens," he said in a voice as firm as his hands. "Fate will ordain our bonding. And there's no use fighting fate. The others understand that, and so do I."

The logic was so childish, so simple, that I couldn't help but laugh. Once I was laughing it was difficult to be afraid. Jax's words and touch were enough to send the worries away. At least, for now.

And despite my relief that there were no expectations, I couldn't help but think about Arthur's healing touch, and the way his crystal blue eyes had stared at me before. He had been thinking about something, but I couldn't understand what it was.

It was like Jax had read my mind. "Why do you ask about the bonding?" he said in an offended tone. "Is a Warrior not enough for you? Perhaps you prefer the sensual love of a Frost Mage instead?"

My jaw hung open as I tried to think of an excuse. Then Jax threw back his head and roared with laughter, a deep sound that reverberated in my chest.

"I'm joking, Aly! Calm yourself. I hope you develop feelings for the others. More so, I hope they develop feelings for *you*. That's the tougher part, in light of... the circumstances." He gave a start. "Not that there's any pressure, of course. I wouldn't want..."

It was my turn to calm him with a touch. "I understand what you mean. We will see what fate ordains."

Jax relaxed, but I didn't. Deep down, I wondered if he had truly moved on from his previous Pyromancer, or if he was only using me to fill the hole in his heart.

"Recovering, I see?"

We both whipped our heads to find Ryon leaning against the doorway. He swung one of his dragon-wing daggers around a finger lazily.

"I am trying," I said. "How is your own wound?"

"Aching, thanks to the half-hearted efforts of the other Quint's Mage," he muttered. "Though I suppose I should feel sympathy for her now that she's doomed to the same fate as us."

Jax's face darkened, but I ignored the dark humor. "You can always have Arthur heal it properly. He did that for my leg."

Ryon's sneer showed teeth, and his grey-and-black hair fell across his eyes. "I prefer the scar. How else is one supposed to remember the mistakes they've made?"

"I find that memory itself suffices," Jax said, deadpan.

"Ahh, memory!" Ryon said as if remembering why he was there. "Such as the memory of our flight through the forest. Perhaps we could have reached the city in time if we'd had proper sorcerous cover."

My breath caught in my throat. He was referring to my inability to trace from horseback. Before I could say anything, Jax answered for me.

"The city survived the attack, as did we."

"Oh aye, *this* time," Ryon said. He pointed at me with the knife. "But the next time, or the time after that? Sooner or later, this girl's *skill*—or lack thereof—will get us killed."

Jax was on his feet in a flash, rounding on the smaller Shadow with massive fists clenched at his side. "The bonding ceremony is at dawn. Are you having second thoughts?"

"We'll see what *fate* ordains," Ryon said, making my words into a curse. He gave me a mocking smile and then left us alone.

6

Alyssa

Jax quivered with anger long after Ryon was gone. He flinched when I touched his arm.

"You look like you're going to punch a hole through the stone wall."

Each of his muscles relaxed individually. An army of soldiers throwing down their weapons one by one. Finally he exhaled and turned to me. "Do not pay him any mind. You are a convenient scapegoat for his frustrations, not the root cause."

"He seemed to be warming up to me during our journey here," I said. "Before things got crazy, I mean."

Jax closed his eyes and pinched the bridge of his nose with two thick fingers. "Ryon's temperament has become more volatile in the past week. I fear the madness affects him more than the rest of us. Hopefully the bonding ceremony will cure such an ailment."

"Which is tomorrow, apparently?"

"Sorry. I meant to tell you as soon as you woke. The Archon's personal runemaster, who performs all Dragon bonding ceremonies, sent word only hours ago."

The tingle of anticipation returned tenfold. On the way to the city, the bonding had been an event to look forward to in the future. Knowing it was tomorrow morning was like being pushed to the edge of a cliff without warning.

"What did you mean?" I asked. "When you warned Ryon about jeopardizing the ceremony?"

Concern flashed across his bloody eye for an instant, then was gone. "A long story." He gestured at the tray, which had been picked clean except for one pitiful chicken leg. "Are you done with supper? Are you sufficiently stuffed?"

I held up a hand as if to shield myself. "If I eat another bite I think I might burst like a *fireball!*"

Jax sat on the edge of the bed, looming over me. In a suggestive voice he said, "I wasn't talking about the food."

As soon as I realized what he meant, I erupted in a fit of giggles. That sent him into a bout of laughter until we were both wiping away tears.

"That's the most foolish line any boy has ever given me!" I said.

"I'm a man, not a boy."

"After that line, I'm not so certain."

"I did feel awfully foolish saying it," Jax admitted. He leaned forward, his hand finding mine. The smell of him was wonderful, a spicy musk that reminded me of oiled leather and steel. "You haven't answered the question."

"My breath probably smells like mustard!" I said, only protesting a little.

"I like mustard." He kissed me to prove it, his strong nose pressing against mine while our lips met in a wonderful embrace.

I broke the kiss, feeling playful. "I haven't bathed since the battle. I'm dirty!"

"I like dirty, too."

His tongue invaded my mouth and he made a noise deep in his throat, destroying my remaining protests. The bed lurched from his weight as he crawled on top of me, surrounding me with his heat. I wrapped my arms around him, running fingers through his hair as we kissed.

Flames, I wanted him. And I had no patience.

Grabbing his hair, I pulled him sideways off me until he was on his back, and then I crawled on top. I pushed my hips down onto him, rubbing up and down against the bulge in his uniform, his *Dragon* uniform, a source of power and sexiness. My recently-healed wound was a distant memory. Jax looked up at me, lust filling his good eye.

"You like this?" I asked.

"Steel save me, I do!"

I slid down his body, straddling one of his massive legs, until I reached his belt. The Dragon symbol buckle came away easily, then the laces down the front, opening his black trousers to reveal what was underneath. What I *wanted.*

His cock slid out like a sword from a scabbard, huge and thick and begging to be touched. I ran my fingernails along the underside and giggled as the Warrior squirmed.

"Maybe I'd rather go to sleep..."

"Oh, don't tease me, girl!" he growled.

"I'm told sleep is crucial after healing..."

He sucked in a breath, and I could tell he was on the edge of taking over and ravaging me. That was tempting too, but tonight I wanted to be in charge.

Gradually, with deliberate slowness, I moved my lips toward his manhood while maintaining eye contact. I kissed the underside of his tip, which finally made Jax clench his eyes shut and moan. Then I ran my tongue across the left side, then the right, before parting my lips. Only a finger length, enough to caress the edge of his tip, feeling the ridge between my lips. Tasting him. Underneath me, his massive thigh muscles went rock hard, tensing from the pleasure. I rubbed against him harder.

Finally I opened my lips and leaned forward, taking all of his head in my mouth. The rumble of pleasure that escaped his chest practically shook the bed.

"Mmm," I moaned into him, pushing lower. He was so *thick* I couldn't take more than an inch of him into my mouth, so I kept my lips tight and moved up and down on what I could. Judging by how he grabbed a handful of my hair and squeezed it in his fingers, it was plenty.

Up and down I went, Jax's pleasure mirrored into my own. I loved that I could turn the massive, powerful Warrior into a quivering mess with only my lips. It made me feel powerful the way a runetablet did.

Jax reached down to squeeze my breast, untying the laces of my blouse so he could slip a hand inside. His fingers found one of my tender nipples, pinching them with just the right amount of pressure. I moaned louder, wanting more of him. I wished I could take all of him in my mouth, down to the hilt, to feel him spasm and scream.

I couldn't do that with my mouth, but I had other ways.

I gave his head one final stroke before pulling away, breathing heavy from the tingling sensation climbing up my body. Jax grabbed my arms firmly and pulled me forward until I was kissing him, rough and hard and needy. He grabbed the edges of my pants and pulled them down, the laces coming loose from the force. I was frantic for him then; I felt like I would die if I didn't kick off my trousers and undergarments as quickly as possible, our attraction as sharp as a perfectly-traced spell.

I straddled his body and prepared to lower myself onto him, but Jax was already thrusting upward, guiding the tip of his cock against my wet slit. It hit the right place and slid inside with ease, the tip, then a few degrees more. Jax exhaled and I sucked in air, filling my lungs with his breath.

Before he could give me any more of himself, I shoved my hips down on him, impaling myself on his throbbing sex.

We both screamed with simultaneous ecstasy, not caring who might hear. My vision went white for a moment, the feeling in my pussy so powerful I thought I might pass out. Jax kept his grip on my arms strong, holding me in place. He drank the sight of me with his eyes, then finished unlacing the front of my blouse, loosening it enough for him to pull over my head until we were both bare. A bead of sweat trickled down my back and between my cheeks, and the cool air on my skin felt almost as wonderful as the man beneath me.

I put a hand on his chest, pressing him down into the bed. "You're not allowed to move," I commanded with a wicked smile.

Jax narrowed his eyes. "Is that so?"

"Mmm hmm," I said, slowly riding him. My entire body rippled up and down, just like riding our horses at a gallop away from the Silithik. The memory disappeared as I pressed back down as far as I could go, feeling the tingle of his hair rubbing against my lips and thighs as I swallowed all of him.

"The Warrior is traditionally in charge, you know," he said, arching an eyebrow.

"Not tonight."

Up and down I went, his manhood spreading my walls wide with wonderful pressure as he grew impossibly hard. I arched my back and moved faster, and faster, wanting to take my time but not being able to resist the heat between my legs, the desire to have him as quickly as possible.

"I don't think I can hold back," Jax said, teeth clenched.

"Well you must." I slowed down a fraction, teasing him more.

"I don't think I *can*..." He moaned with pleasure, tilting his head back into the pillow. The apple of his throat bulged, so I leaned down and gave it a quick flick of my tongue.

And then the passive Jaxon was dead, replaced by the powerful Dragon Warrior who killed Silithik by the dozens. With a roar he leaned forward into a sitting position, wrapping his arms around me tight, kissing me on the breast. I craned my head back and

54

moaned to the ceiling as his lips found a nipple, sucking on it the way I'd sucked on the tip of his cock.

Jax's hands slid down and cupped both ass cheeks, moving me up and down on him. I surrendered to his strength and allowed him to control me, moving my body up and down on his cock. I tried to let out a low moan but it came out like a ragged scream, and it went on and on as Jax's arms pumped up and down, crashing my body down onto him, almost violent with passionate desire. I opened my eyes wide because it was my turn to drink in the sight of him, the tension in his chiseled face and the sweat beading at his temple. I ran a hand across his cheek, touching his ear, wishing I had a thousand hands with a thousand fingers so I could feel every bit of him at the same time, never letting go.

Jax's roar of climax triggered my own breathless gasp. The muscles of his arms bulged and tightened, squeezing my behind as he thrust up into me one final time, shuddering and spasming as he filled me with his seed. I muted his cry by kissing him, pressing my lips over his to taste him as we trembled together on the bed, joined by our bodies if not yet by a sorcerous bond.

7

Arthur

Flaming die.

The curse stuck to the inside of my head like an infestation all through my bath, and then supper, and even now while walking back to our rooms. I continuously prodded the thought the way one prods a sore in their mouth, pestering it too much to allow it to heal.

Flaming die.

It wasn't an unusual curse, I told myself. Logically, I'd probably heard it countless times from a hundred different tongues. But there was something in the way Alyssa had said it during the battle. It was too similar to my dream. The dream that had tormented me for longer than I could remember.

Flaming die.

Was the memory of the battle genuine, or had I imagined it? I'd read studies surrounding the complications of memory, how the mind could convince itself it had witnessed something when no such experience had occurred. Perhaps that was what happened here: I only remembered bits and parts of the battle outside the capitol, and my mind had filled in the gaps with memories from my dream.

It made sense. I should have accepted it and moved on. Yet the nagging feeling persisted.

Moving about the capitol was difficult with a crutch, but I didn't mind. It allowed me extra time to think. Nobody took the time to *think* anymore. People rushed to conclusions, voiced them in arguments and debates, and then acted upon the spurious decision. I missed the days when Dragons, and indeed other powerful leaders, spent time in quiet reflection. Cleaning their mind in a bath of swirling thought.

Flaming die.

As I entered the hallway that housed our six bedrooms, I decided to speak to Alyssa once more. I could begin by asking how her wound was feeling, which was a silly question after less than an hour but would provide me the opening I needed. Most people didn't like being asked a question bluntly. Formalities were a waste of time, but they helped soften the blow.

But when I reached her room, I found the door closed. I raised my fist to knock, then hesitated. The hour was late; as tempting as it was to knock, waking her would probably not help me get the information I needed. And it would likely annoy Alyssa. I found myself not wanting to do anything to make her unhappy.

I turned away from her door and came face to face with Ryon.

"Looking for your Pyromancer?" he rasped.

Embarrassed at being ambushed, I used my crutch to hobble around him and down the hall. Ryon followed along, turning his gait into a slow stroll to match my own debilitated pace. I knew I shouldn't engage him when he was like this, when the madness was scratching at his brain from the inside and he was looking for a fight, but I couldn't stop myself.

"She's your Pyromancer, too."

Ryon spun one dagger around his finger. "*My* Pyro died in the

Academy. *My* Pyro's name was Danni. *My* Pyro could runetrace from horseback."

"Tracing at a gallop is difficult," I said.

"You do it."

"Difficult things can be done with years of practice. Alyssa has had only a handful of days."

Ryon's dagger fell to the floor with a clatter. He scowled and picked it up. "That's my point. We shouldn't be stuck with a fucking *rookie*."

I stopped in front of my room. I could have gone inside and shut the door. I didn't need to engage him.

Flaming die, the words taunted me.

"I don't disagree," I told Ryon. "But it must not be easy for Alyssa, either. Have you considered her feelings?"

A dark expression came over Ryon's face. "She's not the one getting the bloody end of the sword. We are."

"She's blameless in all this," I said, hoping it would end the argument.

"Don't tell me you feel bad for her," Ryon said. I hobbled into my room. "Don't tell me you're on *her* side."

"We're all on the same side," I said, closing the door.

*

I couldn't sleep. Too many thoughts ran through my head: memories of the battle, the words Alyssa had said, anticipation for the bonding ceremony in the morning. The itching of my wound as it finished healing.

And the voices that returned.

They'd been coming and going like mosquitoes for the past few days. At first it had seemed like my own internal monologue, giving voice to the thoughts inside my head. But then a second voice had joined in, and the two of them began arguing over actions. They were whispers at the edge of my hearing, like if I only whirled around quickly enough I could catch them.

The madness from the Dragon bond being fractured. Danni's death echoing forward into the future.

Do it, one of the voices purred to me, seductive and intoxicating. *Pick up the rune. Put out the fire.*

I opened my eyes with horror: fire crawled up the walls of my room, spreading faster than was natural. The wood walls popped and cracked, and a tapestry fell away from its mount in a heap of embers. In the blink of an eye the flames moved across the ceiling, nearly enveloping everything.

Use your frostwave rune, the voice insisted like a lover. *Save yourself, save all of them, before the blaze consumes the entire city.*

The hallucination looked so real that I almost surrendered to it. Every instinct demanded I scramble to my runepouch on the ground and trace. It was practically a compulsion. Only with great willpower did I manage to pick out the details that ruined the illusion. The walls couldn't crackle because they were made of stone, not wood. Flames didn't move like liquid. And I couldn't feel the heat, which should have been roasting me like a winter goose.

It's not real, I insisted, and I wasn't sure if I was arguing with the voice inside my head or myself. *I am imagining it.* I blinked, and the flames were gone.

I lay in bed for a long while, waiting for my pulse to quiet. When my mind finally returned to some semblance of calm, I knew I wouldn't be able to sleep.

My leg was stiff as I hobbled back out into the hall. By the time I reached the outer courtyard of the city, nestled between the keep and the massive outer walls that ringed the capitol, I almost felt normal again. The city was alive despite the late hour. Crowds of Archenon citizens walked among the shops and stands. Children weaved in and out of the throng, their bedtime a mere suggestion. Music drifted from two different taverns, and the air was filled with the smell of spiced meat. Two men stumbled into a wine sink while laughing and singing along with the musician inside, content to continue their merriment until they ran out of coin or were told to leave.

I picked a direction and walked aimlessly for a while, savoring the chaos of it all. Despite the thousands of rotting Silithik husks outside the walls, people went about their chores and tasks. No matter how many soldiers or Dragons had perished in the defense of the city, life moved on. The people were eager to celebrate living to see another sunrise. It was a sobering reminder of why being a Dragon was important.

After a while, I realized I was searching for something. Not a distraction from the madness creeping closer in my mind, but something specific. A place where I could relieve the urges crowding my brain.

Once I realized what I was doing, I felt silly for looking. It was downright embarrassing for one of my profession. If any other Frost Magi saw me, or learned of what I intended...

I shook my head. I needed to stop this. Considering my options was fine, but only to plan ahead. Obsessing over what could not be controlled was a pointless affair.

But this can be controlled, said a voice, and I couldn't tell if it was the madness or my own voice. *You can return to your room right now. You can give up this foolish errand.*

The crowds thinned as I moved farther from the district filled with taverns and wine sinks. I was somewhere on the west side of the city, but I wasn't exactly sure where. I scanned the rows of shacks and lean-tos attached to the outer city walls, reading the signs hanging above the doors. An apothecary. Next to that was a discount jeweler who dealt entirely in second-hand brass. The next two structures were abandoned, followed by a leather worker. None of them were the establishment I desired.

A cluster of young women in evening dresses giggled as they walked by, sending sideways glances my way. I should have worn an inconspicuous robe rather than my Dragon uniform, allowing me to avoid such stares. Attention was something I typically abhorred, along with crowds. If given the choice, I would choose a quiet corner in a library over a raucous tavern every time.

I was definitely lost, I decided. A man leaning against a trash barrel smoking a pipe met my eye; he nodded approvingly. He looked like the kind of man who would know where to find what I was looking for. I could ask directions, but that would mean telling him where I was going. I'd rather continue wandering than give voice to my destination. As if that made the entire ordeal more palatable.

I was about to give up when I saw it.

I ducked into an alley, then slowly peered around the corner. The dilapidated brick-and-beam structure across the road sent an excited flurry through my gut. A light glowed inside the single bubbled glass window, flickering faintly in the night. Dangerous and inviting.

She is home.

Only a handful of citizens occupied the street, and most of them looked drunk. Too drunk to care what a single Frost Mage was doing with his free time. Despite that, I needed several minutes to work up the courage. I hobbled out of the alley and across the cobblestone road, the click of my crutch announcing every step. I kept my eyes on the building as if that could shield me from suspicious eyes. As if that could hide the dark sin I courted this night.

I reached the door. The woman inside took customers at all hours of the day, and the candle in the window meant she was not with anyone now. I knew this from the first time I'd called on her, long ago. When I was a younger, weaker man.

All I had to do was knock. Rap my knuckles on the door. The wind blew my robe around my ankles as I hesitated.

"Blessed are the Dragons!"

I whipped my head around as a drunk woman approached. Her dress hugged her hips nicely and showed too much cleavage, and her cheeks were rosy with cheer.

"I..." I began.

She grabbed my face with two hands and kissed me on each cheek, then pulled back to get a better look at me. Her heavy eyes and sour breath spoke of an evening full of wine. "The city is saved!" she slurred. "Tell me, Mage: how many of the bugs did you slay yourself? A hundred? A thousand?"

"Only Shadows count their kills," I said curtly. "Now if you will excuse me..."

The woman looked around, realizing where we were. Her eyes lit up. "Paying a visit to Lady Anis tonight?"

"No!" I sputtered.

"Never seen one of your kind visit her, I haven't."

"I was only passing by when you accosted me."

"There's no need to be embarrassed." The girl put her hand on her ample bosom. "I myself visit Lady Anis once a month, when I have the itch. There's no shame in it. What do you desire from her this night? A palm reading? Or perhaps you need her to peer through the aether to speak with a deceased relative?" Her eyes sparkled. "Or a dead lover?"

I took a step back. "Frost Magi have no need to visit fortune tellers. All of them are frauds, and show only what the customer desires to see. Men and women of my profession pride themselves on *logic*."

"Frauds?" the girl said, playfully offended. "Last month, based on the alignment of the stars and the direction of the wind, Lady Anis predicted tragedy would befall my brother. Three days later, Orren fell from a tree and broke his arm." She nodded as if that was all the proof she needed.

"I need to go," I said.

"Hey, wait! Let me buy a hero a cup of wine. And maybe a dance..."

I hobbled away from the woman and the fortune teller's shop, upset at myself for even entertaining the idea.

8

Alyssa

"I'm sorry for pouncing on you last night."

Jaxon's voice rumbled in his chest, a whisper and a roar all at the same time. I liked the way it vibrated through my nude body, which was pressed against his underneath the bed sheet. The hair on his legs tickled mine as he shifted slightly.

"Is that a joke?" I purred back.

"I... Why would it be?"

"Well," I said, "if you failed to notice, I didn't exactly mind you pouncing on me."

He chuckled. "I've always possessed a ravenous lust after battle. Food, melon wine, and then coupling with a woman." He stroked my hair. "A gorgeous woman with hair like fire."

I grinned at the compliment, ignoring that his past memories of such things were with other women, or occasionally his former Pyromancer Danni, whose hair wasn't red at all. I didn't care about any of that. As desperate as Jax had been for me, I was equally hungry for him. Perhaps he was right: a brush with death made one yearn for base desires. Taking solace in each other's bodies was a reminder that we were *alive*. I'd read about such things in books, and other students whispered about it in the various Academies, but I had always thought it was an exaggeration.

"I'm also sorry for not obeying your command," he said.

I paused. "What command?"

His fingertips caressed down my spine, then back up. "You commanded me not to move. I did my best to obey, but in the end relented to the beast inside my loins."

I giggled. "The beast inside your loins? You should write poetry."

The jerk of Jax's body was immensely satisfying. "Poetry? Me?"

"Why not? The toughest men often possess the most tender minds." I shook my head gently. "Regardless, I accept your apology. Truth be told, I loved the way you took me in the end, guiding me with your arms. I love how strong you are." I traced my finger along his chest.

Jax sighed as if relieved. "So you did enjoy it?"

"I thought the volume of my cries made it obvious, but yes, I enjoyed it very much so."

"You weren't wishing I was a slender Frost Mage with hair as fair as a maiden?"

I threw myself up onto one elbow to frown down at Jax. "Why would..." I sputtered. "That's... I don't..."

"You and Arthur seemed to share a moment earlier. How was his touch?"

"He was healing me! Nothing more!"

It was his turn to laugh at my reaction. "Only a joke, sweet one. You are easy to tease."

I punched him in the arm. "And you're not funny."

He pulled me back on top of him, kissing me on the tip of my nose. Then he grew serious. "I meant what I said last night. I am not a jealous man. If you develop feelings for my Quintmates, as is common after a bonding, then all the better." He poked me in the arm. "And like I said last night, that is *not* meant to pressure you in any way. Only a reminder to follow your heart with what feels natural."

None of this felt natural. Well, being with Jax did. But nothing else. The idea of being with more than one man at a time filled me with unease.

Yet his suggestion sent a tingle of curiosity up my spine.

"So," I said, looking for a change of subject. "Your eye." I pointed to the bloody orb, which held not a speck of white.

"It's impolite to point out one's flaws," Jax said with a smile.

"I thought Warriors reveled in their battle wounds, a story behind each one."

"Fair enough. What about it?"

"You've never told me how you got it."

"Because it's not an exciting story," he said.

"I'd like to hear it all the same."

His eyes focused on the ceiling for a moment, and then he let out a deep breath. "It occurred at Ranjupai Stronghold. On the border to the north-west. The Silithik had sent a quick skirmish across the border, and had managed to capture the Governess while she was touring the outer defenses. Silithik do not *capture* us alive, and we did not know why they wanted her alive. Our Quint intercepted the cluster of beetles as they carried her toward the Borderlands. We cut through them to reach her, and I lost my sword in the fight. When we arrived at the beetle carrying the Governess, it dropped her to the ground and raised its claws high, determined to slay her if they could not capture her alive. I threw myself in front of the blow, which caught me on the side of the head and bruised my eye. And then I was awarded a medal of valor upon returning to Ranjupai Stronghold. The Governess erected a statue in my honor."

"Flaming hell," I whispered. "That's unbelievable!"

Jax barked a laugh. "Of course it's unbelievable—it is not true! The actual story involved one of Maze's steam contraptions exploding unexpectedly while we were patrolling a forest to the east." He lightly smacked his cheek with a palm. "A piece of brass debris hit me here and broke my jaw and orbital bone. Those wounds healed, but the eye did not."

I playfully shoved him. "You flaming fool! I believed your first story."

That only made the massive man laugh harder. "I don't know how you did! How would a beetle even carry a Governess away?"

"Perhaps it could hold her upright in its claws? I don't know! Stop making fun of me!"

Jax patted the air with a palm. His face was still an amused shade of red. "Yes. Fine. Of course. I would never make fun of you. That is terribly rude."

"While you're confessing things: you still haven't explained what you meant last night," I said. "Regarding Ryon jeopardizing the bonding ceremony."

In the blink of a bloody eye, Jax's face became serious. "It was nothing."

"Tell me! Are Dragons supposed to keep secrets from one another? Or do I need to pull every speck of information from you, like the story about your eye?"

"It's not a secret," he said.

"Then you can tell me." I punched the bed with a fist like an angry toddler. "Tell me tell me *tell me!*"

Jax stretched his arms behind him, his joints popping like snapped twigs. "The bonding can be rejected if one of the members does not accept it."

"Wait, *rejected?* You mean the bonding ceremony isn't guaranteed to succeed?"

Jax blinked rapidly, suddenly embarrassed as if he'd revealed too much information. "No. I mean, not really. The vast majority of ceremonies are successful. Only in the rarest of occasions, if one harbors anger or resentment in their heart, does it fail."

"Such as a Shadow resenting a girl for replacing his previous Pyro?" I pointed out.

"I did not intend to make you worry, Alyssa. I'm sure it will be fine."

I swung my legs to the side of the bed and grabbed my clothes. "Why did you have to tell me that right before the ceremony!"

Jax made a choking sound. "You asked! Demanded, even!"

"You still didn't have to tell me!" I threw on my clothes. "I'm going to take a bath before the ceremony, then change into a clean uniform."

"Alyssa..."

I slipped from the room on bare feet. The grey sky outside the window hinted at the coming dawn. As I walked down the hall, I replayed last night's interaction with Ryon. He probably *wanted* the bonding to fail so he could go on his Honor March. So he could avenge Danni.

Deep down, I wondered if Jax secretly wanted the same thing.

I made my way to the bath, hoping the scalding water would calm my mind.

9

Arthur

I sat on the edge of my bed and pulled on my boots, tying the laces around my ankle. Every action this morning held exaggerated importance. Fetching my morning tea from a servant, stirring two spoonfuls of rose honey into the murky liquid. Rinsing my face and neck from the cool washbasin to remove the grime of sleep, then brushing the knots from my long hair. Hanging my clean Dragon robe from a peg on the wall. Retrieving a flat steel iron, heating it in a coal brazier, and then using the flat stone of the wall to run the iron across the uniform to remove the wrinkles.

I could have asked Alyssa for help with the latter. One spell from her would be far easier than heating the iron with a brazier. But seeing her prior to the ceremony felt... invasive. As if we were a pair of adolescents avoiding one another on the day of our wedding.

Had it been this way with Danni? I couldn't remember how I felt, but the ceremony itself was fresh in my mind. We had all been so young, then. Scarcely older than Alyssa was now, with only a few years of combat under our belts. Each of us had been immeasurably excited to be bonded into a Dragon Quintelaide. We didn't know each other before the bonding, except for Maze and Harry, who had spent a year together patrolling the coast of the Sunrise Sea. We were all strangers.

Today felt different. I knew everyone in the Quint intimately. Even though Alyssa was new, we had gone to battle together, and nearly perished together.

And instead of excitement tinged with fear, the way I'd felt all those years ago, today I felt relief tinged with acceptance. Our previous Dragon bond was tainted. The missing piece was like broken glass mixed in with a bowl of oats, ruining every bite. I was relieved to cure the part of me that was broken. If such a thing *could* be cured, which remained to be seen. Alyssa gave me hope.

Flaming die.

I opened my runepouch and checked the individual tablets, ensuring everything was in its proper place. I'd had the dream again last night. Galloping across a ridge line toward a mountain peak, smoke from a thousand fires tainting the perfect sky. In the dream I dismounted, and then a Silithik driller hit us with a barrage of chitinous spikes. I tried to buy time for my wounded Quintmate, a fire-haired Pyromancer who had taken a jagged spike to the shoulder. "Flaming die!" she screamed, a curse and a taunt all at once while she traced with her wounded arm and launched balls of smoldering death from her fingertips.

In the past, the Pyromancer was someone I didn't recognize. It was never Danni. But when I dreamed last night, I was nearly certain that the woman was Alyssa. It *felt* like her. Was reality mixing with the dream? The familiarity of a recent battle fitting roughly into the groove of my memory, creating a self-fulfilling prophecy? Because if that dream was a prophecy, destined to come true, then the other dream...

I wished I'd been able to visit Lady Anis without interruption. As embarrassing as it was for a Frost Mage to visit someone who told fortunes, I wasn't sure how else to approach the problem. I didn't know if books on the subject even existed. I'd never looked for them in the libraries. Such superstitions had existed longer than the Archenon itself. Surely someone had taken the time to put ink to paper. Perhaps I could bribe a servant to search for such a book in the library so I wouldn't risk getting caught myself.

The knock on my door was soft, yet still made me flinch. "Is it time?" I called.

There was a hesitation. "It's me," Alyssa answered. "May I come in?"

Her voice excited me in a shocking way, and I leaped from the bed to open the door. Alyssa's hair was so wet it was almost black, hanging on her shoulders and sending rivulets of water down her arms. She wore only a towel, which revealed a splay of her bosom and legs that were long and smooth.

"Hello," I said, feeling myself blush.

"Hi yourself," she said. My blush must have been obvious, because she casually lifted the towel to cover more of her chest. "Can I ask a favor of you?"

"Of course," I immediately said.

"I hope I don't offend you..."

"You couldn't offend me if you tried." I kept my eyes firmly on her face. *Stars above, what could she want from me?*

Her mouth pressed into a thin line. "Do you have a hairbrush I can borrow?"

A hairbrush? The request was so simple that I almost didn't understand. "Of course," I said, leaning into the room to grab the brush next to the wash basin. "Why would that request offend me?"

She shrugged one shoulder, which made the towel slip a few inches. "I only assumed you have a proper brush because your hair is so silky and flawless." Alyssa smiled. "That is not the kind of compliment men typically expect to receive."

"I would hope my hair looks flawless," I replied. "I take care to brush it every morning! Pointing out such a thing would not offend

71

me, Alyssa."

"Thank you." She lifted the brush appreciatively. "I have to get ready. Wouldn't want to be late to my own flaming Dragon ceremony, huh?"

Before I could think of something clever, she was gone.

I peered out into the hall to watch her tip-toe back to her room, closing the door softly. Her feet had left wet footprints on the stone floor. Did she honestly think flattery of that kind would *offend* me?

Flaming die, I heard the woman in my dream say, similar to the curse Alyssa had just used. The two voices sounded identical.

I shook my head. I needed to focus on the immediate future first: the ceremony, then our marching orders. Only then, if I had the time, could I worry about a dream and whether or not it was a prophecy.

I left the door open and went back to arranging my runetablets, finding comfort in the simple ritual.

10

Alyssa

A fist banged at my door for the third time. "Alyssa..." Jax warned from the other side.

"Almost done!" I said, peering at myself in the mirror.

"You said that the last time I asked. The others are already waiting."

I dipped my hand in the rosewater and touched the left side of my neck, then the right. I hated girls who obsessed over their appearance. I'd been surrounded by them at the Academy, especially the fourth and fifth, when many of the girls in my class cared more about the opposite sex than they did about their own training. So long as a woman was clean and tidy, any effort beyond that felt like an unhealthy waste of time.

But today was different. This was my Dragon bonding! An event I was so unlikely to experience that I'd never even allowed myself to fantasize about it. And now that the day was here, I felt inadequate in every way: physically and emotionally and *sorcerously*. I was replacing their old Pyromancer. Ryon, and maybe some of the others, still looked at me with skepticism. And since I couldn't fix any of those doubts, I focused on what I could control: my appearance. Because if I looked extra professional, extra beautiful, it just might make up for my shortcomings as a runetracer.

I took one final look in the mirror, decided I'd done enough, and opened the door.

Jax had his fist raised like he was about to bang again. He lowered it and looked me up and down, his bloody eye widening along with his good one.

"Alyssa," he breathed. "You look stunning."

I turned around to close the door so Jax wouldn't see my silly grin. By the time I turned back around I had hidden it. "You don't need flattering compliments anymore. You've already taken me to bed."

"No flattery, only truth," he said. Then he hugged me, squeezing me to his chest with strong arms. He pulled back and said, "The bonding ceremony is going to be fine."

I couldn't tell if he sounded worried, or if I was projecting my own concerns onto him. He took me by the arm like we were a couple leaving for a formal ball. But we walked in mutual silence as we mentally prepared for what was to come.

We weaved through the stone corridors of the keep, passing servants and other Dragons who had returned to defend the capital city when the Silithik bore down upon it. Every hallway and room looked identical to the last, and I wondered how Jax could tell them apart. We climbed three flights of stairs and entered a part of the keep that held fewer servants, and that had walls adorned with older, yet more extravagant tapestries. Finally, we came to a massive wooden door, jet black and smoothed with age. A guard stood on either side, razor-sharp halberds held at the ready.

"Hail, Ninety-First!" the one on the left intoned.

The other guard added, "Be welcome, saviors of the Archenon!"

Their adoration was so enthusiastic and raw that it almost

seemed sarcastic. They stared straight ahead, as if not worthy of meeting our gazes.

"We arrived late to the battle," I said, feeling uncomfortable. "Our contribution was minimal at best."

The one on the left flicked his eyes at me, then away again. "My apologies for not being clear, Pyromancer. I was referring to your discovery of the Silithik tunnels burrowing through our territory. And your defense of the fifth Academy."

"We won a battle for the capitol yesterday," the other added. "But your Quint won a battle for the entire Archenon!"

I didn't much feel like a hero. Technically, I wasn't even a bonded Dragon yet. But their compliments filled me with pride nonetheless.

"May the Archon watch over you," Jax said, opening the huge door.

The bonding room was circular, possessing only a pale stone pedestal in the center. A single window in the shape of a five-sided pentagon occupied the far wall, and high overhead was a dome made of brilliant colored glass in shades of orange, red, and purple. Stone tiles comprised the floor of the room, all of them grey except for the area near the pedestal itself. The tiles there were shiny black like obsidian, with gold stones forming perfect circles. Six gold circles arranged symmetrically around the pedestal. One for each profession.

I'd been here once before, under completely different circumstances. On the night I'd intended to flee the capitol, and my responsibilities. Instead, I'd been caught by the others, forced to pretend it was my intention to travel north with them. That was when I realized they intended to abandon me as well and go on their own.

It had worked out for the best, but the pain I'd felt that night was as fresh as a *fireball* burn.

"Do you remember the first time we were here?" Maze asked. I turned to find him and Harry against the wall by the door, with

Arthur staring at the ground in thought. Ryon was missing, though the others didn't seem concerned by his absence.

"Of course I remember," Harry said. "How could I forget?"

Maze shook his head. "No, I specifically mean the thing you'd said to the bonding runemaster." He chuckled. "That comment kept us laughing for days."

Harry's confusion deepened. "I have no idea what you mean."

Maze looked to Jax for confirmation. The big Warrior smiled and pointed to the window. "You blurted out that the window should be a hexagon, not a pentagon, so as to match the number of professions in a Quint."

"I did no such thing!" Harry replied.

Maze was already sputtering with laughter. "Aye, you did! The bonding runemaster asked if you'd actually graduated from the Academies, or if you were an impostor who'd snuck into the room!"

Harry's mouth hung open as we all shared in the laughter, even me. The history of Dragon Quintelaides was one of the first things students learned at the Academy. The six professions were originally five, before runetracer was split into two specialties: Pyromancer and Frost Mage. Despite the change being made more than a century ago, remnants of the old way were everywhere, whether in the word *Quint* meaning *five* in the root tongue, or Pyromancers and Frost Magi sharing a wing in the Academies, or in the five-sided window here in the bonding room.

Maze put an arm around Harry's shoulder and patted him on the chest. "Fear not, brother. I'm sure I've blocked out plenty of my own embarrassing memories."

"Such as the time you tried inventing a faster spider mine?" Arthur said, the tiniest smile crossing his face.

"I remember that incident just fine!" Maze jabbed a finger in his direction. "And I paid the farmer for the damage done to his barn."

"And half his field of melons," Jax said.

"Don't forget the nine chickens!" Harry added.

"Oh aye, the chickens," Jax nodded. "Nothing left but charred feathers blowing in the wind."

Maze glowered at everyone playfully, which made them laugh harder. The mood was light and fun. Friends teasing one another before going to battle.

"If you're going to treat this as a joke," Ryon said as he strode into the room, "then maybe we can hire a court jester to perform the ritual instead of the runemaster."

All levity disappeared as if he'd sucked it from the room. Maze cleared his throat. "A Shadow I once knew liked to claim all the world was a joke, as long as you were willing to laugh in the face of death."

Ryon's face was a mask behind a mop of charcoal hair. "Sounds like something a young, naive Shadow would say."

"There is deep truth in humor," Jax rumbled softly.

"And deep foolishness as well." Ryon crossed his arms and paced the room as if we weren't there.

We all milled around while waiting. It was only a few minutes, but felt like hours, until the Archon's runemaster arrived. He was a portly man whose baggy robe fit snug around his barrel of a belly, and with a narrow crown of hair that left most of his head bald. A leather satchel hung from one shoulder, bouncing against his hip. He closed the door behind him and turned to face us.

"The Ninety-First Dragon Quintelaide," he said in a surprisingly high-pitched chirp. He spread his gloved hands. "It feels as though it was yesterday when I first bonded you."

"Time has passed quickly," Jax said at the same time Ryon muttered, "A lifetime ago."

"The past four years have been noteworthy in many ways," Arthur said amicably.

"Hmm. Yes." The runemaster locked onto me and stepped forward. "You must be Alanna. I'm honored to have heard much about you, dear. I'm Runemaster Altonio, personal runetracer to the Archon."

"The honor is mine," I said, glancing at Jax. He gave a small shake of the head to indicate it wasn't worth correcting the man. Even at arm's length I could smell the sour wine on his breath, and I realized his good cheer was actually a result of still being tipsy from the previous night. *I hope his current state does not affect the ceremony.*

Altonio clapped his hands together. "It is time. Please take your places." He gestured at the pedestal in the center of the room. I followed the others, who seemed to know which gold circle belonged to which profession. I approached the remaining one, where I saw a jagged flame carved into the stone circle, so faded with age that it was almost invisible. My legs tingled as I stepped on the surface. Only my imagination, surely.

"Will the ceremony be different than last time?" Harry asked.

"Oh, not at all! No difference whatsoever," Altonio said, approaching the pedestal at the center. The six of us were arranged in a ring around him. "And no need to worry. I have supreme confidence this will be as routine a ceremony as has ever been performed in this. If *any* bonding ceremony can be called routine, that is."

He carefully lowered his satchel to the ground and opened the flap. With his two gloved hands he removed a single object from inside: a sphere of dark grey stone. Slightly larger than a human skull, it was covered with lines like a maze. Altonio lowered it heavily to three silver prongs jutting upwards out of the pedestal, rotating it until he was satisfied with its position. Then he removed his gloves, tucking them carefully into his robe pocket.

"There will be no complications?" Arthur asked. "From our... situation?"

"None whatsoever!" Altonio repeated, giving us a reassuring nod. I wasn't sure if his confidence was genuine, or merely a facade to keep us calm.

"How can you be certain?" Arthur insisted. "We were told this has never been done before."

"If you are not confident in the ability of the Archon's own runemaster," Altonio said bluntly, "then you are free to leave this place."

Arthur looked like he wanted to ask more questions, but then Altonio cleared his throat ceremoniously.

"The bonding procedure is simple," he said, now speaking directly to me. "I am but a conduit for the ceremony, initiating the runemagic and nothing more. The bonding is up to you six, and you six alone. The analogy I typically use is that it is similar to taming a wild horse. Do not force it. Relax, allow it to happen, and then everything will be done." He gave a final nod. "You have three hours."

Three hours? I opened my mouth to ask how it could last so long, but before I could, he touched the orb on the pedestal with both hands.

The surge of runemagic was tremendous, several orders of magnitude more powerful than anything I had ever witnessed. It gushed from the ground like a geyser, up into the sphere before splitting into six branches, streaking across the ground and around the gold circles. Then the runemagic was a torrent invading through my feet and into my body, and every muscle I possessed tensed, and the air rushed from my lungs. My nerves were on fire, my skin lanced away and my body dipped in salt water, a blinding pain that blocked out all other thought, and then the runemagic clenched me in a massive fist and threw me into the air.

In an instant, the rush of runemagic was gone.

I blinked.

The ceremony chamber had been replaced by a white room. No, not a room: there were no walls, no ceiling, no *anything* at all. The white extended endlessly in every direction. I looked down at my feet and couldn't see the ground on which I stood. Everything was calm and quiet. A peace fell over me more complete than anything I had ever felt in my life.

Was I dead? Was this the afterlife, where our souls flew into the night sky to become stars? I wanted to call out, but disturbing the beautiful silence felt obscene.

"Alyssa."

I turned to find Jax to my left, smiling faintly. I sighed with relief.

Arthur appeared next, stepping out from behind Jax as if he'd been there the entire time. Maze followed behind him, then Harry. Lastly, Ryon strode into the white space, glowering at everything.

"Incredible," Arthur whispered, eyes wide like a child's as he looked all around. "Even the second time, it takes one's breath away. Simply incredible."

"Ryon, what—" Jax said, cutting off suddenly. The Shadow was leaning over something that hadn't been there a moment before: a grey stone slab laying on the not-ground, roughly two paces long. Intricate flowers and vines were carved into the slab, beautiful in a haunting way that confused me. Harry stepped up to it and put a hand to his mouth. Maze gasped and removed his welding goggles from his forehead.

The five of them clustered around it, blocking my view.

"What is it?" I asked. My voice echoed strangely in this place. Too faint and too loud at the same time. "What are you looking at?"

I took two steps before Ryon jabbed a finger at me without looking. "Don't come any closer!" he hissed. I stopped dead in my tracks.

"Ryon..." Jax began.

"No, Jaxon! Not here. Not now."

Jax shifted, and I caught a glimpse of what had horrified them so. A body lay on the stone slab, the black and gold Dragon uniform clearly visible over the curve of breast. I knew who it was instantly.

Danni. Their previous Pyromancer.

"Why is she here?" Maze whispered. "Why are we tormented so?"

Arthur stroked his chin with scholarly curiosity. "Perhaps her body represents the part of our previous bonding that is tainted."

Harry took a shuddering breath, and held his head in his hands to steady himself. "I wasn't prepared for this."

"None of us were," Jax said, steeling himself. "But it is time to move on. With the ceremony. With our lives."

Slowly, each of them turned away from the body of their deceased Pyromancer. Ryon was the last, still leaning over the stone with his fingers gripping the edge tightly. His shoulders rose and fell with each deep breath.

"Ryon," Jax said gently.

"I cannot," he said, an admission rather than his usual defiance. "Jaxon, brother. I cannot do this."

"*You* cannot," Arthur said, his normally cold voice surprisingly soothing. "Any one of us individually would be unable to stand it, that is certainly true. But we can suffer it together if each of us shares the burden."

"Aye, each of us sharing the grief," Maze added.

Ryon pushed himself away from the stone, finally turning to face the others. The five of them moved together, spreading their arms in a group hug. They held themselves there, heads bent together, for a long moment. The silence of their pact spoke volumes.

Then they broke apart and arranged themselves in a line facing me. I stood very still as Jax strode forward by himself. The others watched silently. I was afraid of what that meant.

"Alyssa," Jax whispered, taking both of my hands in his. I was shocked to see that his left eye was not filled with blood: in this strange place, it was as white as if it had never been wounded. "I already have a stronger connection with you than I ever had with... anyone else. For me, this bonding is nothing more than a formality." He kissed me softly on the lips, smiled, and then returned to the others.

Harry came forward next, a determined look on his face. He paused at arm's length. "You can never replace Danni. You *can't*. But I'm beginning to realize that is fine. You don't need to replace

81

her. You're your own woman, your own Pyromancer. And I hope you will succeed with us. No, I *know* you will."

Maze was next, walking on two legs of flesh instead of a mechanical one. Seeing him approach with a normal stride, rather than his unnatural gait, made me smile.

"I, uhh..." He stared down at the not-ground like a boy sheepishly trying to ask a girl to dance. He ran a hand through his mop of blond hair. "I already know we make a good team. Expect we'll kill a lot of bugs together. Looking forward to it." He clapped me on the shoulder, then moved aside with a relieved sigh.

Only two remained. Arthur looked at Ryon, waiting for him. The Shadow took a single step forward, then abruptly stopped. He shook his head back and forth.

"No," he moaned, voice thick with pain. "No, you can't make me, I don't want to forget *her*..." He turned back to look at Danni's body.

"Ryon, you *must*," Arthur insisted. "If the bonding fails..."

Ryon trembled where he stood, head still twisted to look at the dead Pyromancer. He looked like he would stand there forever.

So I stepped forward instead.

"Ryon," I said gently. I touched his arm and he whipped back around, but instead of anger in his eyes it was pain. "I know I am not her. I'll never be anything close to what she was. But if you'll let me, I can try to be something new. Maybe a sister instead of... Instead of what she meant to you."

The words were ridiculously inadequate, a droplet of comfort falling into an ocean of grief. As soon as they left my tongue, I wished I could have them back. I knew Ryon would rage against them, against me, against the entire unfair situation.

But Ryon blinked, and a single tear rolled down his cheek from the eye hidden by his wave of hair. His head trembled in a nod, and that was enough. I took his hand in mine, squeezed it once, and stepped away to let Ryon be by himself.

And then there was Arthur.

The Frost Mage stared at me, a curious look on his face. Like he'd been considering a puzzle for the better part of an hour and was close to figuring it out. He approached, his black Dragon robe swishing around his legs and his yellow hair swaying against his shoulders.

"I think you have great promise," he said, for all the world sounding like a professor giving a student their grade after an exam. "I look forward to helping you grow." He leaned forward and kissed me on the cheek, his lips leaving a cool, wet sensation.

Warmth filled my chest like a ball of flame, accompanied by a feeling of success. I swung my gaze around me, looking at the five men who accepted me, who were—

The white light changed, shifted, broke apart. A howling sound rose all around us, filling my ears.

Something is wrong.

The endless white nothing had been replaced by walls of black, walls that closed in and sucked away the light. I looked to Jax but he was nothing more than a lifeless statue of himself, the features of his face smooth and frozen. Then cracks appeared on his hard cheeks, spiderwebbing down his marble neck, and the pieces crumbled and became dust that floated away on an invisible wind.

I reached out a hand to catch the pieces, but my own fingers were grey and lifeless. I was a statue as well. With horror, I watched cracks appear along my hand and wrist. The black walls were closing in rapidly, and the smell of decay was so overpowering that I thought I would gag.

I opened my mouth to scream.

11

Alyssa

The sensation was like coming up for air after being submerged for too long: I gasped, and shivered, and listened to my heart drumming in my ears.

We were back in the bonding chamber, arranged in a circle around the pedestal and Runemaster Altonio. Sunlight streamed through the single five-sided window, illuminating the pedestal. I sensed the runemagic retreating back into the sphere, and then dissipating into the air all around us until it was no more.

I put a hand to my cheek and was happy to touch flesh. I could still feel Arthur's lips there. It had all been so real.

"It worked?" Altonio said, relieved. "Thank the runes, it actually *worked.*"

I blinked and gazed around the ceremony room. I felt... different. Not bad, or good. Just different. I couldn't tell why.

And then Jax moved.

He stepped out of his circle to the left, wrapping an arm around my waist to steady me as if I might faint. I didn't just feel his hand on my back: I felt my own body *through his hand.* He looked into my eyes and smiled, warm and loving and happy all at once.

Except the feelings didn't come from his eyes. They came from my head. A part of my mind I hadn't known existed; a door that had been opened and was letting new feelings inside. I could sense his emotions as if they were my own.

"Yes," Jax said. "Relax. It can take some getting used to."

One by one, I looked at my Quintmates, each time feeling the invisible bond settling into place. Arthur was the bundle of curiosity in the back of my head, examining me for my reaction. I could also sense he was over-analyzing the kiss he'd planted on my cheek, whether it was too forward or not personal enough for such a moment. Maze looked down at his mechanical leg: a trickle of sadness blossomed, which quickly shifted into acceptance. Harry's eyes were closed; he was relieved that this was over, or maybe relieved that it had been successful.

And then there was Ryon. The Shadow was a maelstrom of anger and pain and loss. His grief was so strong that it made my chest ache; it felt like he'd just lost Danni all over again. He stared intently at me, searching for something in my eyes I couldn't understand. The emotions pouring from him through the bond made me want to fall to my knees and weep.

Stars above, how can he stand it?

He shook his head and turned away, the hard mask returning to cover what he felt.

Maze stepped toward the Runemaster, his mechanical leg clicking on the tile. "What do ya mean, it actually worked? You told us there would be no complications whatsoever."

"And there weren't!" Altonio said happily, wiping sweat from his brow.

"Your confidence in the procedure is not as strong as you led us to believe," Arthur said. "Are we to assume you had no idea how we would react to a second bonding ceremony? That it may not work at

85

all?"

Altonio frowned. "You are the first Dragon Quintelaide to ever experience a second bonding! Of course we had no idea what to expect."

"We were told you had theories..." Harry said.

The Runemaster barked a laugh. "Oh, aye, I had *theories*. But a theory is only as good as its ability to stand up to rigorous testing, which is why..."

I closed my eyes as he droned on. I felt dizzy. Jax's hand patted my back and he asked, "Are you well?"

"I am, actually," I said. "The sensation is unusual. I'm sure I'll get used to it." I looked up at him. "I *will* get used to it, right?"

"Soon it will be like a second sense," Jax replied. I could feel his desire to stand close to me, as if his proximity could shield me from any trouble. It was comforting knowing that he felt that way about me.

"Does the ceremony usually take longer?" I asked. "He claimed we had three hours, but that lasted only three *minutes*."

Arthur approached us. "The answer to that question is complicated."

"Really? It seemed like a straightforward question."

He smiled knowingly.

I cocked my head at him. "Well? Are you going to explain what that's supposed to mean, or are you being intentionally cryptic?"

The Mage's smile deepened. "Tell me, what is different about the room?"

"Well, for one thing, I'm bonded with five men. Harry is annoyed right now, which is making *me* annoyed. And since I don't have a target for that annoyance, you'll have to do. Tell me why the ceremony only lasted a few minutes."

"Look around the room, Alyssa. Truly *look*."

Instead of arguing more, I sighed and obeyed. There wasn't

much to see. Ryon leaned against the wall by the door, arms crossed and head down. Harry and Maze clustered around the Runemaster, who was talking about runetracer consensus prior to theoretical experimentation. The orb was the same, except for the sunlight bathing it and the lingering echo of the immense amount of runemagic that had just been traced.

I gave a start. *Wait a minute.*

The light on the stone orb was wrong. I followed the beam up to the window. Slanted downward into the room, the light was so bright that it showed every mote of dust that passed through. I had to squint; it made it difficult to focus on other objects in the darker room. I pictured where the sun would have to be on the horizon to create the angle of light.

"She understands, now," Jax mused.

"I'm not sure I do," I said slowly. It felt like someone was pulling a prank on me. "The ceremony was quick, in that strange white place. Yet several hours have passed here? How is that possible?"

"Behold the magic of the unknown." Jax put an arm around me and guided me away from the window. "Best not to think too hard on it just yet. Suffice to say, the power of the Dragon bonding ceremony is mysterious."

Arthur returned to the runemaster and began grilling him about the procedure, and his curiosity ignited my own. I approached the dark sphere on the pedestal. Up close, I could tell it was made of the same grey runestone as the tablets in my pouch; even the grooves carved into its surface were the same shade, slightly lighter than the exterior. I circled the orb, following the lines with my eyes. The desire to trace it with my fingertips was strong. Overwhelming. There had been so much runemagic in the room during the ceremony, a cyclone of it, more than I had ever experienced. I reached out with a hand—

"No!" Altonio snapped. I quickly retracted my hand. "That is immensely powerful, Alanna. It must be traced with both hands simultaneously."

"So it *is* a type of runetablet."

He held up one finger. "A runesphere, to be precise. There are only five in existence. Like runetablets, the effects of an unskilled hand tracing it can release an unstable amount of runemagic. If you attempted to trace it, even for a second, the result would be disastrous. That is why I am entrusted with its protection."

"I've never heard of such a thing," I said. "Why are students not taught this in the Academy?"

"Because there is no need." Altonio pulled on both of his leather gloves and carefully lifted the runesphere off the pedestal. When it was back inside his satchel, he closed the flap and hoisted it onto a shoulder. "Only I possess the skill and training to trace it. Announcing its existence needlessly would only tempt lesser runetracers with its power." He gave me a pointed look.

That didn't make much sense to me. What was the point of keeping it secret if it was eventually made obvious during the bonding ceremony? Secrecy for the sake of secrecy was pointless to me. Knowledge was always valuable. Besides, if there were five such runespheres, where were the other four?

"Come!" Altonio said, cutting off any other questions. "The feast awaits."

*

We were served enough food to feed an army.

The table was built to hold 20 people, but the six of us crowded down at one end, which was covered in bowls made of delicate porcelain so tightly I couldn't see the table surface. Meatballs rolled in cornmeal and fried in oil. Fluffy rice spiced with jasmine and garlic. Chicken loins pounded flat and charred black on the outside, yet so juicy on the interior that grease ran down my lips with every bite. Braised pork shoulder in a melon wine sauce that was tart and sweet on my tongue long after I'd swallowed. Three different types of beans in varying colors of sauce, green and brown and red.

And the bread! Buttery supper rolls, slices of black bread, and crusty trenchers for sopping up gravy. Flaky pastries filled with savory meat sauce. Farther down the table were half a dozen plates of dessert pastries. Maze had gone straight for those; I didn't think he'd eaten anything else.

The room was as ornate as any I'd seen in the capitol. Nestled on the top floor of one of the high towers, the walls were mostly glass showing a wide view in every direction around the city. Even with distant clouds covering the sun, the clear glass filled the room with brightness.

My hunger wasn't only my own: five other ravenous sensations tingled in the back of my head, amplifying my appetite. *This is going to take some getting used to.*

"So," I said after finishing a slice of pork. "What was that place?"

Jax asked, "What place?"

"The place from the ceremony." I gestured with a fork. "With the endless white nothing in every direction."

"White nothing?" Ryon chuckled while slicing a shank of beef.

I felt a mixture of confusion and amusement from the men in my Quintelaide. Maze swallowed his pastry and said, "Oh, it's different for each person."

"What do you mean, different?"

"No two people go to the same place," Jax explained. "They are locations deep within our minds. Created by our imaginations."

I frowned. "But I spoke with you while I was there. Each of you. That wasn't real?"

"Aye, it was real," Harry said. "Arthur, what was it you said about it? Your theory on human subconscious? Arthur?"

The Mage was staring at a bowl of beans like it hid the meaning of life. He blinked and looked up, suddenly aware that everyone was looking at him.

"Oh, I don't remember," he said, returning to the staring contest with his food.

Harry frowned at him a moment longer, then waved a spoon. "Every place is different. Whatever *you* need, the ceremony provides. For example, the ceremony transported me to the archery range at Terrian Stronghold. I shot arrows at a target from an endless quiver for an hour, falling into the relaxing motions. Then the rest of you appeared and remarked on the accuracy of my shooting."

"That starved for compliments, are you?" Ryon teased. Harry elbowed him in the ribs, and Ryon playfully threatened him with his knife.

"I was on a battlefield," Jax announced. "I slew wave after wave of Silithik, and my arm never tired. Yet on they came, each one cut down by my sword."

He looked at the others, waiting for them to chime in. When they didn't, he turned to me and said, "You were in a white place?"

"Yes," I said. "It was like a blank canvas waiting for paint."

"And we were there?" Harry asked. "But nothing else? Nothing at all?"

I didn't need the bond to see how unnerved the others were; each of them had paused their meal to study my face. Like there was something wrong with me.

"Every experience is unique," Arthur said softly. "It is best not to spend too much time analyzing them, or comparing one to another." He looked at me with those crystal blue eyes. "What matters is we are bonded now. Our Quintelaide is once again whole."

I mentally scolded myself. I'd been so focused about my own experience that I'd forgotten the most important reason for doing this in the first place: to stave off their madness. I didn't need to ask: the others nodded along with Arthur, relief pouring through their bonds. I knew it with the same certainty that they did: the ceremony had worked.

"I, for one, am looking forward to our future together." Jax raised his wine glass. "To the Ninety-First Quintelaide."

90

Each of them raised their own, even Ryon after a heartbeat of hesitation. I hoped the blush crawling up my cheeks wasn't obvious as we touched glasses and drank to the future.

"We're something of a battle cry around the capitol," Harry said, refilling his cup from a pitcher sweating with condensation. "Everywhere I go, the guards call out to me, praising the Ninety-First."

"Aye," Maze said. "I went drinking last night at a wine sink. Met up with the Tinkers from the Forty-Eighth and the Hundred-and-Eleventh. When they found out I was the Tinker for the Ninety-First, they shouted my praises to all that would listen, until the entire room was cheering me! I didn't pay for a drink the rest of the night, and I swear I danced with every girl."

"Your rhythm's still intact with that jousting lance for a leg?" Ryon teased.

"Oh," Maze grinned back, "I managed just fine." A burst of sexual lust poured through his bond for a moment, causing me to blush.

"Speaking of the future," I said, "I have another question."

"Alyssa, this isn't the Academy," Harry said. "You don't have to raise your hand before asking a question."

"Although it's a refreshing bit of tact, especially compared to our Shadow's predisposition for interruption," Maze added.

"We're a Dragon Quintelaide," I said.

"Is that what we're doing?" Ryon muttered. "Stating obvious facts?"

"It's also not much of a question," Maze added.

I rolled my eyes. "The beasts we're named after. *Dragons.*" I looked around the table. "Were they real, or just part of mythology?"

Arthur blinked at me. "What leads you to believe we know the answer to this question?"

"Everyone at the Academy believes the truth about them is

learned upon being promoted to a Dragon," I said. "Now that the bonding ceremony is over, and I am an official member of the Quint, I thought you would tell me."

Jax gave me a sympathetic smile. "It is good to know some things never change. Such rumors passed around the Academy when we were students as well. I am sad to say that it is not true. We know as little as you do."

"They're stories to scare children," Ryon said, brushing back his hair. "Who has ever heard of a great winged beast soaring through the air?"

"Gryphons are quite real," Arthur pointed out. "As well as Silithik wasps."

"And dragons were supposedly long enough for a hundred men to ride on their spine," Ryon retorted. "With wings so large that they blocked out the sun. There is a difference between a gryphon and a beast *that* size."

"True," Arthur admitted.

"I believe they were real," Harry suddenly said. "Years ago, I was on a patrol with another Ranger who claimed to have seen the bones of a great winged beast in the borderlands. He said the talons were as long as this table."

I gazed up the length of the table and struggled to imagine something so large.

"I once patrolled with a soldier who believed Father Winter would curse us if we disturbed a patch of freshly-fallen snow," Jax said. "Men exaggerate. Women, too." He smiled at me.

"You don't know whether Dragons were ever real," I teased. "And you don't know anything about the bonding ceremony. Is there anything you *do* know that I haven't already learned at the Academy?"

"I know I'm sick of sitting in the capitol while the war rages on," Ryon growled.

Maze toasted the air with his melon wine. "I'm looking forward to blowing up some bugs!"

"When will we be deployed?" I asked.

Jax sipped his wine. "Field Marshal Tyronix will be giving us marching orders this afternoon, along with the other Quints currently stationed in the capitol. I don't know when we'll leave, but I expect this will be our last luxurious dinner for the foreseeable future."

I chomped into a butter roll and said, "Better get my fill, then."

Everyone dove back into their food with enthusiasm. After finishing my roll and reaching for another, I noticed that Arthur was staring down at his beans again, lost in thought. I tried to think of some conversation to pull him back to the present, but nothing interesting came to mind.

"Where do you suppose they'll send us?" Harry asked.

"Perhaps the east?" Jax said, chewing on a bite of chicken. "That seemed to be where the largest thrust of the Hivemind's attacks are focused."

"I heard the north-west border is crumbling," Maze said. "They'll send us there, mark my words."

"Planning on halting the entire Silithik advance with a single well-placed spider mine?" Harry asked with a grin.

"Oh, aye. Nothing to it. Though perhaps it will take *two* mines."

"Wherever they choose to send us," I said, "the region will be better for it. It's a shame the Silithik lack higher intelligence, or our Quint might have the same fearsome reputation among them as we do among the citizens of the capitol!"

"I wouldn't be so sure," came a voice.

I didn't recognize the thin figure standing in the doorway of the dining room. His withered face ended in a sharp chin, and his eyebrows were like bushy grey caterpillars below an egg-bald head. His cobalt robes were interlaced with silver swirls around the hem and sleeves, and the gaze he swept across the room exuded power. Only when he took another step into the room did his robes shift, giving me a view of the amulet around his neck. An amulet adorned with six separate gems, which only one person in the Archenon wore.

"Lord Archon!" I blurted out. I wracked my brain for the proper way to greet the leader of our nation. Citizens of the Archenon were required to go to one knee, but was the same true for Dragons? None of my Quintmates moved from their seats, although Harry shifted in his chair before stopping himself. *Why do they not show him respect?*

"You wouldn't be sure of what?" Jax asked in a measured tone. "Our reputation among the Silithik?"

The Archon walked into the room slowly, his robes swishing on the floor. He stopped at the head of the table as if it was his place, and his eyes passed over us, never focusing on anyone individually. The smile he wore held no warmth. "I wouldn't be so sure the Silithik lack higher intelligence. They are a Hivemind, after all. Somewhere, deep beyond the Borderlands, is the source of their tactics and larger strategy."

"Not to mention the runetracing Queen," Harry said. "And their ability to trace portals from one location to another."

The Archon waved a thin hand. "I am skeptical of such reports."

"Skeptical?" Jax asked, incredulous. "We brought the Queen's own skin carved off her back to the fifth Academy. It was plain for everyone there to see." A moment later he remembered to add, "Lord Archon."

"Extraordinary claims require extraordinary evidence, *Warrior.*" Somehow the leader of the Archenon made Jax's profession into a curse. "Some scabbed-over swirls on a pus-covered roll of carapace are hardly evidence of anything. Only when my runemaster can reproduce what you *think* you saw will I believe such an impossibility."

"Your runemaster performed the bonding ceremony admirably," Arthur chimed in. "In spite of his doubts that it would work at all."

"Hmm. Yes." The Archon swung his head in a slow nod. I got the impression he was disappointed the bonding was a success, but that couldn't be true. Why would he have ordered it if he thought so? "Now we know such a bonding is possible. This is valuable information. I want to commend you for being so cooperative in this experiment."

"Experiment?" Jax growled. "That is what we are to you?"

"*Jax*," I hissed, shocked that he would speak in such a tone.

"You are loyal servants of the Archenon," the Archon said haughtily. "In spite of your failures—which are indeed considerable—your Quintelaide's strength is needed for the war. But only so long as you obey your commands. For example, if you were given a direct order to bond with a new Pyromancer, and you departed the capitol without doing so, that would be an act of tremendous disloyalty."

Jax lifted his chin. "A simple miscommunication with our marching orders, as we've explained."

"And if your orders were to defend Bracknall Stronghold?" The Archon asked, voice dangerously soft. "It would be difficult to misunderstand such a simple, specific command. Tell me again, Warrior Jaxon of the Ninety-First Quintelaide: how was it that you found yourselves in a Silithik tunnel deep within the Borderlands?" A ghost of a smile touched his thin lips. "Answer carefully. Disobeying a direct order so you could complete an Honor March would be treason."

The tension in the air felt thicker than the carrot gravy from our meal. Jax felt like he was about to explode with anger.

"It was my fault!" I blurted out, jumping to my feet. The Archon's head spun toward me, and I shivered under his intense gaze.

"Aly," Jax warned.

"I was examining the terrain outside Bracknall Stronghold, to determine if any of it could be used to our benefit. My horse was spooked by a scouting beetle, and I was unable to soothe her. She sprinted away with me still on her back. By the time she finally stopped, we were miles from the stronghold."

The Archon held his hands behind his back and narrowed his eyes at me. I returned his gaze as calmly as I could; it felt like he was weighing and measuring me on a set of invisible scales. "Your name?" he asked icily.

"Alyssa."

"Pyromancer Alyssa," he said, looking down his nose at me. "It is a great crime to lie to your Archon. An even greater crime if such a lie conceals another treachery. Perhaps you misspoke? I will give you a chance to amend your statement, if so."

I thought back to that night at the stronghold. I'd visited the battlements, staring out into the unknown. The guard on duty saw me. More in the stables, too. All witnesses who could tell the Archon I was lying. All he had to do was send a single *runemessage* and inquire.

"I did not misspeak," I said, encouraged by the feelings of support pouring through the bond I shared with the five men at the table. "I'm lucky my Quint followed me into the Borderlands and saved me. We were even luckier to stumble upon the tunnels leading into the Archenon. The Academy would have fallen had we not killed the Queen. Our discovery likely saved the capitol itself."

"Do not presume that the victory outside this city was your doing. You are hardly more than a girl." The Archon's wrinkled face twisted with distaste. I braced myself for his rebuke, but instead he regained control of his emotions. "Your Quint has gained quite the reputation in the city. You especially, Pyromancer. They say you slew a Queen, the first human to do so in... well, since anyone can remember."

"An exaggeration," I said. "All of us killed the Queen together. I merely was lucky enough to strike the killing blow."

He nodded smugly. "Ahh, yes. That certainly makes more sense. A Pyromancer fresh from the Academy managing to kill a Queen?" He snorted, then turned to face the others. "I'm sorry Alyssa here was the best graduate we had to offer as a replacement for your Quintelaide. I do wish you the best of luck in the war to come. Hopefully such an unseasoned Pyromancer does not hinder you any further."

The words were more piercing than any wasp stinger. I thought back to Ryon's admonishment regarding my inability to runetrace from horseback, and the shame from the memory was fresh. No matter our success in the end, the Quint was undeniably weaker with me than with a more veteran Pyromancer. Any joy I'd felt from the celebratory feast disappeared.

The Archon nodded as if he'd accomplished what he came here to do. "I'll leave you to your meal."

"Won't you join us?" Ryon said, deadly calm. The hatred coming from his bond was strong enough to frighten me, and his fingers were white on the hilt of his dagger. "The beans are cold by now, but filling."

The Archon's smile was thin. "Another time. Perhaps when you return from wherever your marching orders take you. I wish you good fortune in the battles to come. Keep your blades sharp, *Shadow*." He took one last distasteful look at our group, and then his blue robes swished across the floor as he left.

12

Arthur

I watched the Archon leave the room with a calmness not shared by my Quintmates.

"Bloody fool," Ryon cursed. "I'd love to show him how sharp my blades are." He unsheathed one dagger and used it to spear a roll.

"Don't say such things," Jax warned. "Not aloud. Someone might overhear, and they won't know you are joking."

"Who's joking?" Ryon shot back at him, eyes full of fury.

"What was that all about?" Alyssa asked. "Do you all have a history with the Archon?"

Jax put a hand on her arm. "It started after the first attack on the Academy. The Archon blames us..."

"Where is he going to send us?" Harry asked Maze. "There was a strange tone to his voice. I have a bad feeling about what our orders will be."

I ignored them, staring at my food without seeing. I wasn't concerned where he would send us because I already knew. It was a place I'd seen in my dreams a hundred times before, since I was a child.

It was the same place I'd visited during the bonding ceremony.

The memory was still so fresh and strong that I fell into it easily. The moment the Runemaster had touched the runesphere, I was transported into the middle of a battle. We were in the mountains, on a high plateau looking down into a long valley. A river split the valley in two, and on either side was an endless swarm of Silithik approaching our position.

"Behind you!" Jax shouted. Maze whirled, swinging his sledgehammer in time to catch a beetle across the head, caving it in. Harry was shooting arrows to our right, keeping most of the wasps at bay, but every now and again one got close enough to harass our group. When they did, Ryon leaped into the air and removed their stingers with two rapid swipes of his daggers.

I was focused on tracing, my *blizzard* spell forming in the air above the valley. The jagged bolts of ice that emerged fell heavily to the ground, creating a killing field among the army below. Somewhere to my left was our Pyromancer, a ball of runemagic releasing waves of flame down a tilted approach to our plateau, holding off an entire beetle advance by herself.

"Maze, they're in position!" Jax roared, pointing at the mountain peak with a gauntleted finger. "Do it!"

Maze knocked away another beetle and then hobbled over to the object we guarded: a metal box no larger than a boot, with a slender plunger sticking out of the top. A coil of copper wire ran out of its base and up the mountain ridge toward the peak above, the explosives having been carefully placed in a mine shaft. The Tinker gripped the plunger with both hands, shouted, "Hold on!" and then slammed it into the box to trigger the explosion.

Nothing happened.

Maze stared for a moment, then pulled back the plunger to try again. There was a clicking sound from the box, but no more. He turned a crank on the side of the device, which made a high-pitched *whirring* noise.

"No!" Maze wailed. "It's not working. Why isn't it working?"

"Maze," Jax grunted as he cut a beetle clean in half. "If this is a joke, you've chosen a poor time for it!"

"It's not a joke, damn it all! Something must have cut the cable." He tossed the device down with disgust. "I need to check the line."

The constant pulses of weaponized runemagic to my left abruptly ceased. "Let me go instead," our Pyromancer said, mounting her horse. In past dreams I had assumed it was Danni, but now I could see Alyssa's face clearly. "If I can't find anything wrong with the wire, I can always set them off with a *fireball*."

Jax whirled, his face masked by the steel helm. "Triggering the explosion that close will kill you."

Alyssa brought her horse around. "Not if I aim my *fireball* from a safe distance!"

"I'll help." I ceased my own runetracing and strode to my horse.

"We need your *blizzard* putting a dent in that army," Jax said.

"It won't matter if we can't bring down that mountain," I said. "And Alyssa needs backup!"

I kicked my horse into a gallop, following Alyssa up the path that wound along the ridge line toward the peak. I knew none of this was real; this was a construct of the bonding ceremony, a creation of my subconscious. But it was identical to the dream I'd dreamed a hundred times since I was old enough to have memories, and I could smell the smoke from Alyssa's spells tainting the fresh mountain air. It was difficult not to be swept up in it all.

I wished I could stop myself. I wished I could stop *all* of it. But it always played out the same.

As in the dreams, Alyssa slowed her horse when we were halfway to the peak. She leaped from the saddle and grabbed the length of copper wire, showing me the frayed end.

"That explains why it didn't work," she said, searching the area nearby. "But what caused..."

I knew the Silithik driller was going to emerge from the path ahead, but was unable to do anything but watch. It had a body nearly identical to a Silithik beetle, but instead of four clawed arms, it possessed only two stubby appendages with a single joint each. It needed no such claws because its weapons were hidden within its mouth. The split jaw opened to reveal two fluted teeth, like horizontal fangs that stuck out of its lower mouth. There was a soft hissing noise as the driller launched a volley of spikes, each one as thick as my thumb, and twice as long.

Alyssa dodged them as best as she could, but three of the driller spikes smashed into the boulder next to her, *CRACK CRACK CRACK,* and the fourth caught her on the arm. She screamed and spun sideways, falling to the ground in a heap.

"No!" I yelled, as I always did in the dream. My finger traced the quickest *frostbolt* of my life, striking the driller directly in the chest, impaling it on the rocks behind. Its high-pitched screech drifted down to us as it flailed around with its stubby arms.

"Flaming hell!" Alyssa cursed, getting back to her feet. A chitinous spike stuck out from her shoulder, just beneath the collar bone. She touched it and fell back to the ground, screaming in pain.

"You have to remove it," I said, turning back to the mountain path. Three more drillers appeared over the ridge, pausing when they saw one of their kind speared with a bolt of ice. The *frostspike* I traced struck the boulder, exploding and encasing all of them in a sheen of ice.

"I... I can't remove it," Alyssa said. "Help me!"

I turned to my right, where 50 beetles climbed the slopes toward our position. "As soon as I dispatch these," I said, knowing no such moment would come. I knew this dream like the lines of a sad song: after them would be another dozen drillers at the top of the ridge, and then another wave of beetles up the slope, and by then the wasps would be on us and it would all be over.

But part of me insisted I could win, that maybe this time would be different, so I traced as fast as I could, sending *frostbolts* and *frostspikes* like our lives depended on it. And as the beetles neared us, with the distant wasps growing larger by the second, Alyssa let out a constant stream of curses.

"Die. Flaming die! *Flaming die!*"

*

"Arthur?"

I jerked as if I'd been struck, spilling a spoonful of beans out of the bowl in front of me. Harry had his hand on my arm, and was leaning forward to look up into my face. I was back in the dining room, in the high tower in the capitol. Far from the mountain with the drillers and beetles. Far from my doom.

"Sorry, I was lost in thought."

He nodded at the bowl in front of me. "You gunna eat the beans, or stir them together until they're mushy?"

I let go of my spoon. "I've had my fill." In truth I hadn't eaten much at all, but then again, gluttony wasn't one of my vices. I didn't like the way a heavy stomach dulled my mind.

"I've had my fill and then some." Alyssa leaned back in her chair and patted her belly. "I'm pregnant with food. I feel like a pig."

"You couldn't look like a pig if you tried," I said, trying to rejoin the conversation. Alyssa blushed and warmth trickled through our bond. I didn't know why; I was only speaking the truth.

Jax rose from the table. "We need to leave for the Field Marshal's briefing."

"That's clear across the keep," Maze moaned. "How about I curl into a ball so you can roll me there?"

"I find a long walk helps with digestion," Jax said.

"Easy for you to say. You've got two good legs."

Chairs scraped as we all rose and filed into the hall. The guard posted outside the room hailed us as we passed.

"Arthur," Alyssa said, falling back to walk alongside me. "I meant to tell you. My leg feels almost completely normal now."

"Of course," I said. "Didn't I say it would?"

"Yeah, yeah," she said. "I just wanted to thank you again. For healing me the right way. Even if it did hurt worse than when I earned the wound in the first place."

I imagined her falling to the ground, a driller's spike lodged in her shoulder. "You're welcome."

"Jax told me about the Archon," she continued. "The way he treated you all when Danni died. How he's used you as a scapegoat for his own failings. Hopefully we can change his opinion."

"Oh, yes," I said. I didn't much care what the Archon thought of us, although I was flabbergasted to learn he didn't think much of the Queen's runes we'd brought back. I would need to speak with Runemaster Altonio later to ensure he was giving it the proper study it deserved.

I didn't want to ramble on to Alyssa, though, so instead I said, "The bonding ceremony. You were in a white room? Like a blank canvas?"

She nodded. "It was the strangest thing. My feet were obviously standing on something, but there was just... *nothing*. And not in the way a dream is fuzzy at the edges. I was very aware of the nothingness in every direction."

We reached the narrow stairs spiraling down into the keep proper. I let her go first, glancing down at her slender body automatically. Alyssa was shapely in her Dragon uniform, with her long legs and curvy hips, and her fiery hair was tied back in a braid today, which showed off the smooth skin of her neck. It reminded me of the way the skin of her thigh had felt when I healed her, warm and supple and beautiful.

I shook off the thought and asked, "And the five of us were with you?"

"Yes," she said after a flicker of hesitation.

I frowned as we descended. "What are you leaving out?"

She looked back over her shoulder with a wry grin on her face. "You know, I'm not so sure this Dragon bond is a good thing. I'll never tell a lie again."

"This is not necessarily a bad thing. What else happened in your version of the ceremony?"

"You five were there... Plus Danni."

"Oh," I said.

"Her body," Alyssa clarified. She looked around to make sure the others weren't within hearing range. "She was dead on a slab. You five mourned her, then came forward to speak with me individually."

"That was it?"

"Yep," she said. "Then I was back in the room. The whole thing lasted no more than a few minutes."

"What did I say to you?" I asked.

We reached the bottom of the stairs and turned down a hallway. Jax, Maze, and Harry were striding ahead, while Ryon was well behind us. At first, I didn't think Alyssa had heard my question. Then she slowed so I could walk next to her, and she eyed me sideways.

"Why don't you tell me what *you* saw in the ceremony?"

"I asked you first," I pointed out.

"And if I don't want to tell you?" she asked. "I'm new to this entire thing, but the bonding ceremony seems like a very personal experience."

I must have said something embarrassing to her. I wanted to know about the ceremony from an academic perspective, but I cared more about her privacy than my own curiosity. I turned so that I was looking directly at her, so she could see how serious I was.

"Alyssa. If you don't wish to tell me, I completely understand. I will not bother you about it further."

She flashed a strange look. "That's kind of you. But it's nothing unusual. You were actually quite sweet. In the ceremony, you told me I had great potential, and that you were looking forward to helping me grow."

"Oh," I said. "That's not embarrassing at all."

"And then you kissed me."

I almost tripped over the rug that ran the length of the stone corridor. Alyssa was polite enough to pretend she didn't notice as I regained my stride. "I kissed you?"

"A polite kiss, on the cheek. It suited the moment, actually." She snapped her fingers. "And then we were back in the bonding chamber."

"Oh. Very well, then." I thought about that a moment longer, then asked, "What did the others say to you? Did any of them... you know. Did they show similar affection?"

Now she gave me a sly grin. "Why, Arthur. If I didn't know any better I'd say you were snooping."

"No! I only–"

She cut me off with a laugh. "Relax, Frosty. I was only teasing you."

Relief turned to confusion. "Frosty?"

"Yeah. You know, what we call Frost Magi at the Academy sometimes." We walked in silence for a few steps. "Nobody's ever called you that before?"

"No," I admitted. "Is it a bad thing?"

"I mean..." She waffled a hand. "Depends on the context. I've seen it used as a friendly nickname by some. There was this Frost Mage in my class who was a terrible jerk. I used to call him *frosty fartmouth*, back in the first Academy when such a name was actually funny." She chuckled at the memory. "But when I call you Frosty, I intend it as a friendly nickname."

"I'm glad," I said, and meant it.

We turned at the end of the hall and approached the door to the briefing auditorium, the same one where we'd received our orders from the Field Marshal last week before our trip to the Borderlands. Alyssa stopped outside the door and turned to me.

"No."

"No?"

"I'm answering your question. None of the others in the ceremony kissed me. Only you." She shot forward to give me a peck on the cheek, then smiled. "Let's go find out where we are being sent!"

She went inside. I stood out in the hall a few moments longer, touching the spot on my cheek where her lips had been, and wondering why it felt so good.

13

Alyssa

I felt a burst of excitement as I passed through the door, and I wasn't sure if it was Arthur's or mine. I wasn't usually that forward, even if it was just a kiss on the cheek. But like the kiss he had given me during the strange bonding ceremony place, it felt right in the moment.

The sight of Field Marshal Tyronix standing at the front of the room, majestic in his battle armor save for a helm, cast aside all other thought. We had been here only days ago to receive our orders —my *first* orders in the Quint—but that felt like a lifetime ago. I'd been in battle since then. *Several* battles. I'd earned the respect of my Quint. And of course, I'd been bonded to them.

I was a *real* member of a Dragon Quint now.

The room wasn't as crowded as the first time, but at least nine Quints were here today to receive their orders. They milled around, chatting with one another. I spotted Jax over against the wall speaking with a stout female Warrior. Yet before I could join him, Tyronix turned his head and met my gaze, his eyes as hard as the steel covering him from head to toe. Then he did the worst thing he possibly could have done.

He smiled.

"Hail, Pyromancer Alyssa!" he called, loud enough to silence the entire room. "Slayer of Silithik Queens!"

My heart sank; he was mocking me. His praise was sarcastic like the Archon's. And why not? It was ridiculous to believe a mediocre girl straight out of the Academy could accomplish such a feat.

But then the other Quints in the room were turning toward me, holding their fists over their hearts in salute. "Hail!" they shouted, a chorus of voices. "Hail, Pyromancer!"

"I'll want to speak with you later," Tyronix said. "Bragging rights aside, we haven't had a Quint face a Queen in battle since the Third Era. If there's anything you can tell us, any tactic that might give us an advantage in the future, I want to hear it."

"Of course," I said. Realizing his compliment was genuine made me more uncomfortable than if it was mockery. I lowered my head and made my way to Jax by the wall, ignoring all the nods and smiles given to me by the other Dragons I passed.

"Uncomfortable being the center of everyone's attention?" Jax whispered when I was beside him.

"Something like that."

"Success is better than failure," he said, and I felt a trickle of humiliation come from his bond. "Trust me on that."

Tyronix cleared his throat. "Let us begin. We all have a tremendous amount of work ahead of us. But first, all of you deserve commendation for your steadfast defense of the capitol yesterday. When we learned the Silithik were descending on the city from behind our battle lines, you were recalled to defend the heart of the Archenon. Your swift return is the only reason this keep, and the city that surrounds it, are not full of bugs."

Every Dragon in the room stood a little bit taller, myself included. Praise was easier for me to receive when it was done as part of a group, apparently.

"The discovery of the Silithik tactic of burrowing into our territory is proving invaluable," Tyronix continued. "Obviously, such knowledge allowed us to recall all of you to the defense of the capitol. In addition, we have also dispatched teams of runetracers to the border with dowsing runetablets to ensure no new tunnels are created."

Next to me, Jax beamed with pride. Maze gave a subtle nudge to Harry, grinning.

The Field Marshal's face grew serious. "It is important we savor such victories, because they are becoming increasingly rare." He turned to the board behind him, which held a map of the entire Archenon. It was shaped like a crescent moon, with the two ends pointing north and the Borderlands a concave bulge in the middle. To the south-east, below the Sunrise Sea, was the Gryphon Kingdom, with the capital of Oorani nestled safely behind the Sarandrelle Straight.

"This is what we controlled at the end of the ceasefire." Tyronix grabbed a rolled-up map from the table next to him. "And here is what we control today, to the best of our knowledge." He unfurled it and pinned the corners over the existing map.

A gasp passed through the room.

The western half of the scythe, jutting north alongside the Borderlands, was a patchwork of bubbles. Huge swaths of the Archenon were now behind a black line marked "Captured/Lost." The circles indicating Quints and armies of traditional soldiers were fewer, and spread out among the remaining bubbles of territory. The borders to the east also bulged with the might of the Silithik Hivemind, but it still remained one continuous front, if barely.

Tyronix let out a deep breath. "I will not sugarcoat the situation. The war is proceeding poorly. As you can see, the Silithik have shattered our forces to the north-west in the first week. We are presently regrouping to give the bugs a unified front, but it is slow going, and we lose contact with more pockets of soldiers every day. Civilian evacuation is all but impossible. Losses are in the tens of thousands, and growing."

Murmurs of anger and shock passed through the room. One Warrior to my left, a man as large as Jax and with a vicious scar on his face, trembled with rage or grief. I counted myself lucky that my home village lay to the south, safe from Silithik swarms.

But safe for how long?

I remembered the refugees from Stronghold Bracknall. Men, women, and children of all ages crammed together like cattle, dirty and starving, shuffling along in the hopes of reaching some place safe. That had only been a speck of dust on the map, a map which now looked nothing like the nation I remembered. I tried to imagine how many civilians were fleeing the Silithik there, desperately trying to find safety behind armies and Quintelaides who were dying just as quickly. The ache in my heart made me want to sit down and weep.

Jax felt the same way. With a clenched fist he whispered, "I hope we are sent to the north-west."

"Aye," Ryon agreed.

"Our armies to the east fare slightly better," Tyronix barked. "The mountain terrain allows us to funnel the bugs into manageable choke points. We still lose ground every day, and we are outnumbered more than I would like, but we're giving better than we're receiving. The Silithik are paying a price for every square of land they take."

He paused as if he'd hoped the room would cheer, but there was only somber silence.

"The central front, just north of the capitol, has seen relatively little action." He pointed to the one section of the border that looked identical to the previous map. "It appears the majority of their hives here were focused on the subterranean attacks. Sixteen of the seventeen Quints assigned there are being redeployed to the other fronts as we speak."

"And if the bugs attack there once more?" a wizened old Pyromancer asked. Wrinkles tightened as he frowned. "They will have a clear shot all the way to the capitol, will they not?"

110

Tyronix smiled. "We have reason to believe that will not occur." He turned to a man standing against the wall, who I had not noticed until then. "My men and women would be honored to receive your briefing, General Caretaan."

The man who took Tyronix's place at the front of the room was tall and slender, with sharp cheeks below eyes that were slanted. His skin was olive instead of the paler complexion of Archenon citizens, and he looked like he wore a permanent scowl behind his hawkish nose. His plain white robe shifted as he gestured to the map.

"Dragon Quintelaides," he said in a voice like ice. "Thank you for receiving me today. My name is General Caretaan."

"From the Gryphon Kingdom!" Harry whispered.

I looked at the slender man with new eyes. He did look similar to the gryphon who had flown me from the Academy to the capitol.

"Field Marshal Tyronix has put my gryphon scouts to good use patrolling the Borderlands," Caretaan said in a slow, lecturing voice. "We also have three scouts dedicated solely to monitoring hive activity within the Hivemind itself. As overwhelming as the invasion has been so far, our information indicates the Silithik have committed nearly the entirety of their strength to the attack. Current hive strength is lower than we have ever seen."

"That's his important information?" Ryon whispered. "That most of the bugs are currently in our territory? What a surprise."

"Be quiet," Jax hissed.

"So," a female Tinker at the front said. Her right arm was a mechanical prosthesis like Maze's leg, with some sort of array of tools at the end instead of fingers. "We'll be transported by gryphon into the hives to kill their Queens while they're vulnerable? Is that it?"

"Nothing so heroic," Tyronix answered. "Even with diminished strength, the Silithik hives are too dangerous to attack."

"Much is unknown regarding Silithik breeding and larvae development," Caretaan went on, "but we estimate the Hivemind will not have new armies ready for battle for at least another month.

Their strength in the field is all the strength they have."

"Oh, fantastic news!" one Shadow in the front said. "Our dead citizens will be overjoyed when I tell them."

"Shadow Alurin," Tyronix warned.

"I just don't see how any of this matters, sir." Several other Dragons murmured their agreement.

"It matters," Caretaan said in an icy voice, "because it shows the Hivemind resources are finite. Even if we lose territory, every Silithik killed puts us one step closer to surviving. If we can slow them down, we can win a war of attrition."

"That's an awfully big if," Shadow Alurin said.

Another person I couldn't see shouted, "You speak of *we* and *us*. But it is Archenon blood spilled fighting the Silithik! Not gryphon!"

"Why does the Gryphon Kingdom send only scouts?" another yelled. "When will you send troops to stand alongside us?" Cheers greeted the outbursts.

"Settle down," Tyronix growled.

"Could use more gryphon support for sure," someone complained. "In the last war, we had an aerial scout assigned to every Quint. Every one! Now you feathery fluffs hide on your peninsula, guarded on three sides by water!"

Another angry voice, this one a woman: "If we perish, they'll come for you next! You'll have no one to fight alongside you then!"

Caretaan narrowed his eyes. "We are sending more than what is fair."

"Not nearly enough!"

Caretaan crossed his arms stubbornly against the crowd, which grew angrier by the second. Even Ryon's hand was on the pommel of his dagger as if he wished to use it. I looked around with wide eyes, shocked at the insubordination from such seasoned soldiers.

Tyronix turned and smacked his steel gauntlet on the table. The smacking sound cut off the protests from the room.

"Enough!" he commanded into the silence that followed. "You are Dragons. It is your duty to obey orders that are given. Neither myself nor Caretaan need your feedback, as *constructive* as you may think it is." He stared around the room, daring anyone to argue further. Only when he was certain no one would did he relax. "It may not be the good news you want, but our winged allies have brought us vital information. No bug reinforcements are coming any time soon." He tapped the map on the wall. "This is it. This is what we have to fight, for now. This knowledge allows us to redistribute the troops north of the capitol to the east and north-west fronts with confidence."

He paused again, the intensity in his eyes shifting from anger to determination.

"Yesterday, we had no paths to victory. Today, we do. If we can wear down the Silithik assault, we can win by attrition. Every man or woman we lose must take a thousand bugs down with them. No risky endeavors, no overextension of our strength. From this point forward, our overarching strategy is one of slow retreat. Make the Silithik pay for every speck of land they taint with their slithering scales. If you fight with heart, and trust this strategy, the Hivemind will run out of beetles before we run out of land to give."

Tyronix put a hand on Caretaan's shoulder, gripping it softly. "Thank you for the briefing, General. If you'll meet me in my quarters, there are details of the Archenon's defense I would discuss with you."

General Caretaan nodded to him, then swept his eyes across the room. With his arms held behind his back, he strode through a door behind the map. Tyronix waited until the door closed before speaking in a dangerously soft voice.

"Dragons, hear my words plainly. I do not have to tell you every detail of every order. Field Marshals before me certainly preferred to give marching orders without so much as a hint of context. I prefer to give my Quintelaides as much information as possible because I want you going into battle knowing our overall strategy. Knowing that there *is* a strategy. I believe such an approach makes us all stronger." His face hardened. "But if a foreign dignitary, a bloody *ally* of ours in this war, is ever treated that way again..." He shook his head. "I will change my approach so fast you'll be on the front lines without realizing what happened. And that is a truth as strong as any steel. Are there any questions?"

The Shadow to my left licked his lips like he wanted to say something, but remained silent like everyone else.

Tyronix looked relieved. And, it was impossible to ignore, exhausted. He picked up another scroll of paper and unrolled it on the previous map, using tacks to pin down the corners. "Your marching orders are here. Please see the quartermaster for details and any supplies you may need. And if you have any questions about your orders, then bloody well consider keeping them to yourselves!" A few men and women chuckled. "And then, if you still think the questions are valuable, you may bring them to me. Dismissed."

He crossed his right fist over his heart. I quickly joined the other Dragons in returning the salute, lowering the fist only when Tyronix had left the room.

Everyone scrambled to reach the board to see the marching orders. Jax held me back and pointed to Maze, who was shoving his way through the crowd saying, "Make way! Make way for the cripple! Hey, now! Show some respect for the wounded! Don't you know I'm a hero? I've paid a price for my bravery!"

"I bet you blew your leg off stepping on your own mine!" someone teased.

"More likely he did it on purpose!" a female Ranger yelled. "You Tinkers are too cavalier about replacing your flesh with steamwork nonsense."

Maze said, "Don't be jealous, dear. If you're extra nice, maybe I'll build you a metal leg if ever the same fate should befall you."

"I'd rather die where I stand, thank you very much."

Ryon scowled at the door Tyronix had exited through. "I don't like how much boot-licking the Field Marshal did back there."

"The gryphon *was* a general," Harry said.

"A general of what? The few dozen birds who fly high above the battlefield while we bleed and die?" Ryon spat on the ground. "Better to fight the war alone than to beg for their help, meager as it is."

"Aye," said the big Warrior woman Jax had been talking to before the briefing, her voice full of bitterness. "I say we go beyond that. Once we beat back the bugs, we should turn our attention to the south-east. Storm the walls of Oorani, knock whatever gryphons remain out of the sky. Show them what a real war looks like."

Ryon gave her an approving nod. "If we're still alive then, come look for our Quint and we'll join you."

Jax frowned, but said nothing. Arthur looked thoughtful. I wasn't sure what to think about such open discussion of betraying our allies. It filled me with unease.

The other Quintelaides checked their orders and dispersed, yet Maze had not returned to us. When the crowd had thinned, we saw him staring at the paper tacked to the map, shaking his head with confusion.

"What is it?" I said as we all approached. "To which front are we being sent?"

Maze said nothing, so Ryon leaned toward the paper. "Eighty-Second, Eighty-Ninth... Ninety-Second. Where is our marker?"

"We're not listed," Maze said.

I saw that he was right: the Quints in the room were listed in order, and there was no Ninety-First.

"Surely a mistake," Harry said.

"Mistake?" Ryon snorted. "Or an intentional cruelty?"

I looked around the room for someone to ask; Tyronix was gone, and so were the rest of the Quints. The only other face I saw was a young boy's, standing in the doorway wearing a messenger's uniform. He held a tiny scroll in one hand. When he saw me, he winced apologetically, then came forward.

"Forgive me," he said, "but I was instructed to wait here until the end of the briefing."

"Who instructed you?" Arthur asked.

The messenger extended the scroll, which bore a wax seal I didn't recognize. But my Quintmates surely did.

"The Archon," Jax said, half realization and half growl.

"Apologies again," the messenger said before retreating back into the hall.

Jax stared at the scroll in his fist as if it were a poisonous snake. Finally he cracked the seal with his finger and unrolled it, reading silently before looking up.

"We're no longer the Ninety-First," he breathed.

Ryon snatched it out of his hand and read it out loud. "...taking into consideration the death of your former Pyromancer... new bonding ceremony... Hundred and Thirty-Third?" He looked up. "I don't understand."

"You heard what he said at the feast," Harry said bitterly. "The entire capitol is singing the praises of the Ninety-First. So he's decided we are no longer the Ninety-First."

"Changing our number because the city adores us?" I asked. "Is the Archon truly so petty?"

"I told you he was," Jax said, resigned. "He blamed us for the attack on the Academy, used us as scapegoats to protect himself from any political failing regarding the invasion. When we discovered the Silithik tunnels and portals, it showed that the blame was not ours to bear."

"And now he's punishing us?" I said. "For discovering something that has *saved* the Archenon?"

"As I said, he is a petty man."

Arthur cocked his head. "It is an interesting thought experiment, since we are the first Quintelaide for this to be a consideration. Given our reconfiguration, should we retain our original unit number, or be assigned a new one?"

"I don't give a steaming shit about *thought experiments*," Maze said. "We're the Ninety-First, no matter what the ink says."

"This is an insult," Ryon growled, running a hand through his grey hair. "A vile insult."

I went to the map while they argued, following the list of orders to the bottom:

ONE HUNDRED AND EIGHTEENTH: TERRIAN STRONGHOLD

ONE HUNDRED AND TWENTY-FIFTH: TERRIAN STRONGHOLD

ONE HUNDRED AND TWENTY-NINTH: VALNU STRONGHOLD

ONE HUNDRED AND THIRTY-THIRD: RESERVE

"Hey, everyone?" I said. "It gets worse."

14

Arthur

I knew what the sheet would say, and what orders we would receive. I knew because I'd dreamed of the place. I'd been there during the bonding ceremony. The future was as clear as if it were drawn on the wall with chalk.

Reserve unit.

I stared at the words. I looked at the other marching orders, then back.

"I don't understand."

"Reserve?" Jax said in disbelief. "We are to remain here in the capitol?"

"Steaming son of a..." Maze cursed.

New possibilities opened in my mind. Perhaps my dream was only a dream. A vivid delusion with no bearing on reality. That place in the mountains with the smoke all around, and the spike in Alyssa's shoulder, and the screams as we were overrun...

She shook her head at me. "Can you believe this, Arthur?"

"I cannot," I said, though I meant it in a different way than she did.

"Maybe it's meant to be an honor," Harry said. "Extra recuperation after the battles we've fought."

"We're not different than any other Quint," Jax said. "Every Quint, except for those who just arrived, has been in constant combat since the ceasefire ended."

"We're too valuable to be left sitting on our asses," Maze argued. He gripped his welding goggles in an angry fist. "Especially while the Archenon crumbles around us."

Everyone was upset. They weren't relieved the way I was. I licked my lips and chose my words carefully. "There are tactical purposes for holding some units in reserve. If the Field Marshal believes another attack on the capitol is possible..."

"That's not what he said in the briefing," Alyssa pointed out. "They're pulling forces away from the central front to bolster the flanks."

"Fuck theorizing," Ryon spat. Both of his daggers were in his hand, the knuckles pale as bone. "I intend to find out for myself."

We followed him out of the briefing room and into the hall. The Shadow leaned forward while he walked as if he were marching to battle.

"It makes no sense," Jax was saying. "It is highly unusual to be held back from the deployment. Tyronix would have spoken to us directly, to ensure we understood why."

"Or," Maze said, "he's too busy helping his gryphon friend preen his feathers to care about our orders."

"Or lack thereof," I said, hoping to inject some levity into the situation. The attempt failed. *I never was good with humor.*

"Slow down, Ryon," Jax said. "You should be calm when you—"

"I don't *want* to be calm," he hissed, still facing straight ahead. "I want him to see my anger."

We climbed one flight of stairs and entered a wing of the capitol keep reserved for nobles and important dignitaries. The rugs were plush and vibrant, and every wall sconce held a marble bust or elaborate candle girandole. Ryon slowed when he reached a door flanked by two guards.

"I'm here to see the Field Marshal," Ryon demanded.

"Honorable Shadow..." one of the guards began.

"If you don't let me in, I'm going to slit both your throats," Ryon said with deathly quietness. "It will happen so quickly you won't have a chance to even *think* about raising your halberds in defense. You'll be dead before you hit the floor. So I will say again: *I'm here to see the Field Marshal.*"

Rather than let him pass, the guard on the right extended a note in a gauntleted hand. It trembled in the air, along with his voice: "He... he said to give you this! Read it!"

"I'm sick of ink and paper," Ryon snarled. "I want to talk to a damn *person.*"

Jax took the note and then placed his body protectively between Ryon and the guards. "Think, Ryon. There has to be an explanation for this." He held up the note, which was nothing more than a piece of paper folded over once.

"Aye, the explanation is that this is all a bloody mistake." Ryon snatched the note from Jax's hand. "If these words say anything else, I'm charging through that door, just try and stop me."

"The Field Marshal said to read it elsewhere." The guard no longer trembled, though his voice still held an edge. "Somewhere private."

"His chambers are private!" Ryon pointed with a dagger, which made both guards flinch.

"Thank you for passing it along," Jax said with finality. He stared Ryon down, waiting.

Although Ryon was a brother to me, I'd always disliked his quick temper and unpredictable nature. I believed that every action had a purpose, or reasoning, behind it. Surely a man such as the

Field Marshal had a good reason for holding our Quint in reserve. And he'd left us a note to explain why.

But I was afraid to say so out loud without emboldening Ryon's wrath, so like the others I waited in tense silence.

Finally Ryon strode back down the hall, shoving past me and Alyssa on his way. The two guards visibly relaxed.

We followed him through the keep until we reached the hall with our own quarters. Since we didn't have a common room, we used Jax's bedroom, cramming into the small space until we could barely close the door. Ryon opened the note and began reading.

I noticed that Jax's room barely looked used; the washbasin towel was still folded dry, and the bed had not been slept in. I eyed Alyssa, standing on the other side of the large Warrior. They had shared a bedroom again last night. The feeling swirling in my stomach was... confusing. Almost jealousy, I thought. I had never been jealous before, not with Danni or any other woman. Why did I feel this way now?

I could still feel the place on my cheek where she kissed me, tingling with memory. Were her lips always that full, or was she pouting right now? They looked so supple. So *kissable*.

She twisted her head to look at me, and I quickly turned away. She could sense what I was thinking now, of course. Most of us had gotten used to our bonds, pushed them into the back of our head where they wouldn't be a distraction. To Alyssa, those sensations were still fresh and new. I needed to remember that. Alyssa smiled at me, and I felt my cheeks redden.

Thankfully, Ryon helped change the subject. He threw down the note and said, "I'll kill him."

"The Field Marshal?" Alyssa asked.

"No."

The note fluttered closest to me, so I grabbed it and held it up. It was not addressed to anyone.

121

There is much occurring at this moment that I cannot explain. Many decisions are out of my hands. The decision to keep you here in the capitol was one of them.

I plead with you: be patient. Put your heads down and wait for your orders. I'm doing everything in my power to resolve this.

-Tyronix

I handed the note to Jax, who then read it out loud for the group.

Ryon's face was a swirl of fury. "The Archon is behind this."

"You don't know that," Harry said.

The Shadow held his dagger like he wanted to slash at the air, but it was too crowded in the room. "Who else is above Tyronix?"

"It is possible the actions are related to the Gryphon Kingdom," I said. "These orders coincide with General Caretaan's presence."

"*Coincide* is another way of saying *coincidence.* This has the Archon's stink all over it."

"Perhaps," I admitted.

Jax leaned against the wall and crossed his arms. "I trust Tyronix."

Ryon brushed back his hair from his eyes. "You would. Warriors stick together, no matter how *idiotic* the reason."

"Why wouldn't I trust him?" Jax shot back. "He didn't have to leave a note. He could have given us the order and told us to obey in silence."

"So?"

Jax rolled his eyes. "So why warn us at all? Clearly there is more going on behind the scenes than we can see. The Archon is playing a game."

"Which is why I said I want to kill him."

Jax pushed off the wall, grabbed Ryon by the collar, and

slammed him against the door so hard the wood groaned. He held him there, staring down into his face.

"Enough," Jax whispered. "Whether the threat is serious or idle, I will not hear you speak such words about our leader. Not out loud. Not here in the capitol, where ears are everywhere. Our madness is cured, brother. You have no such excuse to fall back on."

I wondered if Ryon would argue about that point. My own madness had not returned, but it had only been a few hours since the bonding. I wouldn't trust that it was gone completely until more time had passed.

Finally, Jax let go. Ryon stared up at the Warrior with shock.

"I'm as frustrated as you are," Jax said. "You know I am, because you can feel it. But we must not allow this war to erode our sense of loyalty and order. We are a Dragon Quintelaide, not a sloppy group of foot soldiers. We are beholden to the Field Marshal, and above him, the Archon.

Ryon's face was blank, but he exuded shame through the bond. That wasn't an emotion I was used to feeling from the man.

"I won't say it out loud anymore," Ryon said. "But I meant every word." He opened the door and disappeared into the hall.

*

The Archon gave an address that night.

We gathered in Maze's room, huddled around his cube-shaped *runemessage* receiver on the bed. Ryon and Jax were the only ones missing; neither were anywhere to be found. I hoped that the latter was looking out for the former.

He couldn't truly be serious about killing the Archon, I told myself. They were only words, spoken in the heat of anger. He would never do something so treacherous.

"*Citizens of the capitol,*" the Archon began, voice hollow and tinny from Maze's device. It was a local address, meaning the *runemessages* were not repeated beyond the walls of the city. "*Tonight, our city sleeps peacefully. Despite surprise attacks from two simultaneous Silithik hives. Despite the walls of the capitol being tainted by beetle mucous. Despite a swarm of wasps so thick the sky was more black than blue. Our great city will see another day, another night, another sunrise.*"

"We already saw another day," Harry said quietly. "He should have given this speech *last* night."

"*It was no easy feat,*" the Archon went on. "*Some Quintelaides were unable to reach the city in time, and some arrived so late as to make no difference. But still, we prevailed against the might of the Hivemind's greatest forces.*"

I snorted. Armies of only beetles and wasps were hardly the Hivemind's greatest. If we ever had to fight the enormous, hulking bruisers, or the drillers from my dream...

"Late Quints? He'd better not be referring to us," Alyssa said.

"*Although an experienced runetracer myself, I have not set finger to a runetablet in many a year. Yet the defense of the jeweled city of the Archenon was so vital that even I strapped on my runepouch and sent what* fireballs *I could into the fray.*"

"Hah!" Maze said. "I'd wager gold against brass he never left the safety of the inner keep."

"*But I was not the only one to join the effort. Countless citizens took up arms, ready to fight the bugs in the streets. Many more aided our troops by carrying weapons and supplies to the walls. Refilling quivers and pitch barrels. Handing out water skins and bandages. Where many of our Quints failed the city, you filled in the gaps with your courage. It will never be forgotten, so long as...*"

"Many Quints failed the city?" Maze said, incredulous. "We fought an entire hive on the way here! We fought them again by the south gate!"

"He may not be speaking about us," Harry said doubtfully.

Alyssa waved a hand. "Quiet! He's talking about the war."

"*...certain this is a turning point in our struggle against the* *vicious Hivemind. Up and down the battlefront, brave Archenon soldiers are pushing the Silithik back into the Borderlands. They perish by the thousands, their carapaces shriveling in the sun like raisins. Rest assured that we are doing everything we can to end the war as swiftly as possible..."*

"Everything except deploying one of your best Quints," Maze muttered.

"...for the only outcome that we will accept: the complete destruction of the entire Hivemind. With the bodies of their beetles surrounding our city as witnesses, I promise this: we will make them pay for breaking the ceasefire, for their cowardly attack on the sovereignty of the Archenon. I promise you!"

His voice rose to a crescendo as if expecting a crowd to erupt in cheers. Instead, the *runemessage* ended.

"That explains why his address was sent only through the capitol, and not throughout the Archenon," Alyssa said. "The citizens of the capitol may believe we're pushing the bugs back, but everywhere else the lie would be obvious."

"Such propaganda is understandable at times," I said. "Necessary, even, if unfortunate."

"A leader should not lie to their people," Maze said definitively.

"Come now. You know it's never so simple," Harry said.

"Why shouldn't it be? One can bend the truth or avoid certain details without telling outright lies."

"Is bending the truth any better?"

As they argued about the details of the address, I sat on the bed and thought about how Alyssa's knee was currently brushing against mine. The dream was still so vivid, watching her scream and crumble to the ground with the spike in her shoulder. The panic in her voice. The way she looked up at me, desperate for me to save her.

But if the dream is real, why are we being held back?

I needed to determine if it was only a dream, or something

prophetic. Or else I feared I would go mad in a completely new way.

15

Alyssa

The last week had been the craziest of my life. First, the attack on the Academy, then being rushed to the capitol to join a Dragon Quint. Then traveling to Bracknall Stronghold, and the Borderlands beyond... and then back into the Archenon by way of sorcerous Silithik portal. We had a day of rest at the Academy before being ordered back to the capitol... which turned into a mad rush to beat the hive armies descending upon the city. We'd hardly had time to breathe. Flaming hell, even the week *prior* to all of that had been a stressful blur of Academy lectures and final practices before the Graduation Assessment.

Waking up with nothing on my schedule was like being transported to a strange and distant world. For once, I had *downtime.*

The first thing I did was visit the bath, sponging every inch of skin with a thick lather of soap. I even washed my hair twice, squeezing the water from it with slow luxury.

The dining area held a scattering of city guards in between

shifts. I didn't see any of my Quintmates, so I piled my plate high with wedged potatoes and sausages in cream sauce and sat at a table by myself. A few soldiers greeted me with salutes and, "Hail the Ninety-First!" calls, but many more watched me out of the corner of their eyes. They probably wondered why we remained in the city instead of being deployed to the front. I wished someone would ask me, so I could tell them I didn't know.

After that, I retrieved my runepouch and made my way to the practice courtyard. The capitol boasted one solely for runetracers, made of thick stone blocks banded with iron to keep stray spells from damaging the city walls. The courtyard was disturbingly empty. I almost wondered if it was closed before remembering nearly all other runetracers had been deployed. Arthur and I were the only remaining ones.

I thought back to my first day here, riding on the back of a gryphon and then being forced to display my skill in front of my new Quintmates. If they'd brought me here, the place where one *should* runetrace, I wouldn't have accidentally set the gardens on fire. Though of course, that was their intention at the time: to embarrass and humiliate me.

I took my place at one end of the courtyard, aiming at one of the steel poles standing in a row at the other end. *Flares* first, I decided, moving my finger over the runetablet until I felt the wonderful intoxicating power trickle into my chest. The first *flare* fizzled out unsuccessfully, but the next two I traced without issue.

As I practiced, I thought again about what Jax had said regarding the makeup of our Quintelaide. Maze and Harry still felt like friends, but Arthur... There was something about the thoughtful Mage that made me tingle inside. While Jax made me feel physically safe, Arthur stimulated me intellectually. I loved the way he always paused, cocking his head in thought, before he said something out loud. I could tell his mind was a tome, filled to the brim with opinions and logic. I wanted to curl up with two glasses of melon wine and talk to him long into the night.

I sent a *flare* arcing across the courtyard, missing the pole by a full stride. I set my feet and tried again.

Did I feel anything for Arthur beyond an intellectual connection? He had an attractive face, with sharp cheekbones that demanded touching and eyes that pierced my mind. Flames, he had hair fairer than my own! He was undeniably one of the most beautiful men I had ever met. I'd never gotten a good look at him beneath the robes, though. Unlike the other Dragon uniforms and armor which left little to the imagination, Arthur's robes concealed the body underneath. His arms were lean and sculpted, from what I'd seen. I found myself imagining what his chest looked like. The curve of his navel, where the hips met the torso. The legs, and other parts...

I blushed as my next *flare* soared well above the targets, striking the top of the wall with a puff of released energy. I gritted my teeth and berated myself. "Come on now, Alyssa. Stop being a stupid girl and *focus*. You have a lifetime to think about your Quintmates."

I traced two more *flares*, both of them striking the target and remaining there with a harsh glow. Then I switched to *fireballs*: two small, two medium, and one as large as I could make it. The last was still smaller than the one I'd traced to kill the Silithik Queen; the adrenaline of the battle must have helped me create one so massive. After *fireballs* came *fireflow*, which I didn't need to aim at all beyond a general direction. Those were easy for me, now.

Flame barrier I spent more time on. The Pyromancer from the other Quint during the battle had been extremely adept, creating the shimmering barrier of flame 20 paces wide. I struggled to create one directly in front of my hand, a curved barrier that appeared wherever I swiped my palm. I had to force it into existence, while the other Pyro's spell seemed to pop into place with ease. Practice could help me do it quicker, but I knew some aspects of runetracing were dependent on the person's inherent talent. Talent I would never have.

I'll just have to make up for skill with effort, I decided, swiping my hand in the air again and again.

I went through the motions as the sun climbed into the sky, losing myself in the comforting familiarity. When my finger was sick of tracing *flame barriers,* I sat down on a bale of hay and looked inside my runepouch. There were a dozen other runetablets of spells I rarely used. Runes for detecting fire, runes for controlling the heat and intensity of flames that already existed. There was even a rune that would shoot a burst of white flame that only *appeared* dangerous, but would pass harmlessly through anyone. I had never understood the purpose of that one.

After a moment of thought, I decided to give one a try: *trailblaze.* All this spell did was spread fire directly beneath one's feet, but functionally it could be used while running to create a trail of fire to fend off followers. There were times it might have been useful—while fleeing through the Silithik tunnels, for example. I needed to have more arrows in my quiver, so to speak. The phrase made me think of Brennan, and smiled sadly for a second.

I jogged in a straight line across the courtyard while tracing, feeling the runemagic seep out of my boots onto the ground. It wasn't easy to trace while running; I had to jog stiffly, legs moving almost like sticks to keep my hips from bouncing, which kept my runetablet more steady. I glanced over my shoulder while jogging: a line of fire stretched behind me, flames licking into the air as high as my waist. I stopped tracing when I was near the end of the courtyard. I watched the fire wink out with satisfaction; it burned for at least fifteen seconds. Just long enough to harass any pursuers.

Again.

Back and forth I went in progressive lines until I'd scoured half the dirt in the courtyard. Sweat matted my hair and trickled down my temple, which I wiped away with a sleeve. Sweating through my uniform would have mattered while we were on the march, but here in the capitol, I could have my clothes laundered overnight. I could also take another bath whenever I wanted.

Those luxuries shouldn't please me, I thought. *We shouldn't be stuck at the capitol at all.*

My hand drifted to my runebelt, and I gave a jerk when it touched leather instead of stone. A runetablet was missing. It must have come off the hooks! A quick scan around the courtyard and I saw it on the ground within a smoldering section of dirt.

Oh no. If it sits too long in the fire...

I crossed the distance and kicked the runetablet away from the fire. My finger burned when I tried picking it up, so I knelt and scooped dirt over the small square. Only after several long moments was I able to pick it up and return it to my belt with a sigh of relief.

"Lady Dragon?"

I nearly jumped out of my boots—a servant boy stood behind me, casting his eyes downward. He couldn't have been older than ten. "Yes?"

"I brought you a water skin, Lady Dragon. It's especially cold and fresh, with ice from the kitchen."

It took a measurable amount of willpower to take the skin slowly rather than snatch it out of his hand. I drank deep, letting the frigid water slide down my throat until my head ached from the cold. I panted when I finally stopped drinking.

"That was awfully kind of you," I said, handing it back. "Thank you so much."

"Oh, it's my job!" The boy gave a sheepish look. "Don't tell nobody, but I was sleeping over in the corner yonder, by the extra hay bales? On account of the practice courtyard being empty. You have a wonderful tracing talent, Lady Dragon! Truly a joy to behold."

I gave a wry grin. "Haven't seen a lot of runetracers, have you?" I waved it off before he could answer. "What's your name?"

"Oliver, but my friends call me Ollie."

"Thank you very much for the water, Ollie."

"Can I ask you something, Lady Dragon?"

I took a seat on the nearby hay bale. "Of course you can."

Ollie pointed at the mound of dirt next to me. "I saw you kick something, then cover it with dirt. Was it a spider?" He shivered. "I *hate* the spiders here in the capitol. Usually smash them with a rock if I see them. But I didn't think a Dragon would be afraid."

I couldn't help but laugh. "Not a spider. Something far more dangerous."

Ollie's eyes widened at that thought. I brushed off the dirt from my *fireball* rune and held it up to him. He frowned.

"A runetablet's dangerous to a runetracer?"

"Oh, sure," I said, clipping it back onto my belt. "Runestone is a volatile mineral. Throw a chunk of raw runestone into a hearth, and it may explode! Runesmiths put some sort of glaze over our runetablets to protect them, but they're still dangerous if exposed to great heat."

Ollie looked skeptical. "Begging your pardon, Lady Dragon, but I still think the city spiders are more dangerous."

I leaned in close. "I'll tell you a secret: I'm afraid of the city spiders too. Don't tell anyone?"

He grinned white teeth. "I wouldn't tell anyone! Your secret is safe with me! I'll let you get back to practicing your magic. If you need anything at all, I'll be right over there by the hay bales, only this time I won't be napping."

I hesitated. "Anything at all?"

"Well, most things. I wouldn't let you use me as a target." His eyes widened. "You wouldn't use me as a target, would you?"

I laughed. "No, no! Nothing like that. Can you fetch me a practice bow and a quiver of arrows?"

He scrunched up his face in thought. "Aye, might be I can get one from the Ranger yard. I'm not supposed to leave here in case any tracers need anything, though..."

"Good thing I'm the only one here then, huh?" I took the water skin back. "Tell you what: if you get in trouble, I'll back you up. I promise."

I watched him sprint out of the courtyard. By the time I'd finished the water skin he was back, a short bow slung over one shoulder and a quiver of frayed arrows clutched to his chest.

"Here you are, Lady Dragon! Bruno wanted to give me one of the frayed bows that hardly shot straight, but I told him it was for a

Dragon, and that you'd light his hair on fire if I gave you anything of poor quality."

"That'll do just fine." I fished out a runetablet that I rarely used, clipping it to my belt. "But it's not for me."

He blinked in confusion.

"Do you know what this runetablet is?" I waited for him to shake his head. "This is an *imbue* rune. It allows me to transfer runemagic to another object. I take all of the power and shove it inside that object, cramming it in there until it can't hold any more! With so much runemagic inside, the slightest disruption causes it to explode. Can you think of a useful object to *imbue* this way?"

"Uhh... Yes?" he said, making it a question.

"I'll give you a hint: you're holding a quiver of them."

He looked down at the bow and quiver in his hands. "Ohh! Like dipping arrows in pitch and lighting them afire!"

"Like that," I agreed, "only much, much more powerful. In order to practice this, I need someone to shoot the *imbued* arrows. Can you do that for me?"

His eyes widened as he realized what I was asking. "Oh no, Lady Dragon! I've always been terrible at archery..."

"Being terrible at something is the first step in becoming good at something," I said gently. "This is a *practice* courtyard. We can both improve together. Why don't you shoot an arrow—a normal one—to show me what you can do?"

Ollie glanced around the courtyard, appearing conflicted, but then dropped the quiver to the ground. He unslung the bow, grabbed an arrow, and nocked it with the exaggerated motions of someone mimicking something he'd seen but had never actually done. His draw was weak, arm trembling from the effort, and the loosed arrow flew only twenty paces before clattering to the ground.

"That was wonderful!" I said before he could feel embarrassed. "Perfect for my testing. If you shot it too far, I wouldn't be able to see the explosion!"

He swelled with pride, then grew cautious. "How will it work with your... *imbue* spell?"

"It's simple," I said. "I need you to repeat everything you just did: ready the bow, nock the arrow, and draw. But instead of loosing the arrow, you'll hold it there until I tell you to fire. Simple, yes?"

"Aye," he said skeptically. Still, he prepared another arrow.

"I'll give the word when you need to loose the arrow," I said as he drew back the string.

My fingertip touched the runetablet. I traced slowly, familiarizing myself with the rune. It had been so long since I'd used it that I had to go over it twice before I could find the right tempo to pull a steady trickle of runemagic from the stone. I extended my hand and focused on the arrow held between Ollie's fingers. Nothing visibly changed, but I could sense the collection of power. Just a little bit, not enough to cause harm if anything went wrong...

"Now!"

He released the bowstring, sending the arrow arcing high into the air. This time it had the range to reach the wall, striking the stone near the base where it met the ground–

CRACK-POP. The arrow burst like a small powder firecracker. It was mostly sound, and the only physical damage was a black ring on the stone and ground.

"Blessed Archon!" the boy shouted, practically jumping up and down. "That was incredible! Amazing!"

I considered telling him that was the smallest *imbue* I could trace. Best not to, lest I scare him for what was to come. "Think you can help me with a few more?"

A grin split his face as he readied another arrow.

This time the trace felt more natural. I let the runemagic collect inside the arrow several heartbeats longer before giving Ollie the signal. His shot was straighter this time, landing halfway to the targets on the other end. The flash was bright enough to blind me for an instant, and the blast sent a nearby bale of hay rolling across the courtyard.

Ollie's eyes were as wide as saucers, and he giggled and prepared another arrow without hesitation.

I was pleasantly surprised at how easy the *imbue* spell felt today. It had never been this easy at the Academy. Perhaps it was the confidence that came from being in a Dragon Quintelaide, or seasoning from battle. This time I traced longer, packing the arrow tight with runemagic. I could feel the wood through the sorcerous connection, sensing it reaching the upper limit of what it could take. Like packing clothing into a saddle bag—I could push the clothes down, making more room, but eventually it became so tightly-packed...

"Now!" I shouted.

Ollie's hand must have slipped, or his muscles were numb from holding the draw. The bow string released, sending the arrow in an unnatural path into the air, tumbling end-over-end rather than straight. I stood paralyzed as I watched it flip and fall toward the ground only a few dozen paces away...

The explosion was tremendous. Instantly, my ears felt like they were filled with cotton. I was lifted off my feet, weightless for a long moment as the sky and walls tilted strangely in my vision, before the ground came up and punched me in the behind. My head whipped back and struck the ground, and then everything went white.

I blinked rapidly as my vision returned, then my hearing. As soon as I was able, I leapt to my feet—a slow lurch, in truth—and scanned the courtyard. Ollie was laying against the wall to my left. He was not moving.

"Ollie! Oliver!" I crouched over him. "Ollie! Oh flames, tell me you're not hurt..."

His face and servant uniform were covered with black soot. I was about to go find a healer when his eyes opened, white islands within the dark sea of his face.

Then he started laughing.

"That was fantastic!" he said, rising to a sitting position and shaking his head. "It blew me straight across the courtyard. I flew for a moment, Lady Dragon! Did you see me fly?"

I put a hand on the side of his head to steady him. "I did not, because I was flying through the air myself. Ollie, I'm *so sorry*. I shouldn't have traced an *imbue* that powerful. I lost focus."

He grinned. "It's my fault, don't you worry. Fired the arrow poorly. Told you I was no good!"

His unrelenting positivity in the face of what had nearly been a tragedy made me laugh, which quickly turned into a raspy cough. I wiped my face with a hand and realized I was covered with as much soot as he was.

Ollie tried to get to his feet, then sat back down hard. He put a hand to his head and said, "You don't need my help any more, do you?"

"You've helped me plenty," I said. "Let's go find a Frost Mage who can heal you. Just to make sure everything's in the right place."

I helped him to his feet. He looked up at me with curious, embarrassed eyes. "After that... Do you mind coming to the servant quarters?" He looked down at himself. "It's just that this is the third robe I've soiled this month, and I don't think master Porio will believe my story."

16

Alyssa

I led Ollie to the keep's infirmary while he explained how he'd soiled his other two robes this month. Apparently the boy was prone to playing seek-and-flee with the other servants, and his favorite hiding place was the soot-filled kitchen hearth when it wasn't in use. The healer—an old woman with a visible callous on her runetracing finger—verified that nothing was broken or badly bruised, then scowled at me while Ollie excitedly explained what had happened. I promised it would never happen again, and then we went our separate ways, Ollie waving before running down the hall.

I berated myself the entire way back to our rooms. Tracing that much was a stupid risk; I should have only *imbued* a small amount rather than escalating each time. I wasn't a student at the Academy anymore, where a careless action would get me in trouble with the headmaster. Here, someone could get injured, or worse.

But the experience also showed how I needed to practice more. Maybe I would get Harry to help me, or some other experienced archer in the capitol. Anyone other than a servant boy.

My Quintmates were gone from their rooms when I returned. A relief, since I didn't feel like explaining why I looked like I'd spent the last hour cleaning out the inside of a hearth. I retrieved a fresh change of clothes and carried them to the bathing room, grateful for the solitude.

It was a fleeting feeling.

The bathing chambers were comprised of adjoined changing rooms with baskets for storing belongings. Two stone archways led into the bathing rooms themselves, men on the left and women on the right. The last two times I'd bathed, I'd had the chambers to myself. Tonight, a man sat in the changing room facing away from me. He wore a towel around his waist, and his hair was a deep brown sticking wetly against his shoulder blades. He leaned forward to use another towel to dry his feet and legs, an action which made the muscles of his back ripple.

"Oh, I'm sorry!" I said when I saw the stranger. "Hope I'm not intruding..."

I must have surprised the man as much as he surprised me; he leaped to his feet and spun around. His front was as chiseled as his back, abdominals like puffy supper rolls leading up to a lean chest. Rivulets of water trickled from his wet hair down his chest and arms. He held the other towel around his waist, and his eyes softened when he saw me.

Eyes that were crystal blue orbs.

"Alyssa!" Arthur said. "You're, uhh, not intruding one bit. I'm not used to seeing others in here."

I stared at the Frost Mage I thought I knew. His hair had thrown me off; it was much darker while wet. And his body...

"Me neither," I said. "It's been deserted of late."

"I find that long, hot baths are good for more than just cleanliness," Arthur mused, shifting from one leg to the other. "They help one relax during an especially stressful time."

"Absolutely." Flames consume me, there wasn't an ounce of fat on him. How could someone looking like *that* hide his form underneath a robe? I hoped he couldn't sense what I was thinking through our bond.

What I felt from *him* was a flash of concern. "What happened?" he asked, frowning.

I remembered why I'd come here, and how I must look to him with a face full of soot. I tried to think of an excuse but nothing convincing came to mind. "I was practicing in the courtyard."

"Ahh," he said as if that explained everything. He folded his arms—which were wiry with muscle rather than bulky—over his chest. "Trying a new spell?"

"I rarely use my *imbue* runetablet," I admitted. "So I commissioned the help of a servant boy. Suffice to say, I should have requisitioned an experienced archer instead."

Rather than berate me, Arthur surprised me by grinning. It made his cheekbones pop out even more. "There is nothing wrong with stretching one's boundaries. Nothing risked, nothing gained."

"Next time I'll risk someone other than a child."

"Nonsense. I'd wager that boy is bragging to all his friends about helping a Dragon with her runemagic. You probably made him prouder than he's ever been."

"You don't know if I injured him or not," I pointed out.

Arthur shook his head. "I know you wouldn't, Alyssa. You're more skilled than that."

I wanted to point out that it wasn't a matter of skill but a matter of *carelessness* that could have led to Ollie being injured, but the confidence in which he'd made the statement filled me with pride. A compliment given without intention. Arthur was the kind of man who said things because they were true.

"I'm going to get cleaned up," I said, dropping off my change of clothes into a wicker basket. "Thank you, Arthur."

He looked puzzled, and said, "You're welcome," as if he didn't know why I was thanking him.

The women's bathing chamber was a long room with bathtubs in a row, and privacy curtains that could be extended. Even though I had the room to myself, I chose a tub at the far end, using the metal brazier of coals to heat the underside of the tub until it was a scalding temperature before returning it to its spot. Although my morning bath had been luxurious and relaxing, this one possessed a specific purpose. I retrieved a bar of hard soap from the shelf, peeled myself out of my uniform, and dipped down into the water, hissing with pain and then pleasure at the scalding temperature.

It must have taken me an hour to scrub every speck of grime and soot from my skin. Even lathering and rinsing my hair three times didn't feel adequate; when I was done I still imagined I could feel flakes of ash on my scalp. *It will have to do.*

That night at dinner, I struggled to keep my eyes from glancing at Arthur every few minutes. Flames consume me, that body! There was no hint of it underneath his robes. Just that cool, thoughtful face.

He glanced at me. I quickly looked away.

"I did speak with Tyronix today," Jax was saying. "Only for a minute, but long enough. He confirmed the orders came directly from the Archon."

"Did you ask him why?" I said.

"He told me there was no explanation." Jax gestured with a chicken leg. The food tonight wasn't as extravagant as the feast yesterday, but it was still filling. "And he said that based on the Archon's attitude, he *shouldn't* ask. But he believes the reason is political."

"We provide a convenient scapegoat," Arthur said. "Blame us for why the war is going poorly, without ever coming out and saying it directly. And refuse to allow us a chance to redeem ourselves. It's almost clever."

"I learned some new information today too," Ryon said. He leaned forward on our table with conspiracy gleaming in his eyes. "One of the guards I spoke with heard a rumor that our Quint was supposed to keep the southern Silithik hive from reaching the city.

That we failed in our endeavor, and now we are being held back as punishment."

"I heard something similar," Harry said with more bitterness than I'd ever heard. "Archers on the practice range claim we were supposed to arrive a day prior to when we did."

"But none of that is true!" I said. "We were ordered back to the capitol, and came as quickly as we could. Our orders never even mentioned fighting the Silithik hive. If anything, they're lucky we stumbled upon it and did what damage we could."

Jax smiled at me sadly. "What's happening is clear. The Archon is smearing our name. The real truth does not matter to him."

I stared down at my food. My Quintmates had all accepted how petty the ruler of the Archenon was, but it was still a shocking revelation for me. It filled me with frustration and anger. And now I recognized the sideways glances from the other soldiers in the dining hall for what they were: looks of animosity. I wanted to stand up and announce to the room that we were *heroes*, not a disgraced Quint.

Maze finished a bite of food and leaned back in his chair, idly bouncing one of his mechanical spheres on his palm. "Did any of those rumors mention how long we're going to be held back? Because I'm not too keen on listening to reports of the front lines falling apart left and right while we sit on our asses."

Ryon tossed down his fork with disgust. "We don't have to remain here, you know. We can find our own fight. Kill some bugs. Do what we're *supposed* to be doing."

Jax carefully put down his fork and knife. "Such a thing was a mistake once, decided with our hearts instead of our minds. Even if it weren't a terrible mistake, I doubt we would get away with it a second time."

"We barely got away with it the first time," Maze pointed out.

"I suspect the Archon doesn't only want to humiliate us," Jax went on. "He may also be hoping to bait us into disobeying orders again. Our treason would be more public, then. He could have us discharged. Thrown in a dungeon deep beneath the keep. We cannot give him the excuse, no matter how tempting."

Ryon sat back and crossed his arms, but nodded. Although he still had a stubborn streak, he seemed more reasonable after the bonding. I wondered if that was the madness subsiding, or just my imagination.

"I'm going to walk around the city tonight. Buy some soldiers a cup of wine, see what I can learn." The Shadow tossed his napkin on the table and stood. "Ultimately, I doubt we would be held back for long. Once the Archon realizes we won't do anything rash, he'll send us out to battle. He can't afford *not* to."

After dinner, I struggled with boredom. I wasn't in the mood to walk around the city, so I went to the keep library and found a historical text on the formation of the Gryphon Kingdom 300 years ago. Normally, books and tomes weren't permitted to leave the library, but the shriveled library keeper insisted I take it with me, commenting that she trusted a Dragon to return it undamaged. I still didn't feel deserving of such special attention, but I happily accepted her offer.

I only read four pages in my room before becoming restless. My mind was a flurry of thought: the war, the Archon's strange focus on our Quintelaide, and where we might eventually be sent. I thought about Arthur's body, lithe and wiry in stark contrast to Jaxon's massive bulk, both of them beautiful and strong in their own different ways.

Still, thinking about Arthur in such a way felt like a betrayal of Jax, no matter what the Warrior had said. I wished he were sharing my bed that night so I could discuss it with him; thinking about it without him only made me feel more guilty. When I did finally sleep it was in restless bouts, turning and shifting on the bed throughout the night.

With nothing else to do the next day, I returned to practice my runetracing in the morning. A bright-eyed girl with hair the color of pitch smiled at me as I strode into the courtyard.

"Where's Ollie?" I asked.

The girl frowned. "Oh, you mean Oliver? He's working the archery yard today. If you need anything, Lady Dragon, you may ask it of me instead."

I felt a pang of sadness. I'd spent all morning looking forward to working with the boy.

I went through the motions as the sun climbed into the sky: *flares* first, then increasing sizes of *fireball* until I could barely control my trace. *Flame barrier* and *fireflow* came after that, then another round of *trailblazes* back and forth in the courtyard. The servant girl was excited to run and fetch me a water skin when I asked, although it wasn't as cold as the one Ollie had gotten me.

"Taking a break?"

Arthur strode into the courtyard, arms hidden inside the pockets of his robes. The servant girl ran up to him, but he waved her off politely.

"Only for a minute," I said. "*Trailblaze* is exhausting. Have you come to get your own practice in?" His yellow hair was pulled back into a tight tail, which I'd come to notice as something he did prior to runetracing.

"Actually, that is not why I'm here. I..." He hesitated. "I hope I'm not being too forward."

I licked my lips. "Not at all."

"There is a skill I would like to help you learn. Specifically, tracing from horseback."

I gave a start. "You want to help me?"

"Of course, Alyssa. Why wouldn't I want to?"

The burst of elation in my chest was so powerful I was certain he could tell even if we *weren't* bonded. I leaped to my feet and said, "Let me change into riding boots and I'll meet you at the stables."

He held up a hand. "Actually, there are several exercises here in the courtyard I would like to perform."

"Oh. Then how...?"

143

"I have found that jumping straight to the end goal is often not the best approach," he explained. "A fellow runetracer taught me the method I will show you today. Although counterintuitive, I think it will work well for you."

I smiled at the Mage, full of warmth. "I'm grateful for any help you can give me!"

"You are able to *trailblaze?*" Arthur asked.

"At a jog, yes. But I fail two times out of three."

He nodded, then led me over to a stack of hay bales underneath a shaded awning. We dragged two of them into the center of the courtyard. He positioned them roughly a pace apart, then gestured.

"Stand on the bales. One foot on each."

I obeyed, standing astride the two bales with a gap beneath me. I felt silly, but didn't question it. Arthur stood to the side, looked me up and down, and nodded.

"Very good. You may trace a spell now."

"Does it matter what runespell?" I asked.

"Something small. A *fireball,* I suppose. Aim for the target there, although hitting it isn't important."

As I readied myself, I wondered what Arthur was going to do. Jump in front of me as a distraction? Shake the hay bales to simulate the chaos of riding a horse? I lowered my hand to my side and touched the runetablet clipped to my belt, then began tracing the simple spell. Even though I had already been practicing today, this time it felt... different. More difficult, probably because I was anxiously awaiting whatever Arthur was going to do. I had to focus on my finger as it ran along the swirled grooves to coax the runemagic into my body, and I failed twice before the third attempt succeeded. The fist-sized *fireball* shot away, missing the target by two paces.

"Good," Arthur said. "Again."

I repeated the process, this time striking a glancing blow at the target. I nodded with satisfaction.

144

"Give me two more like that," Arthur said.

It took me four more tries to hit the target twice. Arthur observed silently, arms crossed and his comely face devoid of emotion. When the last *fireball* hit the target, I let out a relieved sigh and hopped off the hay. Standing with my legs spread for so long was tiring.

"Very good," he said. "Now stand on just one bale." He waited until I did. "Now raise one foot off the ground. Place it against your other calf, if that helps keep it steady."

I wobbled as I stood on one leg. "I can't help but feel like you're pulling a prank on me. Are Maze and Harry watching from some secret place? Will they burst out laughing at any moment?"

Arthur said nothing and gestured at the target.

This was significantly harder than the first test. It took me six tries just to trace a *fireball*, and when I finally did, it shot away at an angle nowhere near the intended target. The second and third *fireballs* were better, but not by much. The fourth I was unable to trace at all, failing eight attempts in a row. I lowered my leg with an exasperated sigh.

"I don't understand," I said. "I'm trying to keep an open mind, but I don't see how any of this helps me. I won't be runetracing on one leg in battle."

Arthur nodded as if he agreed with me. "That's what I thought at first. Come on. Let's try again."

I bit back a curse and went through the process again, balancing on one foot while sending balls of flame randomly across the courtyard. Arthur had me switch legs after that. Then, when he allowed me to stand on both feet, he made me raise up on my tip-toes while tracing. *That* was the toughest, resulting in only one successful trace out of six attempts while I trembled on my toes.

Finally I sat down on the hay bale and wiped sweat from my forehead. The servant girl came running to give us skins of water. "Arthur. I know you're a lot more experienced than I am. And I trust you. I do. But I need to understand how this will make me better at tracing from horseback."

I looked up at Arthur. His head blocked the sun, creating a nimbus of light around him. He waited for me to drink from the water skin before answering.

"Horseback riding is all about motion. Moving in rhythm with the horse while you're in the saddle." He spoke as if it were simple. "The Academy only trains us to runetrace while motionless, or perhaps at a walk. Anything beyond that is unnatural. In order to runetrace while at a gallop, we must build up our runetracing ability in situations that are uncomfortable, or situations where we are distracted. Runetracing must be something you are able to do second-nature. While you are only half-aware. Standing with one foot on each bale, legs spread, helps you runetrace while under uncomfortable strain. Runetracing while standing on one leg requires a mastery of balance, as does standing on the tips of your toes. Slowly, agonizingly so at times, your ability will adapt to these distractions. When you've mastered them, we will try runetracing at a full sprint, and then perhaps move on to horseback. It takes time."

Part of me was skeptical that anything I'd just done would help with the end goal, but I nodded. It was comforting having someone focused on helping me. Someone to trust.

"I'm a hard worker," I told Arthur. "What I lack in talent, I make up in effort."

He smiled. "Some of the longest-surviving runetracers were those with less innate talent than their peers."

Thinking of other runetracers made me pause. "Was it Danni?" I asked.

"What?"

"You said another runetracer taught you these methods. Was it Danni?"

He hesitated, then nodded. "Aye, when we were first bonded together. I was like you, unable to do anything but stare at my runetablets while at a gallop. Danni helped me train." He sighed.

"Danni could naturally runetrace from horseback. She never had to try hard."

That explains why Ryon is so bitter about my inability to trace from horseback. "She sounds like she was more powerful than me."

"Perhaps. But it made her cocky. A trait which ended up being her demise." He extended his arm, helping me back to my feet. "Another round balanced on each leg, then I'll let you go."

I returned to the bale, more determined than before.

17

Arthur

Helping Alyssa filled me with deep satisfaction.

I thought about her long after we parted ways from the practice courtyard. She seemed embarrassed to bring up Danni, but in truth my old Pyromancer had been on my mind of late. It seemed fitting that the drills she taught me were now being used to teach her replacement. Danni would have laughed at the circular symbolism of it all.

But although I had been a stubborn Frost Mage when I learned, Alyssa seemed determined to improve herself. Most Pyromancers were haughty and full of self-importance, strutting around with all the power in the world at their fingertips. Alyssa was more humble than most. Less powerful, of course, but I would take humility over power any day. Humble runetracers knew their limits.

As I'd told Alyssa, arrogance was what got Danni killed.

While walking through the corridors of the keep, I thought about the selfish reasons for wanting to help Alyssa. The true purpose for me helping her. The dream had taunted me again last night, being overwhelmed on the mountain ridge with Alyssa, watching a driller impale her in the shoulder. If I could help her improve, maybe I could avoid that fate.

Maybe *all* of us could.

I realized my legs were carrying me to Runemaster Altonio's personal chambers, and a moment later I realized why. When I reached his door I knocked without hesitation, driven by academic curiosity.

He opened the door with a disturbed frown, then brightened when he saw me. "Frost Mage Arthur! A pleasant surprise."

"I'm sorry to bother you," I began.

"No, no, no. Not a bother." He quickly ushered me inside. "Never a bother for a fellow runetracer. Can I offer you tea? Bitterbean juice? I think I have wine..."

"I'm fine, thank you." His chambers were massive but cluttered: the visiting room was filled with six tables, each one covered with stacks of tomes or scrolls held open at the corners with candlesticks. Light streamed inside the bedroom through another doorway, but the visiting room was illuminated from two huge chandeliers hanging from the ceiling and sorcerous torches arranged around the walls.

"How can I help you, then?" he asked.

Not all runetracers chose a life of combat. By the third academy, any Pyromancer or Frost Mage who was not inclined to violence was removed and sent to a separate school outside the capitol, where they were taught a broader variety of runetracing abilities. Such runetracers were often used for tasks like sending *runemessages,* or performing light healing. Others went on to become runesmiths, toiling deep within the Archenon runeforges to create the runetablets from which sorcerous energy was drawn. Many runetracers left to join other professions, utilizing what small runetracing ability they had to become better Warriors, Archers, or Tinkers. Some of the finest leather workers in the Archenon possessed enough runetracing ability to aid in the curing and molding of leather.

The most powerful, and dedicated, of runetracers were eventually raised to the rank of Runemaster. These men and women dedicated their lives to teaching others the runetracing craft, whether specific spells or more broad historical knowledge. Most of the instructors at the fourth and fifth Academies held the rank of Runemaster. Regardless of their specialty, it was the mark of a Runemaster to always keep their door open to any runetracer who may call on them for their wisdom, so that their experience could be spread for the greater improvement of the nation.

But that was not why I was here.

"I may not be permitted to ask such a thing," I said carefully, "but I have come to see how your research has progressed studying the sample we collected. The skin fragment of the Silithik Queen, with the carved runes."

Runemaster Altonio's eyes brightened. "Ah, yes! Come, come. I have it in here."

He led me around the maze of tables to the back corner, where the circle of Silithik skin was stretched wide and pinned to the table with corkscrew vices. The color had darkened from a sandy beige to dark grey. Seeing it again made me shiver.

"I've been holding two sessions per day with fellow runetracers here in the capitol to study the specimen," Altonio said. "I must tell you: many of them are disheartened by the sight of it. Some even believe it to be a forgery, created solely with the intention of sowing fear and discord among the Archenon."

I blinked. "Runemaster, I can personally assure you—"

He cut me off with a hand wave. "Arthur, do not fear! I trust this specimen to be genuine. I was merely sharing the whispers of more paranoid men and women." He scowled down at the section of skin. "However, I do not have encouraging news on its study. See this oval shape surrounding the rest? Yes, even with the indentation here. We believe that to be the starting ring of the rune. Just like ours."

The outer portion of a runestone was a perfect circle. The runetracer could trace only this outer circle to get a feel for the rune, sensing its power and building up sorcerous momentum, before tracing the rune within. Every runetracer had their own routine; mine was to circle a rune exactly three times before tracing inside. Some might call it a nervous tick.

But they were always a perfect circle. Runesmiths who made the circle anything less than perfect found themselves with a runetablet that would conjure only a trickle of power, or none at all. Yet the circle surrounding the Queen's rune was an asymmetrical oval shape.

"I do not understand," I said.

"Then you know as much as we do," Altonio admitted. "As nonuniform as it may be, the scabbing from the outer part here is smoothed with use, much the way our own runetablets become after many years."

"If that's true..."

"Then this entire enormous section of skin is one *single rune,*" he finished for me.

I looked at the rune with a new perspective. Inside the asymmetrical oval were curves and swirls, loops and jagged edges. It was more complicated than any rune I had ever seen.

"How would we ever copy this onto a runetablet? It would be the size of a wagon wheel!"

The Runemaster nodded as if it were his next point. "We've recalled one of the master runesmiths from the south. Hopefully he has some ideas of what to do."

"A runetablet so large it must be pulled by horses?" I joked.

"That is not out of the question," Altonio said. "For the ability to create portals through which entire armies could travel? We would go to great lengths to mirror such an ability. There is still the matter of the groove sizes as well. These are as thick as three fingers placed together. Shrinking it down to accommodate a human fingertip may not result in the same runemagic. We have no way to know. There are a thousand other questions we have yet to ask or answer, as well."

"Indeed."

"You're welcome to join the runetracer sessions to study the specimen. Archon bless me, you've earned the right more than any Mage! The next session is tomorrow morning, an hour after dawn."

"I may do that," I said. *We have little else to do while we sit idly*, I considered saying, but such a passive aggressive comment was below what the Runemaster deserved. Better not to bring it up at all.

"Very good." Altonio nodded as if that concluded matters, but I hesitated. As curious as I was about the Queen's specimen, it still wasn't the *real* reason I had come here.

"Runemaster," I said carefully. "Have you ever considered the meaning, or predictive ability, of dreams?"

"Dreams?" He scrunched up his face. "I had a colleague once, years ago when I taught at the fourth Academy. She found it incredibly enlightening to keep a journal next to her bed, writing down every dream she remembered. She believed evaluating one's dreams could illuminate the depths of one's subconscious. To help understand what you were thinking, and why."

"I'm sorry, Runemaster. What I meant was more along the lines of..."

"What is it, Arthur?"

"Whether you think dreams are merely a creation of our imagination," I said in a rush, "or a potential vision of the future?"

Altonio stared blankly, then let out a lighthearted laugh. "Why, Arthur! You sound like a mystic. Surely you joke."

I made myself chuckle. "A poor joke, yes." I gestured at the Queen's skin. "I'll join one of your sessions tomorrow for certain. Thank you for speaking with me."

I rushed out of his chambers before he could realize my question was serious.

18

Arthur

The days passed slowly.

I was not the only one who felt restless. Ryon sat on a parapet high on the outer wall, sharpening his twin dragon-wing daggers far beyond necessary. Jaxon and Harry sparred with short swords in the practice courtyard, the Warrior giving the Ranger pointers on the best method of deflecting a beetle slash. Maze was nowhere to be seen during the day, although he was undoubtedly fiddling with gears and steam cranks in a workshop within the city. At night we ate supper together, our mutual restlessness accentuated and amplified by the Dragon bond.

Instructing Alyssa was one of the few pleasures of my day. She was stubborn the way all good runetracers were: she refused to give up until she had mastered whatever drill I gave, whether standing on her toes or tracing upside-down with her feet against a wall. She cracked jokes, grinning widely whenever she saw me smiling in return. She told me that even if she never mastered runetracing from a galloping horse, she *would* crack my cold exterior.

And then, at night, she found Jax's bed, or he found hers. And the geyser of love and lust and comfort that poured through the bond—through both of their bonds—left me feeling jealous and alone.

On the fourth day, Jax strode into the runetracing courtyard. Alyssa was sprinting back and forth while tracing her *trailblaze* spell; she was already adept at tracing it while at a light jog, but such a spell was only truly valuable if you could trace it while running for your life from pursuers. Jax approached me while watching Alyssa's long strides. A sheen of sweat covered his face, and his light shirt was stuck to his chest with moisture.

"Is she improving?" he asked.

I nodded. "It may not appear so, but she is. See the small flames licking across the ground behind her? Two hours ago, she could trace nothing at this speed."

"At least one of us is getting something out of this delay," he muttered.

"Have you any news in that regard?"

"None at all," he admitted bitterly. "Tyronix will say nothing beyond vague comments about the Archon's larger strategy. But I can sense his growing concern about the war. It goes poorly, especially in the east."

"The east?" I asked. "I thought we were holding ground there."

"Three days ago, that was true. Now?" Jax shrugged his huge shoulders. "From what I've heard through other sources, the Hivemind has reached the foothills of the Dragonspine Mountains."

An image flashed in my head: galloping along a narrow mountain ridge, desperate to reach a peak where explosives had been housed. Alyssa falling to the ground, crying out for help. Beetles and drillers moving in from all sides, cutting off any escape. *It could be the Dragonspine Mountains. Or it could be a thousand other places.*

"Perhaps the strategy is to fall back to those mountain passes, where the Silithik can be funneled into narrow valleys to fight," I said.

"Perhaps," Jax said, although his tone indicated he didn't believe it was likely. "In any case, men and women die while we lounge around the capitol like prisoners. If we aren't sent somewhere soon, I fear Ryon might pick a fight with a horse just to cut something with his daggers."

Alyssa reached the corner of the courtyard and turned. When she saw Jax she lifted her free hand to wave, the distraction creating a gap in the flames behind her before she regained her focus and resumed tracing.

"Aside from impatience," Jax said, "how are you faring, Arthur?"

"The runetracers in the capitol are clueless," I said.

"How so?" Jax asked. "Not that I disagree, of course. Just wondering in what manner of cluelessness you refer."

"The Silithik Queen's skin. The specimen we brought back. I joined two of the sessions of runetracers examining it. None of them understand how important it is."

"In what way?"

"They only think of this one application: Silithik Queens can create portals, which is something we want to duplicate."

Jax frowned. "That is the most important application. Is it not?"

"Perhaps at first, but there are far greater implications. Did the Silithik learn this ability on their own? What other runetracing spells can they perform? Can other species of Silithik do this, or just Queens?"

"Those sound like questions without answers," Jax said.

"Perhaps, but the other runetracers are not even *asking* them. They're only focused on the damn portals." I shook my head. "I stopped taking part in the sessions because it frustrates me so."

Jax turned to watch Alyssa. "Do they treat you differently?"

The question surprised me, but it shouldn't have. "Yes, actually. How did you know?"

His tone hardened. "We're all being treated differently, now. By the guards, and servants, and everyone else. The rumors spreading through the capitol about our failure in the last battle are working."

I hadn't given it much thought because it wasn't something that could be helped, but now that I thought about it, I realized Jax was right. There was a mood everywhere we went, as if our mere entrance in a crowded room gave everyone pause. Everywhere we went, stares and whispers followed.

"Have you seen Maze recently?" I asked, eager to change the subject.

That brought a chuckle from Jax. "I caught him taking a backpack of food from the dining hall. He says he's found a union of Tinkers who are, I quote, *doing incredible things with dry powder.* I was afraid to ask more."

"Excellent," I muttered. "I was just thinking that we did not possess enough manners in which to accidentally kill ourselves."

Jax turned toward me, a funny look on his face. "Perhaps it is the stress of the situation, but I think I've heard you crack more jokes in the past few days than in the past few *years.*"

"Humor is a known coping mechanism," I said.

"Perhaps," Jax said carefully. "Or perhaps spending your days helping Alyssa are brightening your mood. She certainly has that effect on me."

I opened my mouth to protest, then closed it. I did feel unusually happy when I was helping Alyssa. I thought it was merely the utility of aiding a runetracing colleague. Maybe it was more than that.

Jax was looking at me strangely. "What?" I asked.

He turned to face me directly and put a hand on my shoulder. "You need not fight your feelings, brother."

"I'm not—" I began before he cut me off.

"You cannot hide them from me any more than I can shield mine from you." His voice was gentle. "It would be a mistake to force your feelings before you are ready, but it is a greater mistake to avoid them altogether. Danni is gone. Alyssa is here." He looked over at her again. "And she's special."

The warmth from Jax when he looked at her was strikingly similar to my own emotions, if stronger. *Love.* That's what it was. More than just a friendly emotion. It shocked me to feel something so strong from the big Warrior after only knowing Alyssa a scarce two weeks.

"I'm going to go hit something with my sword," Jax announced. He gave me a final look before striding away, waving goodbye to Alyssa while she continued sprinting around the courtyard.

Love. A complicated, yet powerful feeling. When I looked at Alyssa, I felt a flurry of thoughts and emotions. Pride in her sorcerous improvement. The desire to protect her from the enemies to come. Attraction to her body, long legs gliding across the ground, her flame of hair flowing behind her. The swell of her breasts, heaving with every labored breath when she paused between practices. Thoughts of what she looked like *underneath* her uniform. She'd seen me half-nude in the bath, but I'd left before she changed. The lingering curiosity was overwhelming.

I still missed Danni. It was a deep ache that remained wherever I went. Yet with each passing day, Alyssa occupied a greater and greater part of my mind...

I looked away. A servant boy in a white robe stood in the doorway of the courtyard, his path blocked by the fire from Alyssa's *trailblaze* spell. I held up a finger to tell him to wait a moment. Alyssa should be done soon.

Jax's words echoed in my head. Was I fighting my feelings? I had not acted on them yet, but neither had I tried to suppress them. Although every time I let my thoughts drift around Alyssa, I ended up thinking about that dream...

"What's wrong, Frosty?" Alyssa said as she jogged up to me. "You look like you've single-handedly lost the war."

I shook away my thoughts and hoped she couldn't tell what I was thinking. "Nothing's wrong. I was merely lost in thought. You completed your laps?"

"All five," she said, making the number sound like a curse. "I need to catch my breath or I'll be spreading as much vomit onto the ground as fire."

I chuckled at her joke and waved to the servant. He eyed the smoldering ground hesitantly before hopping over it and running the rest of the way.

"Ollie!" Alyssa exclaimed. "I thought I'd scared you off."

The boy skidded to a stop and handed her a water skin. "No, Lady Dragon! I've been stuck serving the *sparring* courtyard. The fighters there are terribly sweaty. I should bring them a trough of water rather than a skin!"

She smiled at him. "That sounds like our Warrior, Jaxon. Did he have one eye that was filled with blood?"

Ollie's eyes widened. "That was him! He caught me staring yesterday, and he gave me a look that could peel the bark off a tree. I thought I would be punished for certain."

"Jax has a kind heart beneath his intimidating exterior," Alyssa said. I sensed a pulse of affection from her bond. It made me jealous.

"Do you need anything else, Lady Dragon?" The servant looked nervously over his shoulder. "I'm s'posed to be back at the archery range next, and master Porio won't be kind if I'm late."

Alyssa looked at me and said, "You can run along. Will I see you later?"

"Of course!" With that, Ollie ran off the way he'd come, leaping over the dark ground marking the remnants of Alyssa's last spell.

"Later?" I asked.

She watched him go with a smile. "He's going to show me something in the city. He said it was a surprise." Alyssa giggled. "I think he has a crush on me."

"What boy wouldn't?"

The words left my mouth automatically. I quickly realized the indirect compliment held within. Alyssa blushed, and smiled at me, and a feeling came from her bond that was similar to what she felt after succeeding at a difficult trace.

"How long until we can try on an actual horse?" she asked. "I can be as patient as I need to be, but it helps if I know how far away the goal is."

"I was planning on telling you at the end of today's practice, but now is as good a time as any," I said. "You've made some swift progress. Tomorrow we'll visit the stables and begin the real training."

"Ahh!" she yelled, leaping forward to wrap me in a hug. Sweat smeared from her cheeks onto my face, but I didn't care one bit. For a few long moments, I savored the way she felt in my arms. "Thank you, Arthur!"

"There's nothing to thank me for. It's not something I'm giving you: you've earned it with your work."

She put her hands on her hips, ready to take on anything. "I think I need to find a new horse while we're there. The one I have now tries to buck me whenever I urge her into anything more than a walk. I miss Fireball."

"Fireball?"

"The horse I was given here two weeks ago," she explained. "The one I rode into the Borderlands. I named her Fireball. I know I would have an easier time with her than with any other horse. It is a shame she probably perished in the Borderlands, far from home."

On a whim, I asked, "What did Fireball look like?"

Her dark eyebrows furrowed. "She was a piebald, white with black splotches. And a reddish mane."

"Did you braid her mane?" I asked. "Four small braids between her ears?"

She cocked her head. "I am surprised you remembered that."

I didn't remember it. *White with black splotches, and with a red mane braided up near the ears...* It was the same horse from my dream. A horse that was dead. I felt my spirits rising. If the horse in the dream was Fireball, then the dream couldn't possibly come true.

"What is it?" Alyssa asked. "You feel... Relieved, I think? The bond is difficult to discern sometimes."

"I'm relieved that you're ready for horses tomorrow," I quickly said. "But first we need to finish today's training. I'd like you to continue your sprints, but this time tracing *flares* with precision."

She groaned. "They might be jogs instead of sprints. My boots feel like they're full of lead, that's how tired my legs are."

"As fast as you can manage, then. I'll call out the targets at random."

As Alyssa switched runes on her belt and jogged away, I admired her attractive form and smiled with renewed hope.

19

Arthur

After training with Alyssa, I declined lunch and made an excuse about needing to visit the runemaster's session to study the Queen skin. But that was a lie, and I slipped out of the keep like a thief.

I walked through the city, listening to the random chatter of citizens. People talked about everything: the weather, the price of mutton or beef, an especially funny wagon accident up on the north side of the city which resulted in wheels of cheese rolling down the street. Many citizens talked about the war. There were whispers spread about the deaths to the north-west, how new cities and strongholds fell every day.

"I trust the Archon more than rumors," one man told his companion.

"Well then you're a damned fool..." the friend said before drifting out of earshot.

I followed the outer walls of the city until reaching my destination. It was the same destination I'd sought several nights ago before running away in fear. And like the previous night, I casually slipped into a neighboring alley to hide first. I still needed to work up my courage before charging in. I needed to convince myself nobody would see me.

Lady Anis's shop was exactly how it had been the other night. It was less intimidating during the day, a single-room cottage with bubbled windows and a door in need of fresh paint. Few people passed down this street; it was the time of day after lunch when most citizens were returning to their jobs. It was time to stride right up to the door and face it. I thought I was ready, although it was easier to hesitate there in my alley than to finally do it.

Before I could take a single step, the door opened and a shriveled woman stepped out onto the street. Lady Anis wore a dress that had once been a vibrant purple but was now faded with age, and she walked with a terrible hunch. She reminded me of my father's mother, who desperately needed the aid of a cane but was too stubborn to use one. A man exited the store with her: tall and slender, he looked like someone out of the Gryphon Kingdom. He certainly had the gait of a gryphon shifter: he walked stiffly, as if he were used to another body and had to move in this one with deliberate thought.

Lady Anis watched him walk down the street, then she hobbled across the road and into another shop. I sighed. Wherever she was going, she wouldn't be telling anyone their fortunes until she returned. I didn't believe in supernatural omens, but that was as much a signal to come back another day as anything. The relief flooded into me like runemagic.

"You gunna stand here all day or visit my shop?"

The woman surprised me so much I nearly leaped into the street. I whirled and found Lady Anis standing behind me, staring up at me impatiently.

"I was just... I don't know what you mean," I said. "I was only standing here. In this alley."

"Hmmph." Her voice was like the croak of a frog dying of thirst. "Just like you were only standing here four sunsets ago, I suppose. Come on, then. I'm too impatient to wait another four nights."

She shoved past me and into the street. Not wanting to be berated any further, and embarrassed about being discovered, I followed her obediently.

Despite being the middle of the day, the interior of her shop was almost as dark as night and it took my eyes several seconds to adjust. Black curtains covered the two windows, fastened to hooks to keep light from creeping in at the edges. The room wasn't at all what I expected: it was clean and simple, with a kitchen to my left and a sitting area to the right. Everything was spotless and smelled like lemons.

"What?" she barked. "You think women like me live in filthy hovels with an inch of dust covering everything?"

"I don't know what I thought," I admitted. "How did you know I was here four nights ago?"

She limped over to the sitting area. "You need to know about your future, do you?" she asked, ignoring my question.

"In a manner."

"Hah! *In a manner.* What you mean to say is *yes,* you need to know about your future. And you're embarrassed about it."

I frowned. "I don't often visit someone of your profession."

"And I don't often receive customers like you. Yet here we are." She lowered herself into a well-cushioned chair and stared at me expectantly. I approached the chair across from her and sat. On the table were two objects: a folded letter sealed with wax, and a crystal orb resting on a three-pronged stand. I eyed the orb with suspicion.

"Oh, pay no attention to that," the old woman said. She took the letter and put it in her pocket. "I've discovered the more complex the theatrics, the less skeptical people are. A crystal orb is useless for what I do, but it is good for business."

"Skepticism is healthy," I said.

"Oh aye, it is. Until you receive evidence that banishes such skepticism. That is what you Magi believe, is it not, *Arthur?*"

I flinched. "How..."

She waved her fingers in the air and widened her eyes. "Maaaagic..." she intoned.

I felt my mouth hang open in shock. This woman didn't know me. I had taken care to conceal my identity. And even if she had noticed me standing in the alley four nights ago, there was no way for her to use that information to discover who I was.

She burst into a cackle of laughs. "Your name is on every tongue in the city. Well, not *your* name. Your Quintelaide's. The Ninety-First. Simultaneously heroes and cowards, it would seem. Quite the conundrum."

"We are not cowards!" I said, more heat in my voice than I intended. I took a deep breath and added, "We had orders. We followed them."

Lady Anis was shaking her head. "Fear not. The Archon's propaganda is strong, but easy to see beyond for those with clear eyes. You'll be glad to know his propaganda is limited in range, too. None outside the capitol much care for what he says about one bloody Quint. Come now, give me your hand. I said give me your hand, stop dawdling."

She reached across the table and seized my tracing hand in both of hers. She gripped it tightly and ran her thumbs over my palm, examining the lines and grooves. Several silent minutes passed.

"There's a girl," she finally said. "She's one of the reasons you're here, but not the *primary* reason."

"Yes," I said warily. This didn't prove anything. I suspected most people who visited fortune tellers wanted to know about a romantic interest.

She rolled her eyes as if she heard my thought. "Very well, then," she said, letting go of my hand and leaning back in her chair. She crossed her fingers together on the table. "Your turn. Ask me what you will, and I'll answer to the best of my ability."

"What... What are the rules?" I asked. "Can I ask you *anything?*

Do I only get a single question, or..."

"Bloody Frost Magi," she rasped, "always over-thinking things! Ask me the damned question! The one you came here to ask. I know what it is, but you need to say the words."

There was only one question I had. A question that had been plaguing me for years, but more so in the last week. Saying it out loud was like releasing a burden from weary shoulders.

"Is my dream real?" I said, like an exhale. "I had another dream once, and it came true. My Pyromancer, my old Pyro, that is, I dreamed she would fall to her death, and then..." I had to clear my throat of the knot that was building. "If one dream can come true, others may as well. Tell me. Is my dream real?"

Lady Anis looked almost sad. She studied my face, frowning as if she could see something there which she didn't like. I felt my heart race as I waited for her answer, though I still wasn't sure if I believed any of this.

A tea kettle began hissing. She got up and went to the stove, removed the kettle, and poured the liquid into two waiting cups next to the fire. Without adding anything, she brought the two cups over to the table and placed one in front of me with a steady hand. The water was a murky brown with bits of tea leaves in the bottom. I ignored the cup and stared at her, waiting for my answer.

She sat back down and took a slow sip of tea. "Normally, I'd give you a long and complex answer. Ask you to drink your tea so I could read the leaves, which is just another theatrical—but ultimately useless—flourish. Customers like to have their fortunes teased out."

"But..." I said.

"But I won't mince words with you," she said with deathly seriousness. "Aye. Your dream is real, just as the first one was."

I blinked. "Is that it? That's all you have to say on the matter?"

"That is all there is *to* say. I am sorry, Arthur."

Despair was my first reaction, despair that I couldn't change this dream just like I couldn't change the first. But it was fleeting. Skepticism returned with years of academic practice, and I made myself frown at the woman. "So you're a fraud, then. You don't know anything, so you give a vague answer without specifics. *Your dream is real.* As if you could know. As if that tells me anything of value!"

Her eyes reflected the light like dark, unflinching marbles. "Believe what you want, Mage. I've told you the truth, whether you wish to hear it or not."

"I do not." I stood up and smoothed out my robe. "Next time you might as well add the useless theatrics."

I strode to the door, feet hollow on her floorboards. I was reaching for the latch when she spoke. "She dies."

I froze with my hand on the latch.

"In the dream. The one where you're on the mountain ridge fighting the bugs, trying to reach that damned peak. You follow her up the mountain on horseback until you discover the problem. A cut cable, whatever the stars that is for. Those foul beasts strike her in the shoulder. She falls, and is unable to runetrace after that." She grimaced. "You are both overrun seconds later."

I returned to the table on numb legs. I sat down. There were tears in the woman's eyes, a shimmering barrier to the white behind. She gave me the barest of nods. I'd never told anyone about the dream. There was no way for her to know.

The dream was true. Alyssa and I would die, just as Danni had.

The weight of it hit me hard, like an anchor pulling my guts down into my legs. It was like Alyssa was already dead, another Pyromancer from our Quintelaide lost. I didn't even care that I was going to die with her. I tried to swallow but found my mouth devoid of moisture. Lady Anis prodded my tea cup. I drank deep of the hot liquid.

"Bitter tea for bitter truth," she said.

I took a shuddering breath. Excuses and denials returned to my mind, refusing to accept what she'd told me. "There's a detail I don't understand," I said. "In the dream, she's riding a horse. A piebald named Fireball. I'm certain it is the same one. But the horse is dead. So the dream cannot be real. It can't."

One of her bushy eyebrows rose. "Are you certain the horse is dead?"

"I am."

But she heard the doubt in my voice. "I'm not sure you are. Regardless, that is your future, no matter what loopholes of logic you cling to. Best to accept it now."

The dream played in my head, images in rapid succession. Riding to the ridge. Alyssa, with a chitinous spike sticking out of her shoulder, red blood staining the black of her Dragon uniform. The Silithik knocking aside my horse, bearing down on me in a slithering stampede.

Lady Anis jerked her head as if she could hear something. "Time to go," she said, hopping to her feet with a spryness that surprised me.

"I have more questions," I said.

She grabbed my arm and pulled me to my feet. "No you don't, dear. Come on. Out you go."

"But I haven't paid." A ridiculous thing to say after learning of my doom.

"No charge for grim fortunes. Just go. *Hurry.*"

She pushed me toward the door and opened the latch. I allowed myself to be shuffled through and into the harsh daylight.

And right into Alyssa.

20

Alyssa

"It's my very favorite place!" Ollie said.

I followed the boy through the city, first down main roads near the inner keep and then through narrow alleys in a poorer section that bordered the outer wall. I would have gotten lost a dozen times along the way, but Ollie seemed to know exactly where he was going.

"How often do you visit?" I asked, sliding sideways between two food carts on the busy street.

"Once a week," Ollie said over his shoulder. "Unless she's busy. She has a lot of customers of late, what with the war."

That made sense. Who would want to learn their future more than a soldier about to march to war?

"I used to come with my sister," Ollie said.

"Does she work in the keep too?"

He shook his head. "No, she's dead."

He said it with a matter-of-fact attitude that shocked me. "Oh, Ollie. I'm so sorry."

"It's fine. I'm not sad anymore. Besides, that's why I like visiting Lady Anis. She lets me talk to her. So she's not *really* dead."

"Ahh," I said. Imagining the poor boy trying to talk to his dead sister filled me with crippling sadness. It was just so sweet.

"What do you think you will ask Lady Anis?" he asked.

I wasn't sure how to answer. Explaining the complications of my Quintelaide, possibly taking a second lover—or even more than that! —was the sort of thing I didn't even want to acknowledge to myself, let alone out loud to a child.

Ollie stopped and turned around, waiting for my answer. I shrugged and said, "I want her to tell me about love."

He scrunched up his face, said, "Eww!" and then resumed leading me down the street.

I thought about Arthur. I knew I had feelings developing, hints of them swirling and tickling my insides. I wasn't sure if they were real, or the results of our new Dragon bond, or maybe just the general desire to have more supportive relationships in my life. I wanted someone to tell me what to think, both about him and the rest of my Quint. I needed cosmic permission that I was pursuing the right thing.

"There," Ollie said, pointing at a cottage up the road. "That's where she—"

The door opened and Arthur walked out.

It was as if I'd conjured him up with thought alone. I now recognized the growing excitement in the back of my mind as the building sensations from my bond with Arthur. A burst of happiness filled me at seeing him at an unexpected place. It was quickly replaced with confusion.

"Arthur?" I said, approaching the door. "What are you doing here?"

He looked at me like I was a Silithik driller. "I'm, uh. I'm sorry," he blurted, then quickly strode away.

"Arthur?" I called. "Arthur!" He turned down an alley and disappeared, a sense of shame and sadness following in his wake.

Ollie didn't seem to notice anything that had happened. His face brightened and he said, "Lady Anis! Lady Anis! I've brought a friend."

He ran into the skirts of the old woman, hugging her lower half tight. Lady Anis was a tiny woman, more wrinkles than anything else, with yellowed eyes that looked like they'd seen a hundred lifetimes of sorrow. She patted Ollie on the back with care.

"I can see that," she told him while eying me up and down. "Come, come."

Still in shock about Arthur's reaction, I followed her into the home. Ollie waved goodbye and waited outside, sitting cross-legged on the ground before the door closed.

"Over here, dear," the woman said. She hobbled to a table which held two tea cups and a crystal ball. On the wall was a jagged piece of canvas art showing a painted sunset, the colors sharp and true.

"What did you tell him?" I demanded. "Arthur. The man who was just here."

"Only what he needed to hear," she said simply. "Come on, then. Don't be shy. For you, the cost is two silver marks..."

I sat across from her and pulled the coins from a pouch on my belt. She shoved them in a pocket without looking, then nodded at me.

"I'm glad you came."

I gave a start. "Do you know me?"

"Can't say that I do." She smiled as if she'd heard a joke and was the only one who understood the punch line. "Now then. Let's begin."

She pushed up the sleeves of her dress—revealing arms that were covered with paper-thin skin—and placed both hands on the crystal ball. The moment she touched it, colors swirled within the glass, blue and green and then faintly orange, rotating from an unseen storm.

"Ohh," she said. "Wow. Oh my." Before I could ask, she let go of the orb and took my hand, tracing the lines of my palm. Her touch was soft and tickled like a feather. Finally, she looked into my eyes and said, "You are here for love."

I wondered how many women came here for romantic advice. Probably all of them. "Yes, Lady Anis."

She closed her eyes. "I see a single heart, torn into five pieces. Not all equal in size, but also not dissimilar."

I flinched, though she kept a firm grip on my hand.

"You know what this means?" she asked.

"I think I do."

"Care to elaborate, dear?"

You're supposed to tell my *fortune,* I wanted to say, but held back. "I have recently joined a Dragon Quintelaide. An existing one who lost their previous Pyromancer. I'm a replacement."

"I heard something about Honor Marches being halted," she muttered. "Always thought that was a foolish tradition. Oh aye, there comes a time when the only option is to *blow the whole thing up* rather than trying to salvage it. But not always. Especially with such talented men and women."

I frowned. "Blow the whole thing up? What does that mean?"

"A figure of speech. *Blow up*, the way Tinker contraptions fly into the sky when they detonate poorly."

"I'm still not sure I understand your meaning. When would it be a good idea to blow the whole thing up, so to speak?"

"Perhaps in the future you will come across such a scenario." She put her hands on the orb again, and the colors swirled. With her eyes still closed, Lady Anis moved her head as if watching something fly above the table. Finally, she intoned: "Only if your heart is whole can you survive this world."

"How can I make it whole?"

She laughed, a dry cackling sound deep within her throat. "You do not need to."

"But you just said..."

"It already is whole!" she said. "What you must avoid is splitting it into pieces."

I took a shuddering breath as her words sunk in. "What you're saying is I cannot share my heart. I must give it to only one man."

"What? No!" Lady Anis looked like she'd bit into something sour. "Think of... of... oh, I don't know. A pie. A pie can be shared without cutting it into pieces. Simply hand out five spoons, and everyone can share in the whole."

She got up and went to the kitchen before I could tell her how ridiculous that sounded. She poured water from a kettle into a cup and then stirred in a giant dollop of honey from a jar. The spoon clinked around the cup as she stirred and brought it back to me.

"Drink."

I took a sip. It was far too sweet and barely warm, but I gulped it down anyway. "You're saying I can share my heart."

She looked at me like I was an idiot. "Weren't you listening? Yes, that's what I said. Stars above..."

I drank the rest of the tea and set it down on the table. "Thank you."

"Don't thank me. I give common sense when only common sense is needed. Oh!" She reached into her pocket and came out with a letter sealed with wax. "This is for you as well."

"Who is this from?" I asked. "Did Arthur ask you to give this to me?"

"It is from me, dear. More advice."

I turned it over in my hands, then began to break the seal with my thumb.

"No!" she shouted. "Do not open it now."

"Then when..."

172

"You *save it*," she said. "For a time of great struggle. When you feel paralyzed with indecision, as if your legs are stuck in a block of ice. Only then will the words contained within help you. Now then, best be off with you. Unless you want to pay for another session..."

I let her usher me outside. Ollie hopped up and brushed off his servant robe, then hurried inside. The door closed with the scrape of wood on wood.

I examined the letter. It seemed suspicious to give something like this to a customer and tell them to open it at a future time, most likely when they would be far enough away from her that they couldn't demand their money back. Most fortune tellers were probably frauds, I knew. The entire experience, especially the crystal ball and the too-sweet tea, was silly. The kind of thing only gullible girls fell for.

But it was only two silver marks, and her words *were* comforting. I could share my heart without splitting it. I didn't even care if she were merely telling me what I wanted to hear.

A slender man with an unusually fair face and long robes approached the door, looked at me, and nodded politely. Then he stepped to the side, presumably waiting his turn to call on Lady Anis's services.

I eyed the letter again. It was tempting to open it now. Whatever words were inside would likely be valuable no matter when I read them. And if they weren't, I'd rather know now instead of a time when I was *really* looking for advice. I slid my thumb over the wax seal, pressing down to crack it in the middle...

The door behind me opened and Ollie came running out. The robed man quickly went inside, and I caught him say, "Lady Anis, I've returned with another question..." before he closed the door behind him. Ollie looked up at me with a big grin.

"Isn't she *wonderful?*" he said.

I shoved the letter in my pocket. "Oh yes, absolutely."

"I told you," he said smugly. "Didn't I tell you?"

"You sure did."

I let him lead me back to the keep, rambling about all the things his sister had told him from beyond the grave.

21

Alyssa

Everyone was in a dark mood at supper, especially Arthur.

He sat at the opposite end of the table from me with a scowl on his face. I hadn't had a chance to ask him what he was doing at the fortune teller's. Considering how embarrassed he'd looked, and the foul mood he seemed to have since then, it was probably best not to ask.

Maybe he was trying to speak to the dead too. The thought drifted across my mind. Arthur wasn't the type of man who believed in such things, but grief made people do strange things. Was he trying to communicate with Danni?

"...the north-west is stabilizing," Jax said. "Slowly, but progress is still progress. However, my contacts tell me the east is losing ground more rapidly with every day."

"We have land to lose in the east," Maze pointed out. "Who cares if we lose ten miles of rocks in the mountains?"

"Aye, but only for so long. Once they're beyond the mountains, there is little terrain remaining to put up a proper defense."

I put down my spoon. "I'm sick of talking about the war. We discuss it at every meal. It's torture since we cannot help one bit. Can we have one night of cheerier discussion? Surely someone has something *pleasant* to talk about..."

Maze sat up straight. "I've been working on a new explosive technology! The Tinker Guild finally shared their experiments." He leaned forward and lowered his voice. "There's this new powder."

"Powder?" Jax asked.

"Aye. Fine and black, and smells like death. Highly volatile. The Guild is still working on the best way to weaponize it, but I have several applications of my own. The potential is tremendous."

"Tremendous power to blow ourselves up!" Ryon said. Maze made a rude gesture, which caused the Shadow to grin.

Harry locked eyes with me from across the table. "Speaking of blowing ourselves up, I heard a rumor about *you.*"

I blinked. "What?"

"I heard from a servant, who heard from another servant, that a Pyromancer practicing in the courtyard the other day nearly blew up herself and a servant boy."

Jax's face split with a massive grin. "I heard the same, but didn't want to say anything!"

"That could have been any Pyro!" I said, blushing. "If you ignore that I'm the only one left in the city..."

"So it's true?" Maze asked.

"Only partly."

"Partly?"

"Yes," I said, struggling to keep a straight face. "I only *partly* blew us both up."

Everyone roared with laughter, which drew stares from the other soldiers dining in the room. Jax wrapped an arm around my shoulder and leaned into me. I shoved him away playfully. It was all good-natured.

Except to one person.

"Enough!" Arthur snapped.

Everyone cut off, shocked. Now we drew stares from the rest of the dining hall for a different reason.

"What are we, now?" Arthur demanded. "Simple soldiers who ridicule each other for our mistakes?"

"Arthur," Jax said, "it was only a joke—"

"Jokes always contain grains of truth." He held his fork tightly as if he intended to go to battle with it. His voice was strained, and he didn't look at anyone in particular during his rant. "Friendly teasing becomes bitter ridicule. Then we are afraid to tell one-another things. Eventually it can tear a Quint apart. We should be helping one another, not cutting ourselves down. Right now it feels like the entire Archenon is against us. We have no allies, no friends. Only each other. And if we're not careful, soon we won't have that."

He trembled and let the fork clatter to the table. His face was crimson with anger. Through the bond I felt a maelstrom of emotions, none of them good.

But the one feeling that came through the clearest was pain. Immense, unbearable pain.

Arthur pointed at me. "*She* is at least attempting to better herself. The rest of you mostly mope around the keep feeling sorry for yourselves, or being angry at our lack of marching orders. *She* is the only one who shouldn't be teased, because she's the only one handling this setback with maturity."

"Brother," Harry said gently.

Arthur's chair scraped as he lurched to his feet. His face was pale, and he suddenly seemed embarrassed by his outburst. Without another word, he whirled from the table, knocking the chair over in his haste to escape our stares.

"Arthur!" I called, but he was already gone.

22

Arthur

What is wrong with me?

I fled down the halls, already out of breath. It felt like I was having a panic attack. I turned down random corridors without looking, desperate to get away from the eyes of my comrades.

Frost Magi were supposed to be the calm, reasonable members of their Quintelaide. Examining information, coming to logical conclusions, then sharing the analysis with everyone else. We weren't supposed to let our emotions control us, and yet that's exactly what I had done.

Everyone teasing Alyssa had sent me into a rage. It was like a pipe had been opened in my chest, the anger pouring out of me in great gouts. Why had I reacted that way?

First being caught visiting Lady Anis, and now this. I was an embarrassing excuse of a Frost Mage.

Eventually I stopped wandering the keep and got my bearings. I didn't want to go back to my chambers, so I went to the bath instead. It was empty, as it usually was since the other Dragon Quintelaides had departed the keep. I heated a tub with the coals from a nearby brazier, stripped my clothes, and stepped into the scalding water.

I sighed while gripping the side of the tub and lowering myself in, every muscle in my body relaxing one at a time. Feet and ankles, then my calves. Up my thigh, my rear, and then my groin—which I hesitated at for a sensitive moment before dipping deeper. And then it was a quick plunge for the rest of my chest up to my neck.

It was wonderful. For several minutes I lay there with my eyes closed, pretending my stress was a physical thing bleeding into the water.

Only when I was fully relaxed, and no longer embarrassed, did I let my thoughts probe the situation again—more logically this time. I didn't think I was upset at the way they were laughing at Alyssa, although that may have been the catalyst. I was annoyed with my Quintmates for other reasons. For moping around the capitol, sure, but also for a deeper reason: they *wanted* to receive marching orders. To them, it was the next step in doing our duty. Fulfilling the purpose of our military unit.

But for me it only meant our doom. Because the dream was real. Alyssa and I would die, and likely the rest of them as well.

I'd been unable to think about anything else all day. It was possible the dream was in the very distant future, but somehow I sensed it was sooner than that. Somehow I knew it was imminent. It felt like a sword hanging over my head, held only by a thread that was beginning to fray. And it frustrated me that nobody else could see it.

I wished I could tell Alyssa. To warn her of what was coming. Maybe the future could be changed. *A futile and childish thought. Almost as childish as believing that one can see into the future.*

"Hi."

I opened my eyes to find Alyssa standing in the doorway. She held her hands in front of her meekly, and hung her head like a child who knew she was in trouble. Her hair was pulled up into a tail that looked like a single flickering flame behind her head, and her cheeks held little spots of red. The sight of her filled me with half a dozen emotions: relief, and caring, and a growing, animal-like attraction.

"I know you probably want to be alone," she said. "Jax told me to give you some space and talk in the morning..."

I rose out of the bath, grabbing the folded towel to cover myself as I did, tying it around my waist. Carefully, I stepped out of the tub. At first, I was angry. Angry at the situation, and at the future which held our mutual doom. But then something new replaced that anger. Where before it had felt like a faucet of rage poured out of my chest against my will, now a new faucet had been opened. A stronger emotion, one which I was powerless to ignore.

If we're doomed, I thought, *then why should I hold myself back?*

I strode toward Alyssa with new purpose.

23

Alyssa

I could feel Arthur's anger through our bond as he got out of the tub and walked towards me, like an animal whose den had been disturbed by an intruder. His hair was dark and damp, hanging loosely across one shoulder, and his scowl was terrible to behold. I had never seen him in a mood such as this. Had I made a mistake in coming here? I opened my mouth to tell him I was sorry.

Before I could, he kissed it.

His lips connected with mine, wet and warm from the bath. He slid one hand to the back of my head, fingers threading into my ponytail and holding me close with desperate need. It shocked me. It was the last thing I expected.

And it was wonderful.

A moan rumbled out of my throat as I returned the kiss, nuzzling his lips with mine. He tasted like the melon wine from supper but I didn't care, it was as intoxicating on his tongue as it was in a cup. I wrapped an arm around him to feel his back, running my fingers along his bare muscles and spine. His entire body was wet and hot, a blanket I wanted to smother me.

He shoved me roughly against the stone wall, sending an excited tingle up my spine. Then his hand moved up my thigh, over my runepouch and to my waist as if he wanted to pick me up. His tongue invaded my mouth and I welcomed it with my own, feeling the wet warmth, imagining it tasting every inch of my body. Arthur's hand moved higher, over the swell of my breast, and I wished my Dragon uniform wasn't inhibiting his needy touch from my skin.

This is what I've wanted, I thought in that moment. *I've needed this desperately.*

"Yes," I moaned, reaching a hand down to his towel, sliding into the seam to feel underneath. His entire body trembled as I found his manhood, hotter than the rest of him and every bit as hard. I began stroking him, and moved my free hand to the laces of my blouse to loosen them, eager to get the uniform off so we would go further, because I could feel his white-hot lust through our bond and it matched my own. This was everything I wanted, especially after receiving confirmation from the fortune teller. He thrust his hips forward in time with my strokes, and I couldn't help but imagine those thrusts *inside* of me, filling me completely...

"I want you," I breathed. "I need you."

With an abrupt jerk, Arthur pulled away from my touch. He panted as he stared at me, eyes wide and fearful.

"What is it? Was it something I said?"

He licked his lips. "We can't."

A vice gripped my heart. "What? Why?"

"I just..." The pain in his eyes increased as he stared at me. Stared *through* me at something else. A distant memory. "We can't. *I* can't. I'm sorry."

He grabbed his clothes and left, bare feet slapping wetly on the stone floor as I stood there, confused.

I didn't understand.

I sat on a bale of hay in the sparring courtyard, watching Jax and Maze take turns driving each other back with the swings of practice swords, the clattering sound echoing off the surrounding stone walls. Both of them were bare-chested and covered in a sheen of sweat, and although Maze didn't possess as much muscle as the Warrior, he was lithe and handsome in his own way. As I watched Jax's shape fall back smoothly, muscular arms moving the wooden sword like a choreographed dance, I realized how much I needed physical release. My Warrior had been angry lately, in too foul of a mood to want to dance with me between the sheets. When he did share my bed, he returned late at night, frustrated after listening to soldiers in the wine sinks complain about the war.

Kissing Arthur had reminded me of what I needed. We had been so *close*. And then he'd yanked it away, leaving me standing in the bath. I didn't understand why he would do that. He'd been the one to kiss *me*, leaving his tub and pouncing on me, shoving me up against the wall. Handling me like a man who could not control what he desired. It was everything I had ever wanted from him without realizing it. I replayed the kiss again and again, failing to decipher anything new each time.

Jax stopped falling back when he reached the end of the courtyard, and then went on the offensive, flowing smoothly from swing to swing as he pushed Maze back. I wished I could pick up a sword and hit something, too.

The problem was that, ultimately, I *did* understand why Arthur had stopped the kiss. I could feel Arthur's pain last night, fresh and bright. Clearly, he was still mourning Danni. That was certainly why he visited Lady Anis, and why he remained in a foul mood long after the visit. Jax might have gotten over the Pyromancer's death quickly, but it was foolish to expect the others to—especially considering their relationships with her went deeper.

I shouldn't have pushed Arthur. I should have given him more space.

Now things were awkward between us. He did not break his fast with us, and was absent from his room when I returned. I wondered if he would come help me train today. If the roles were reversed, I'd probably do everything I could to avoid him. *I should give it a few days.* Flames consume me, we certainly had enough free time to do so.

Jax and Maze laughed and sauntered over to me. A servant—not Ollie—came running up with skins of cold water. I eyed my two Quintmates and wondered if I should ask them about it. That meant giving voice to the embarrassing event, though. My tongue stayed silent.

"Your form is getting better," Jax said. "You did a good job anticipating the moves rather than waiting to see what I would do."

Maze paused to gulp water, then wiped his mouth with a sleeve. "Oh, fantastic. That'll help me if the bugs ever pick up a sword."

Jax frowned. "A beetle claw is quite similar to..."

"I was joking," Maze said, squirting a pulse of water at the big Warrior.

Jax smiled and shook his head. "Sorry. Haven't felt like myself lately. Waiting for orders feels like torture."

"Aye, that it is." Maze looked past me. "Speaking of feeling tortured..."

I glanced over my shoulder at Arthur's approaching shape. His hair was pulled back in a tail, but tufts stuck out around the fringes chaotically, and his eyes were bloodshot. He nodded in our general direction without looking at anyone specific.

"You look like you spent the night with the dungeon inquisitor," Maze said.

"I feel like it, too." Arthur cleared his throat. "Brothers. Alyssa. I would like to address what happened at supper last night. I am sorry for the way—"

"Hey now," Maze said. "No sorries. Not with us."

"There's nothing for which you need apologize," Jax agreed, putting a hand on the Frost Mage's shoulder. "All of us are out of our element sitting on our asses in this damned city."

Arthur nodded sheepishly, still staring at the ground between all of us. "Alyssa. Are you ready to practice?"

"I am," I said, rising. "You boys will have to resume your sparring without an audience."

"Maybe I'll find some ladies down at the market," Jax said. "They stare at me whenever I walk around town, so I might as well let them stare at me while I do what I'm good at..."

I playfully shoved at his chest, which was like trying to move a stone wall. Jax cupped my cheek and gave me a quick kiss. Arthur was already walking away, so I gave Jax a quick smile and then moved quickly to fall in beside my teacher.

"I'm sorry," I said when we were out of earshot of the others. "For last night."

"You did nothing wrong," Arthur said. His emotions were cold and closed off. A trickle of ice.

"But I did," I insisted. I was struggling to keep up with his long strides. "I disturbed you in the bath while you were dealing with some personal issues. I understand the need for solitude as well as anyone, and I am sorry for not leaving you at peace."

Arthur said nothing as we turned down another corridor.

"It won't happen again," I said. I felt like I needed to hear him say something, *anything,* even if it was something I didn't want to hear. "I promise you that."

He stopped and whirled toward me. "I do not wish to discuss this." The pain was there, underneath the layer of ice he was using as a barricade.

I wished he would let me in.

As we made the rest of the trip to the stables in silence, I thought about the note the fortune teller had given me. This seemed as good a time as any to open it. I needed advice. But it was stuffed away in the saddle bag in my room, so I didn't have that option. Maybe when we got back I'd read it.

The first time I'd visited the stables, two weeks ago when both the war and my relationship with the Ninety-First were fresh, it had been a bee hive of activity as countless Quints prepared for battle. Now, it was a shell of its former self. It almost looked abandoned, with rows of empty stalls and an eerie silence in the darkness. It took us several minutes of searching to find a cluster of stableboys huddled around a distant stall. One of them jerked when he saw us, then came running up.

"Sorry, my Lords Dragon," he said in a deep voice despite his size. "How can I help you? Fixing to go for a ride?"

"We are indeed," I said, "but I was wondering if it would be possible to switch horses. Mine has a terrible temperament, and bucks whenever I tighten the reins."

"Do you have any other mounts?" Arthur asked, looking around the vacant stable.

The boy removed his hat and scratched his head. "Afraid not. Low on horses, on account of the war. Only have one spare, but she's so stubborn she might as well be a mule. Broke three of Jarl's ribs while he was reshoeing her."

Down the row behind him, the other two stable boys were nervously approaching a stall where said horse was presumably being housed. There came a deep snorting sound, and then the stall door jerked as if something had smashed into it.

"Looks like there's a Silithik beetle in there instead of a horse," I said.

"Truth, Lady Dragon. While Jarl's out, I'm the one who's gotta *feed* her."

I looked around the stable as if another horse might magically appear. "You must have *something* I can try. It is only for practice. I'll take anything, even a pack animal."

"It will be good to practice on your own horse," Arthur said. "If that's what you're stuck with, then so be it."

Abruptly, the stall door smashed outward in a shower of splintered wood, sending the two stable boys flying. The horse whinnied and lunged through, a plain looking piebald with a rope around her neck. One of the boys grabbed the rope, but the horse was already galloping toward us, dragging him along the ground.

"Watch out!" Arthur shouted, readying his runes at his belt. I did the same, praying I wouldn't have to use it on a horse...

I froze, and dropped my runetablet to the ground. "Fireball!"

It wasn't merely wishful thinking: the piebald with the flaming red mane slowed as she neared us, then nuzzled against my chest. The braids I had made in her mane were still there, confirming her identity. I laughed and stroked her ears. "How in the flames did you get here, girl?"

The stable boys stared at me like I was a witch who'd turned their friend into a frog. Finally one of them said, "She showed up at Bracknall Stronghold. Came trotting out of the Borderlands like she'd been on holiday. Was transferred down here with other supplies."

"Stubborn girl," I said, making soothing noises. "She doesn't know when she's supposed to die."

"Lady Dragon," the other stable boy said warily, "that is the most difficult horse I've ever seen come through here, and that's including the massive Berkshire drafts that the Warriors sometimes ride. You two must have been together for a long time to calm her so."

"No," I said with a smile. "Just one trip. And many more to come. Arthur, isn't this wonderful? My horse survived the Borderlands!"

My comrade didn't answer. His face was as white as bone as he eyed the horse up and down, and he felt alarmed through his bond.

"Arthur?" I said, touching his arm. "Are you all right?"

He gave a start, but his eyes never left the animal. "I am quite fine. The charge startled me."

"Come on," I said to Fireball. "Let's get you saddled. We have runetracing to practice!”

24

Alyssa

Riding Fireball was like being reunited with an old friend. She moved intuitively, obeying the commands with the reins and my heels the moment I gave them. For several minutes I savored simply trotting around the flat ground in front of the east gate of the city. It even helped take my mind off the kiss Arthur and I had shared.

The alarm from Arthur's bond had changed to coldness while Fireball was saddled, and since then it had only deepened. Embarrassment at being startled by the charge in the stable, I assumed. I wasn't going to allow that to ruin my own happy mood.

Riding around outside the city gate brought back bitter memories from the battle that had taken place here. After the fighting had ended, the countless dead Silithik had been arranged in bonfires for burning. Now all that remained were tall piles of ash and soot, which diminished in size each day. Eventually the wind would carry the rest of it away, scattering their remains across the Archenon. I shivered at the thought of some future crop being fed with the ash of a dead hive army.

"First, let's trace from a standstill," Arthur instructed, interrupting my joy ride. "Bring your horse here. Good. Trace a few *flares* while we're not moving."

I obeyed, switching runes and then sending three *flares* high into the sky, exploding like Tinker fireworks.

"Now at a walk," Arthur said, devoid of emotion. "Follow alongside me."

"You got it, Frosty."

He didn't react to my nickname as we guided our horses into a slow walk. My body rocked in the saddle along with Fireball's gait, making it more difficult—but not impossible—to trace. It took me several minutes to trace three more *flares*, with multiple failed attempts between successes.

"That's fine and good, but accuracy from horseback matters too," Arthur said.

I snorted. "Easy for you to say. Your most powerful spell, *blizzard*, can be traced without any consideration for accuracy."

"That's not true," he said coldly. "Many a Frost Mage has traced their *blizzards* haphazardly, injuring nearby structures or people. I myself nearly impaled Jaxon last year when tracing a *blizzard* slightly larger than I expected."

I grinned, hoping to get him to relax. "I suppose I should start tracing a *flame barrier* spell above me during battle, as a shield against any stray *blizzards* you might trace."

He stared blankly, not sharing in the humor. "Switch to *fireballs* for this next round. Aim for that ash pile, over there."

Fine. Wallow in your mood.

He was right: it was tougher aiming at a specific target than merely sending *flares* straight into the air. The first two *fireballs* I traced missed the target entirely, but the third struck the ash mound. Despite the *fireball's* small size, it sent a huge cloud of ash into the air. A gust of wind promptly carried the ash in our direction.

"Eek!" I squealed as I turned away from the cloud of ash. When it had passed, I coughed and eyed my now soiled uniform. "Maybe we should have brought hay bales for targets."

"You had better get used to it," Arthur said. "There will be far more dead Silithik before all of this is over. Again, this time at a trot."

I wanted to laugh at him for being so damn grim, but he was already trotting away on his horse, yellow hair flowing behind him. I followed, bouncing up and down on Fireball's back. What had come over the Frost Mage? Normally, he was cool and calm. The other members of our Quint allowed their emotions to control them to varying degrees, but Arthur had always been able to make himself think and act rationally.

I thought back to the kiss. He had moved with such determination then, casting aside all thought and letting his animal instinct take over. It was incredibly hot. I still shivered with excitement whenever I thought about it. Yet since then, Arthur could barely look me in the eyes.

What happened when he visited Lady Anis? I wondered. *That's when his entire personality changed.*

Arthur pointed at another ash pile. I began to trace.

And promptly failed.

I tried again, and then a third time. There was too much movement bouncing in the saddle. My finger slid across the carved rune, zig-zagging over the groove rather than following them as I tried to account for the jostling. I could feel the runemagic, just out of reach, even when I *stretched* my mind toward it. It was maddening.

Arthur watched silently until I finally gave up. "Your problem is the way you're bouncing in the saddle."

"Oh? I hadn't noticed," I said dryly.

"You have to completely rethink the way you ride a horse," he explained. "Stand up in the stirrups. Not a lot—just enough to stabilize yourself a finger-length above the saddle. Like I'm doing."

I watched him and then tried to mimic it, engaging my leg muscles to bear my weight in the stirrups rather than the saddle.

"It's not suitable for long rides, but it'll get the job done for a few traces. Try again."

I began another trot, this time standing up in the stirrups. It was easier, but not by much: I struggled to keep my finger steady in the grooves of the rune, a trickle of runemagic teasing me before vanishing like mist. I tried again, and again, before finally sitting back down with an exasperated sigh.

"It's not easy," Arthur said. "But it's *easier*."

"It doesn't feel that way."

"Sure it does," he said, bringing his horse around to face me. "I felt your trickle of runemagic that time."

"*Only* a trickle."

"Small steps lead to big ones. Try again."

We repeated the exercise for the better part of two hours, trotting in circles in the shadow of the great city. By the time my legs were too sore to continue, my best attempt had resulted in half of a *fireball* trace.

"Well done," Arthur said.

"Your sarcasm is not appreciated," I muttered.

"No sarcasm. I'm being genuine. The first time I tried this, I couldn't trace a trickle. You very nearly got a full spell off." A trickle of pride came through his bond.

"It's still not impressive."

Yet as we rode back to the city, I felt a tiny bit of hope at his words. Maybe I would get the hang of this eventually.

A messenger girl waited for us inside the city gates. "My Lords Dragon. You're needed in the Field Marshal's chambers."

"Thank you," Arthur said. "We'll be there as soon as we get cleaned off."

The messenger shook her head. "No, Lord Dragon. You're

needed *immediately.* You must go there without delay."

Arthur glanced at me, confused. We both realized it at the same time. There was likely only one reason Tyronix would need to speak with us without delay.

We're receiving our marching orders.

25

Alyssa

"I do not understand why she did not interrupt our practice," Arthur growled as we hurried through the keep. "If Tyronix is delivering our marching orders, then the messenger should not have allowed us to prance around."

"It doesn't matter now," I said.

I was a bundle of excitement. We were finally being deployed. After all the waiting and ridicule, we were being sent to defend the Archenon—the entire purpose of our existence as a Dragon Quintelaide. There was an element of fear involved, but that only made things *more* exciting to me. I couldn't wait to see the look on everyone else's faces.

Arthur didn't share any of my excitement. The only thing I felt from him was a grim resignation. *It's almost like he wants to remain here in the capitol.*

I pushed the thought from my head as we arrived in the briefing room. Everyone else was already here, waiting impatiently. Tyronix was standing in front of the huge map, with the other four members of our Quint waiting with crossed arms. "About time," Ryon said. Jax smiled warmly, while Maze used a rag to polish the lenses of his welding goggles.

"We nearly began without you," Tyronix said. "You'd think you all *want* to remain here indefinitely."

"We're here now," Arthur said.

The Field Marshal nodded, then turned to the map. "The mountains east of the capitol," he announced, pointing. Maze pumped a fist happily, but returned to calmness at a sharp look from Tyronix.

"Two Silithik hives have fallen back from their fronts and are regrouping *here.*" He placed a red thumbtack on the map, just north of the mountains. "They are on the move, according to our gryphon scouts. Their target is this mountain pass *here.* Beyond that pass is the valley where we mine the majority of our sorcerous runestone. We cannot lose those mines, or let them fall into Silithik possession. Your orders are to stop that from happening."

"Are the Silithik aware of the strategic value of the region?" Arthur asked.

"A good question, and one I wish we knew the answer to. I doubt they understand how valuable those mines are to our war effort, or even have the capacity for such strategic thinking. But then again, we never suspected the Hivemind of using advanced strategies like underground tunnels and surprise attacks. In light of the new information regarding the ability of their Queens to runetrace, these mines *cannot* fall into their hands."

Jax approached the map and pointed to the mountain pass at the entrance to the valley. "Understood, Field Marshal. The plan seems obvious. If we can be transported by gryphon here, we can attempt to hold them off at the choke point. I know this pass. We fought a skirmish here three years ago. There are twists and turns to slow the bugs, and we can use runetrace-induced rock slides to funnel them even tighter. With that done, a single Pyromancer could hold them off by herself." He glanced over his shoulder at me.

"A good plan," Tyronix agreed sadly. "But you will not have gryphon support on this mission."

The room was silent for a long moment.

"It will take three days to reach there by horse," Jax argued.

"Two, if you take only short rests and ride through the night," Tyronix said.

Next to me, Arthur moaned, a sound so low only I could hear. It almost sounded like he said, *it's happening.*

"Set up to fail," Ryon cursed.

Jax shook his head. "Field Marshal, I do not understand." He pointed at the map. "In two days we will be fighting them in the open valley, where their numbers will overwhelm us. If we cannot hold them at the first pass, I suggest we fall back to *here*—" he pointed again, "—at the southern exit of the valley. And if we cannot hold them there, we can fall back to the Trondien Stronghold."

"Those are not your orders," Tyronix said stiffly. "Your orders are to keep the mines out of Silithik possession. You are not permitted to fall back under any circumstances."

"Then give us gryphon assistance so we can hold the first mountain pass," Harry said. "Has anyone spoken with the gryphon General?"

"They will not be aiding us in this mission," was all the Field Marshal said.

Ryon growled, his hand tight on the handle of his sheathed dagger. "Is he still in the keep? Give me five minutes alone with the feathered fool and I'll convince him to help us."

Tyronix shook his head. "This was not General Caretaan's decision."

"So we're to ride for two straight days, hopefully reaching the valley before the Silithik," Maze said slowly. "And once we do... We're supposed to fight two full hives by ourselves? In the open? Field Marshal, your orders are sending us to our deaths."

"These are *not my orders*," he said. Every word was thick with hidden meaning. "They are the orders I am told to relay to you. It is out of my hands."

The Archon. He was behind this. My Quintmates were bundles of rage and disbelief in the back of my head. *How could he do this?*

Tyronix stepped forward and embraced Jax's forearm, then leaned in to whisper, "I wish it were different, Jaxon."

"But it is not," Jax said back softly.

"It is not," Tyronix agreed. "Servants are gathering your belongings. Head directly to the stables. You must leave at once if you are to have a chance." He hesitated. "Ninety-First Quintelaide, I hope you are able to carry out these orders and return safely to us. I truly do."

"Ninety-First?" Harry said bitterly. "Don't you mean the Hundred and Thirty-Third Quintelaide?"

Tyronix smiled sadly. "I said what I meant, Ranger. I said what I meant."

*

We walked to the stables in silence. None of us dared say anything. None of us needed to.

Fireball had been prepared rather than my other horse, I saw with relief. She was already weighed down with our saddlebags, along with my Quintmates' horses. We mounted up and strode through the city gates to the east. No fanfare greeted us, nor calls of glory and good fortune from the guards along the wall. They only watched us silently.

Only when we were on the road east, with the hot sun burning overhead, did Maze break the silence.

"Fuck all of this."

Ryon barked a bitter laugh. "Well spoken."

197

"This is the Archon's doing," I said. "Right? There can be no other possible explanation?"

"Undoubtedly," Harry said.

"If the Archon wants us to die," Ryon growled, "then I say we don't give him the pleasure. We can travel farther east, find some other Quints to join. Fight real battles with a real chance of victory."

"Perhaps it is a test," Jax wondered out loud. "To see if we can follow orders to the letter. That would not be surprising, considering our previous mutinous march into the Borderlands."

"This is no test," Arthur said. He was strangely distant as we rode along. Nobody seemed to hear him.

Harry said, "If it is a test, when would they stop us? At the first stronghold we come across?"

"That would be Boxhall Stronghold," Maze said. "We'll reach it by nightfall. Valnu Stronghold after that, before the road turns south."

"At the very least," Harry said, "we should travel to Valnu. If it is not a test, then we can decide what to do."

"This is no test," Arthur repeated. I gave him a questioning look, but he turned away from my horse.

"We cannot disobey an order," Jax announced loudly. "We have done so once, and it was a tremendous mistake. I will not do that again."

"It was a tremendous *success*," Maze said. "We single-handedly saved the war by disobeying orders and marching into the Borderlands."

"Something tells me we wouldn't get that lucky a second time," I said. "We don't have a headstrong, incredibly foolish Pyromancer waiting to ride up and save us at the last possible moment."

A few of them laughed, and I felt small flares of humor through their bonds. It felt good to know I could lighten the mood in an otherwise despairing situation.

"I'm going to follow our orders today," Jax said. "And then again tomorrow. I will do this, because I am a Warrior of the Archenon, and it is my duty. I hope all of you will do the same."

As the sun peaked in the sky and slowly drifted behind us, the mood of our little group slowly changed. My Quintmates began chatting idly. On a whim, Harry nocked an arrow and tried to shoot down a circling buzzard but missed, to Ryon's immense laughter. Maze explained how he'd brought along two kegs of the special new powder from the Tinker Guild. After learning this, Harry and Ryon kicked their horses forward to put as much distance between them and Maze as possible, despite the Tinker's loud reassurances. A map of the mining valley was included in our supplies, and Jax spent a while studying it in his saddle as if it contained a secret he had yet to figure out.

I shared the same mood as them. Despite the circumstances, it felt good to be out of the capitol and on the move. Maybe that's why I didn't feel any deep despair. I was scared, but it was the normal fear that should accompany being sent to battle. Not the crippling fear of knowing I was going to die.

I remembered the letter Lady Anis had given me; I could feel it in the outer pocket of my saddle bag. I examined the round wax seal holding it closed. I considered announcing it to the group, jokingly declaring that we could use some good fortune directly from a woman of that profession. It might get some laughs.

Something stopped me. It felt like the letter was personal, something just for me. That was silly since she was only a fortune teller, but it stopped me nonetheless. I put the letter away and decided to worry about it at a later time.

Jax kept the horses at a steady, ground-eating pace. We came upon Boxhall Stronghold in the late afternoon, a squat castle in a triangle shape with towers at each corner. Aside from the sunlight glistening off a few polished helms manning the battlements, it almost looked abandoned. We waited to see if a messenger would run out and deliver us new orders. None did, and so we continued marching eastward.

The others returned to their nervous chatter on the highway, but Arthur just stared ahead, practically catatonic. I urged Fireball forward until I was riding alongside him.

"Hey."

He looked surprised to see me. "Hello."

"Are you well, Frosty?"

The tiniest hint of a smile touched his lips. "You mean aside from the hopeless battle we're riding toward?"

I smiled. "Aside from that, yes."

"I'm quite fine. Just lost in thought."

Here was my opening to bring up last night's kiss. To apologize again, and maybe get *some* sort of explanation as to why he had acted the way he had. I needed to hear him say that it was fine, that I hadn't done anything wrong. Perhaps that he just needed more time before pursuing a new relationship.

"You want to help me practice some more?" I asked instead. "We've got time to kill while we ride to that hopeless battle, and maybe by the time we get there, I'll be an expert at this."

We both knew I wouldn't be, but it was nice to have something else on which to focus. Arthur smiled.

"I would be delighted to help."

I moved my runes to the clips on the belt, then kicked Fireball into a trot to practice what we had done earlier in the day. We spent the remainder of the afternoon trotting ahead of the group and then back, legs flexed enough to raise my butt off the saddle while I tried to trace. Our Quintmates teased us at first, then ignored Arthur and me as we focused on the drills. I was self conscious of the others watching, which made it more difficult on the first few tries, but soon I lost myself in the practice as my finger flew over the carved runetablet.

"As I told you earlier," Arthur said when we finally stopped, "do not be discouraged. It takes time. You have already progressed rapidly for someone so new, even if you could not complete a single trace."

"I bet you say that to all the cute Pyromancers," I joked to cover my sense of failure. It certainly didn't *seem* like I was progressing rapidly.

"Only the Pyros who *need* help," Ryon said, half teasing and half serious. Jax twisted in his saddle to send him a dirty look. I made myself laugh to pretend like the jab didn't sting.

The road came alongside a river for a time, and we stopped to water the horses and take our own breaks before continuing on our march. The sun was just beginning to dip below the trees behind us, spreading orange and purple streaks across the sky, when Harry suddenly pointed at the sky.

"Look."

We all craned our necks to look: high in the sky flew a gryphon, wings flapping gently as it soared on the wind.

"Wonder where he's headed," Maze said.

"Probably scouting the front," Jax said. "Or else he's heading east for some redeployment."

But as we continued riding along the road, we realized the gryphon wasn't going anywhere. He stayed above us, flying in a wide circle with us always in his sight.

"Like a steaming buzzard," Maze muttered.

I frowned up at him. "You think he's accompanying us to the battle? To give us cover and information from above?"

"More likely he's spying on us," Ryon said bitterly.

Harry's eyes widened. "You don't think..."

Maze gasped. "No."

"I'm inclined to agree with Ryon," Jax said, certainty growing with each word. "I suspect he's ensuring we follow our orders."

"Tyronix wouldn't waste a gryphon on verifying our loyalty to the Archenon," Harry said.

"No, he wouldn't." Ryon sneered. "But the Archon would."

We rode in silence as night descended.

The fields on either side of the road slowly showed more and more trees, dark sentinels in the night. They thickened into a true forest sometime after the crescent moon rose, which blocked our view of the gryphon above. I wondered if he still followed—could he follow without seeing us?—or if he had landed to sleep. I didn't know how long one of his kind could fly before stopping to rest. As I rocked back and forth in my saddle, I wished I was curled up in a bedroll. Practicing tracing was exhausting, even if I couldn't trace any *actual* runemagic yet.

Jax finally called us to a stop when the moon was at its peak overhead. He tended to everyone's horses and took up the first watch while the other five of us rested. I laid flat on the grass next to the road, using a cloak from my saddle bag crumpled up as a pillow. It felt so wonderful to lay down and close my eyes, relaxing my muscles after sitting in the saddle...

"Alyssa," Jax said, shaking me gently. "Wake up. We're riding out."

I groaned and sat up. Everyone was packing and preparing to leave. Flames, it had felt like I'd only just closed my eyes! "If you let me sleep another hour," I whispered, "I promise to do terrible, wonderful things to your body later."

He smiled. "You have no idea how tempting that is."

We continued through the dark woods, wavering in our saddles as the path turned south. Jax had recommended we save our bitterbeans until the next night, when we would need them most. Instead, I reached into my pack and chewed on a piece of dried beef. It didn't help.

Dawn came as we exited the forest, and with it came a sky clear of everything except puffy white clouds. "Maybe we lost him," Maze suggested.

"Maybe he was never spying on us in the first place," Harry said.

I snorted. "Or maybe he's only sleeping, like I wish I was doing."

My theory ended up being the likely explanation, because our gryphon escort appeared in the air a few hours after the dawn. Jax cursed when he saw him.

"They have no gryphons to fly us to battle, but they will spare one to babysit us."

We stopped again when we came to a bridge crossing a stream. Ryon led the weary horses to drink while the rest of us found comfortable places on the ground. Arthur chose a place a short distance from the rest, and after a moment I joined him.

"Is this spot taken?" I asked.

He gestured for me to sit. "It is, now."

I groaned as I folded my legs underneath me. Despite my exhaustion, I didn't think I'd be able to nap with the sun climbing in the sky. For now, sitting felt good enough.

"I never asked you about the fortune teller," I said, voicing the question that had nagged me all during the ride. "Lady Anis."

Arthur tensed. "What about her?"

"What did she tell you?" I asked. "What did you ask?"

He didn't look at me: he stared at a spot on the ground as if he were afraid to meet my eyes. Like an embarrassed child. I studied his face while he sat in silence and wondered if he would ever answer.

"There was a personal matter in which I needed consultation," he finally replied.

"That's an awfully vague answer," I said with a friendly smile.

"It is." I waited for him to elaborate, but then he said, "I hope you won't tell the others. It is not a visit I wish to discuss with them."

"Of course," I quickly said. "I hope you know you can discuss it with me, if you wish. I won't make fun of you. Well, I won't make fun of you *much*."

He met my eyes for an instant. "Thank you." And then he returned to staring at the ground, idly picking at individual blades of grass.

"Aren't you going to ask why I was there?" I wasn't sure if I even wanted to tell him. Maybe I was looking for a way to segue into talking about our kiss in the bath.

"I would imagine you visited a fortune teller to have your fortune *told*," he said with a small smile. "But beyond that, it doesn't surprise me a woman like you would be there."

I frowned. "Why do you think women are more likely to visit a fortune teller? Because we're more emotional than men? You know, maybe I *will* tell the others..."

He grabbed my arm to stop me. His touch was strong but tender, and his eyes sparkled in the morning light.

"Of course I don't mean that," he said softly. "I meant because you're a Pyromancer. Your profession has always been fueled by powerful emotion. It's what gives your fire so much strength."

I let go of some of my anger, but not all of it. "And Frost Magi have no emotions?"

He took a deep breath, holding it. I could tell he wanted to tell me something. He was looking at me intently, as if by avoiding looking at me earlier he'd stored up all of his intensity for now. The fire in his eyes was so hot I wanted to touch him, to kiss him again like we had in the bath...

"No," he finally said. "We don't."

He rose and strode toward the horses, which Ryon was guiding back toward the road. Frustrated, I joined them.

26

Alyssa

The second night of travel was worse than the first, even with the aid of bitterbeans. I fell into a routine of nodding off, hitting my chin on my chest, then jerking back awake in my saddle. Jax smiled at me every time, which prompted me to stick my tongue out at him. On the other side, Ryon had no trouble sleeping while riding: he kept his eyes closed and somehow remained perfectly balanced in the saddle.

I need to ask him how he does it, I thought. *If he will ever talk to me without scorn.*

The gryphon was waiting in the sky the next morning, which prompted a flurry of curses from our party. He was beginning to feel like an executioner leading us to the gallows.

"No use stopping at Valnu Stronghold now," Harry said.

"I told you it was not a test," Arthur said miserably.

"Hello!" Maze called up to the bird, hands cupped to his mouth. "How about you make yourself useful! Fly ahead and scout for us! Tell us how far the Silithik have advanced into the valley!"

If the gryphon heard, he gave no sign.

Maze turned to Harry. "Do me a favor: brush an arrow past his beak. Just to get his attention."

"Don't tempt me," Harry grinned.

"Fucking gryphons," Ryon muttered, brushing his hair back out of his eyes. "It's easy to be peaceful when you can fly above trouble without a care in the world."

"Or when your nation is protected on three sides by water," Harry added, "and has no chance of being invaded."

We rode all morning before the Dragonspine Mountains rose up in the distance. A somber silence fell over the party as the peaks grew higher and higher, blocking out the blue of the sky. Having been pushed at an exhausting pace, the horses were becoming antsy; Fireball constantly tossed her head and tried to pull to the side of the road before I guided her back on course. I knew how she felt. I was exhausted and all I'd done was ride in the saddle. I stroked Fireball's mane and hoped she understood the gratitude I felt for her.

It felt cruel to force her into a trot, so I practiced runetracing at our slow walk. It was more difficult than tracing at a stand-still, but still relatively easy to draw the runemagic into my chest, feeling the heightened senses that came along with it. That gave me a jolt of energy as strong as the bitterbeans, though I stopped after only a few minutes to avoid wearing myself out. Soon we would need every bit of strength we had against the Silithik.

We stopped one final time in the foothills of the mountains, both to rest the horses before climbing into the south-west pass and to muster our own courage. Jax pulled out the rolls of maps tied on the back of his saddle, found the one he wanted, and spread it out on the ground.

I looked over his shoulder as the others gathered around. The map showed the entire valley, with the Dragonspine Mountains running from the south-west toward the Borderlands to the north-east, and other ranges forming the remaining borders of the valley farther to the south. The topography was marked in dark ink—the mountains, foothills, and a river running through the center—while other maze-like features were drawn in red. They looked like the roots of a tree, and spread out through most of the valley.

What are those? Before I could ask, Jax pointed.

"Here, just north of Trondien Stronghold, is the south-west pass. I'll admit, I was hoping we would reach this point to find the Silithik already exiting the valley. Then it would be too late to defend the mines, and we could fight in the choke point or fall back to the stronghold to the south."

"No such luck today," Maze said. "Although maybe we'll come across them in the pass itself."

Ryon stretched. "Nothing stopping us from taking our time, is there? Give the bugs a chance to catch up. Then we'll have no choice but to fight in the pass."

Jax shook his head. "Any slower progression would be obvious. I don't want to give the Archon any excuse to charge us with dereliction of duty, or treason." He pointed to the sky, where the gryphon was circling.

"Would the Archon really do that?" I asked. "Charge a Quint with treason for not marching to their death fast enough?"

"A month ago, I would not have believed so," Jax said. "Then again, a month ago I wouldn't believe he would force us to replace our Pyromancer."

Everyone around the map went stone-faced. I swallowed the bile creeping up my throat.

Jax reached over his shoulder to pat mine. "I am not complaining of your presence here, Aly. I'm only illustrating how I think the Archon will act."

I felt a pulse of jealousy from Arthur's bond, but when I glanced at him he quickly looked away.

"I haven't minded your company," Maze said, elbowing me and giving me a wink. "It hasn't been bad at all. At least, until we get to this valley and all die horrible deaths."

"Remind me never to come to you for a comforting word," I replied.

"In any case, I agree with Jax," Harry said, leaning on his bow like a walking staff. "We know the extent of the Archon's pettiness. We can't delay here hoping the Silithik will overrun the valley."

"So, that's it, then?" Ryon asked. "We enter the valley, see that we have to fight the bugs in the open, and then accept our fate and die in a glorious charge?"

"If you have any other viable options, now's the time to voice them," Jax said.

The weight of Lady Anis's letter hung in my pocket. Now was a time of need if I'd ever seen one. *When you feel paralyzed with indecision, as if your legs are stuck in a block of ice.* Those were her exact words.

"Perhaps we can sneak behind the hive armies," Harry offered, though his tone was doubtful. "Find their Queens. Slay them."

Jax snorted. "Somehow I doubt we'll be able to walk right up to their Queens this time."

"And that's assuming they came along," Arthur said. "Most Queens remain far from battle. The one in the tunnel was only there because she had to trace the portal."

I reached into my pocket, then stopped. There was something else Lady Anis said that was tickling my memory. *There comes a time when the only option is to blow the whole thing up.*

My eyes widened.

"Blow the whole thing up!" I blurted out.

Everyone looked at me. "Care to elaborate?" Jax asked.

"It was something a fortune teller told me. It doesn't matter." I quickly jabbed a finger at Ryon. "Yes, I visited a fortune teller. Save your teasing until we get out of this alive."

Ryon put his hand over his heart with mock adoration. "Alyssa, dearest Pyromancer. If you get us out of this alive, I'll write poetry to sing your praises."

"Damn right you will." I knelt next to Jax and pointed at the map. "What are these red lines?"

"Mining tunnels," Jax said. "They all lead to these three mine entrances."

"Yes! I thought that's what they were." I jerked my chin toward Maze. "You've got those containers of powder? The special stuff you've been bragging about for days?"

"Aye, the two kegs on the back of my saddle. Ryon's been teasing me about them all trip."

"No, I've been *avoiding* them all trip."

"And I've been avoiding the smell of your horse," Maze shot back. "Damned thing smells like he rolled in pig shit before leaving."

"Are you sure it's not your own air you smell?"

"Oh, I know my own stink."

While they joked back and forth, I followed the red lines on the map with my eyes. *It may work. It may actually work!*

"Let's blow the whole thing up," I said again. "We go into the mines. Place trails of powder in strategic areas. And when the Silithik pass through the valley, we ignite it all. Boom!" I clapped my hands together to demonstrate. "It will destroy most of the valley, but it will kill the hive armies, too."

"A creative idea," Harry said, "but it violates our order to protect the runestone mines."

"No," Jax said, eyes widening with realization. "Those weren't our orders. Tyronix told us to ensure the mines didn't fall into Silithik possession."

"Precisely," I said. "This plan accomplishes the orders."

"Are you certain the Archon will accept such an interpretation?" Harry asked.

"I'd rather survive to have such an argument," Jax said.

Ryon was peering at the map. His dagger was in his hand, which he used to gesture from one end to the other. "It's too large of an area. The mines are extensive. Two kegs won't be enough. Not by a long shot."

"I think two kegs will be *plenty*," Maze said. He had the excited look of someone who had solved a puzzle. "In fact, we won't need to place the powder deep underground at all. These are *runestone* mines, and runestone is volatile. If there's enough of the mineral still in the ground, a large explosion at the mine entrance would cause a secondary explosion. And those explosions would trigger even more runestone deeper in the mine tunnels, and those..."

"Not to mention the fine runestone powder in the air down there," Harry added.

"It would be massive. Tremendous." Maze was practically hopping up and down, now.

"Massive enough to kill all of us with it?" Ryon said. "None of this matters if we die in the process. And as much as I'd love to get away from the ugly horse meat you call a face, brother, I wouldn't want you sacrificing yourself so we could escape."

Maze grinned at him as if he'd given him a compliment.

I pointed at the map. "Look here. This ridge, south of *this* mine entrance, has no tunnels directly underneath it or anywhere nearby. We can detonate the powder from there and be completely safe."

"No!" Arthur suddenly snapped. "Absolutely not!"

Everyone looked at the Frost Mage. He was trembling, and his hands were balled into fists. The fear in his eyes, matching the fear from the bond, sent a shiver up my spine. Was he afraid of explosions? Surely not, after the battles we had been in.

"Well?" Harry said. "Are you going to enlighten us as to your reservation to the plan?"

Arthur looked flustered, as if he didn't know what to say. He cleared his throat. "We cannot be certain that map is accurate. There may be mining tunnels under that ridge."

"Then we'll give it a quick scout," Maze said. "In and out. Zip zap."

"But..." Arthur sputtered. "The ridge may still collapse even if there aren't any tunnels directly underneath. We'd be swept away by the rock slide, buried under the weight of a mountain."

"It's still a better plan than fighting the Silithik head-on," I said.

"I've got a coil of detonation cable," Maze added. "We can trigger it from as far away as we please."

"And if something cuts the wire?" Arthur said, strangely insistent. "Then what? We ride up the ridge to detonate it ourselves?"

"That's exactly what I would do, yes," I answered.

It was meant to placate Arthur, but he looked destroyed by the response. His bond was a confusing mixture of despair and anger.

Jax stood up. "Whatever details may arise, this plan is undoubtedly sound. Unless there are alternative suggestions..."

Ryon pointed his dagger at me. "I'm with Alyssa. Let's blow the whole thing up." Maze and Harry both added their agreement.

Arthur hung his head in defeat. I put a hand on his arm. "What's wrong?"

"Nothing."

"I know it's a dangerous plan..."

"The plan is fine," he said, resigned. "There is no way to avoid fate."

He strode away from the rest of us to ready his horse. Jax watched him go and shook his head.

"Fate?" I wondered out loud.

"It may not matter," Jax said, staring off at Arthur. "We might climb into the south-west pass and be greeted by the Silithik long before we can put this plan into motion."

"Maybe so," I said.

It was not so.

We rode through the steep mountain pass against the wishes of our exhausted horses, each switchback bringing a wave of vertigo the higher we went. Parts of the path were scarcely a span wide, with sections that had broken away recently. Soon I'd learned to keep my eyes on Fireball's mane instead of the narrow trail with the steep drop-off dangerously close to where we rode. And falling wasn't the worst thing we had to fear. Each turn brought quiet expectation from the group, wondering if we would come face-to-face with Silithik.

It took us two hours to climb through the pass, ending on a flat plateau in the middle of the south-west ridge of the Dragonspine Mountains. The valley spread out below us, rolling hills descending away from the mountains before giving way to thick forests. A river wound its way at the bottom, the water reflecting the sun like a mirror, before the valley sloped upward in the distance toward more rolling hills and mountains beyond. The ridges that ran perpendicular to the primary mountain ranges looked like the spines of enormous animals laying on the ground, covered in green moss.

The valley was so huge it was difficult to comprehend its size. The beauty of it all made me gasp. I realized just how little of the world I'd seen.

"Well then," Jax said. "There is our answer."

I followed his gaze to the north-east, where more distant mountains stretched in a line. There was a haze in the air between the mountain peaks and in the foothills, like a dust cloud kicked up by a horse, but of course it was much too large to be that.

Unless it is a thousand horses. Or ten thousand.

"Oh," I said as I picked out other details. We were so far away that they looked stationary, but two tendrils of brownish-grey snaked down from the mountains into the valley. Silithik beetles moving down from the pass in single-file, then spreading out into their larger army. It was more than ten thousand Silithik, it seemed. It was a hundred thousand. Perhaps more. I stared at the scene and tried to figure what emotion to feel.

For a long while, the only sound was the chirping of nearby birds and the stirring of our horses. Our doom was shockingly peaceful when viewed from so far away.

"Looks like they are only now descending into the valley," Jax said quietly. "We have three hours, perhaps four, before they reach this pass."

Maze twisted in his saddle to face the rest of us. "I vote for the plan that *doesn't* involve us riding down there and fighting them head-on."

"You'd vote for any plan involving Tinker trickery," Harry said.

"Aye," Maze grinned. "I would. Why do you think I became a steaming Tinker?"

Jax looked around the group for confirmation. Ryon nodded while stroking his dagger. Harry sighed before jerking his head in agreement. I gave my vote with a smile.

Arthur had returned his face to a blank mask. "Looks like my opinion matters not one bit."

"If you have concerns, you may voice them," Jax said. "But do so quickly."

Arthur gave a noncommittal shrug, petulant like a teenager. It was so unlike the man that his dread melded into my own mind. I wished I had time to take him aside and ask him what was wrong.

Maze tilted his head back and cupped his hands around his mouth again. "Hey, feather ass! Which plan do you vote for?" Maze looked back at us. "My new gryphon friend votes for blowing up the mines."

Jax ignored the lighthearted joke, instead focusing on Arthur. "I would like to know you're comfortable with our plan before we begin."

"I'm comfortable," Arthur quickly said. "Let us make our preparations."

No matter what he said out loud, I knew through our bond that it was a lie.

27

Arthur

It was a curious sensation to finally resign yourself to fate.

We galloped north along the ridge toward the nearest mine entrance. It was strange being here in the flesh after seeing it in my dreams for so long. The ridge was as familiar as my childhood home: the triangle-shaped rock to the right, and the boulder on the left which was split down the middle, leaving a flat face one could sit on. The eeriness of it all made me want to pinch my arm to make the dream vanish.

It is no dream, I thought bitterly. *It is finally real.*

The mine was dug into the side of one of the taller mountain faces. The wooden frame of the entrance was cracked with age, the cross-beam tilted as if a giant had come along and sat on it. The depths were veiled in darkness.

"If I ever complain about being a Dragon," Ryon said, "remind me that it's better than toiling in a mine."

"A Shadow?" Alyssa asked, tossing back her red hair. "Afraid of the dark?"

"It's not the darkness I'm afraid of," he said. "Darkness is my ally. Being alive, however..."

"You don't want to help me place the charges?" Maze hopped off his horse. "I hate the idea of dying underground as well, but it won't stop me from doing my job."

Ryon answered with only a glare.

"I'll join you," I said, climbing out of my saddle. *I hope I do not seem too eager.*

Maze opened one of his four saddle bags and haphazardly tossed pieces of metal on the ground behind him. Gears, pipes, steam cranks. A dozen items which didn't seem like they belonged on our trip. Finally he reached the bottom of the bag, pulling out three brass cubes larger than his fist. His spider mines.

"I thought you were using your fancy new powder to blow up the mines," Ryon said.

"These are for our defense." He pointed down the ridge to where the hills met the forest. "Place a few of these down there to warn us when the beetles are near. They'll take out a few dozen of them, if we're lucky."

"I'll deploy them," Jaxon offered. He took the three cubes in one of his massive hands. "Join me, Aly?"

"Sure," she said. "A leisurely stroll through the forest before the battle. Should I pack a picnic?"

They laughed to each other as they began down the hill.

Maze grabbed the map and nodded at me. "Let's go scout the tunnel."

Ryon and Harry remained with the horses while we approached the black maw of the mine. I paused to runetrace a sphere of blue ice above my palm; it wasn't as bright as one of the fiery spells Alyssa could conjure, but it gave off enough illumination to keep us from tripping over our feet. Maze led the way with the map held out in front of him.

I understood why Ryon was afraid; I had heard that mine accidents were common, and generally went unreported. I didn't share his fear, however, because I knew I would survive this part of the dream. We would set up everything fine, placing the explosives and whatever mechanism would trigger them. It was only after, when the Silithik reached us, that our doom would come.

Blue light from my orb sent dark shadows stretching away from every rock. The ceiling was low enough that I had to periodically duck to avoid hitting jagged pieces of rock that hung down like spears. We passed a crusty heel of bread, and the bones of what was probably a recently-eaten chicken. Evidence of the hasty evacuation the miners had made ahead of the Silithik hives.

Motes of runestone dust floated in the air, almost supernaturally weightless. Even though most runestone veins this close to the surface had been exhausted, I could feel the immense power that remained within the mine. The echoing shadow of the runestone that had once existed, it pulsed like a heartbeat, tempting me. The urge to trace more than just my single ball of ice was overwhelming. A dangerous, intoxicating desire.

The path slanted downward, and we walked for a full minute before Maze stopped. "This ought to do it. Four tunnels split off here, creating the primary branches of the tunnel system. An explosion here should ignite the volatile runestone everywhere, causing the chain reaction that we desire."

"And if it doesn't?" I asked.

Maze shrugged. "At the very least, it will destroy the mountain peak above us. The resulting rock slide might kill one or two or ten thousand bugs. Better than nothing."

"Aye," I said, even though it wasn't.

We backtracked toward the square of sunlight in the distance to get the powder kegs. They were like any keg of wine or ale, although lighter since the contents weren't liquid. As Maze untied them from his saddle, I noticed Harry casually sidestepping down the ridge, putting as much distance between himself and the powder as possible.

With the flick of my fingers, I moved my ice orb over one shoulder, where it would remain while I walked. I held out both arms to accept one of the kegs from Maze, who placed it as gently as a mother handling a baby. "Don't drop it," he warned. Then he retrieved a round package as large as Jax's shield. He tied it to his hip, then grabbed the other keg.

We carried the kegs down into the mine with slow, careful steps. Now I couldn't help but feel the danger in our action, even though I knew no tragedy would befall us. An intrusive thought came to mind: what would happen if I dropped the keg? Could my fate be altered? Either scenario resulted in my death, so I was not eager to test the hypothesis.

Maze stopped at the tunnel intersection, slowly placed his keg on the ground, and then did the same with my keg.

"How does it work?" I asked.

Maze grinned. "Not a fire fuse, if that's what you're wondering. The Tinker Guild's got a new trigger method." He untied the round package from his hip. "Do you know what this is?"

"A coil of copper wire?"

Maze flinched. "Steam my soul, how did you know that?"

"A lucky guess."

He tore away the brown paper. "Aye, it's copper wire. Heavy gauge. Not a burn fuse, like most explosives. I'll show you how it works outside." He found one end of the wire and unrolled three loops. With careful precision, he twisted the end, fraying it into several individual wires. He crouched next to one keg and wrapped the wire around a metal knob sticking out of the top. He didn't attach anything to the second keg.

"Out we go," he said, gripping the coil of wire with both hands. Slowly, he walked backwards while unrolling the wire. I led the way with a hand on his shoulder to keep him from tripping.

Outside, Ryon and Harry were staring at the mountain peak above. A winged shape perched there, watching us.

Maze stood up straight to stretch his back. Then he waved at the gryphon. "Glad we have an audience. I want someone here to witness what a Tinker can do with a little preparation."

"Or witness a great failure if it does not work," I said.

Maze only shrugged. "Then I'll be too dead to feel embarrassed. Gather the horses and my belongings. I need to unroll all the wire."

Too numb to try to stop the inevitable events, I packed up all of Maze's mechanical gadgets and then led the horses down the ridge. I gazed to the north-east, where the dust cloud was smaller than it was before. The majority of the Silithik armies had descended the pass and were in the valley. *It will only be a few hours, now.*

We walked down the ridge until reaching a small plateau. Maze had unrolled almost all of the wire, and announced this was as good a place as any to make a stand. *It doesn't matter*, I thought, but I kept it to myself.

Maze pulled a box out of his saddle bag, similar to the spider mines but larger, and with a plunger in the top. He placed it on the ground and gestured.

"This is what triggers the explosion," he said. "Inside are two wheel-like devices called *dynamos...*"

"We don't need a Tinker lesson right now," Ryon muttered.

"Actually, I'm curious," I said. "How does it work?"

Maze gave Ryon an offended look, then smiled at me. There was no creature so happy in this world as a Tinker who was explaining how one of his contraptions worked. "When you push the plunger, the dynamo wheels spin opposite each other, creating a tiny shock. Like a runetracer's lightning, but small. This shock travels up the wire and into the kegs of powder, igniting them instantly."

"Huh," Harry said, rubbing the dark bristles on his cheek. "No fire is required?"

"None at all!"

"What if the cable was cut?" I asked casually.

"Well, it wouldn't work, of course."

"Could it be fixed?" I pushed. "By tying the two ends back

together?"

Maze scrunched up his face as he thought about that. "Actually, aye, that should still work. So long as the copper is connected once again, the little lightning will travel to the kegs."

"Excellent," I said.

We watched as Maze crouched next to the box and gathered the wire. He frayed the end again, took three long breaths, and then touched the wire to a knob sticking out of the box. When nothing happened, he exhaled.

"I thought you said the plunger must be depressed to work," Ryon said.

"This method is new to me," Maze said while he tightened the coil around the knob. "A good Tinker learns not to trust his devices completely."

"I'll stick to runemagic," I said.

"You all won't be making fun of me when we kill two hives in the blink of an eye," Maze said. "My ass will be chafed from all the kissing you'll be doing!"

"Maze," Ryon gestured with his dagger, "if this works, I'll kiss both cheeks. That's a promise."

Maze slapped him on the shoulder and turned to the north-east, where the two hives were drawing closer. The dusty haze in the air was now gone. It was strange knowing that an army was there, concealed by the forest within the valley below us. I almost imagined that I could hear them, if only I strained my ears enough.

She dies, Lady Anis's voice taunted in my head. *You are both overrun.*

Over the past two days marching east, I'd accepted what would happen. I'd had enough time to truly consider it, thoughts swirling around in my head like wine being tasted before swallowed. The idea no longer terrified me.

It made me sad, but that was it.

Still, as resigned as I was to the inevitability of the future, my mind raced. I couldn't help but wonder. I was a man of thought and consideration. Wondering was what I *did*.

Is there a way...?

"Well then," Maze announced. "Time to eat my last meal. Don't want to die on an empty stomach."

Ryon laughed and followed him toward the horses. "I'd rather not die with a *full* stomach. The last thing I want to see is my half-digested supper spilling out of my belly after a beetle slashes me open."

"I'd rather not die at all," Harry said. He turned to me. "Are you coming, Arthur?"

I peeled my eyes away from the incoming swarm and followed my Quintmates.

28

Alyssa

"This valley would be a beautiful place to spend the summer," I said as we picked our way down the ridge toward the tree line. "If not for the Silithik army in the distance, I mean."

Jax laughed, a deep, genuine sound. "They do tend to ruin the scenery, don't they?" He pointed. "Deer scat. I bet there is good hunting here."

"You hunt?"

"I used to," he said. "When I was a boy."

"How often do you get to hunt now?" I asked.

Jax shrugged his huge shoulders. "I haven't since being promoted to Dragon. But sometimes I daydream." He looked over his shoulder. "Daydreaming helps one get through the terrors of the day."

"Oh?" I asked. "What are you daydreaming about now?"

"The things I'm going to do with you when we return," he said.

"The things I'm going to do *to* you."

"Please elaborate."

"Oh, it wouldn't interest you."

"I'm certain it would!"

We reached the edge of the first patch of forest. The canopy was so thick it was like the sun had been covered in clouds, veiling us in darkness. Jax spun on his heel. It caught me off guard and I bumped into his chest, and was quickly wrapped in his arms. He looked down at me with a vicious smile.

"Kissing," he said, planting one on my forehead. "Touching." His hand slid down my back, cupping my ass. "Other things..."

"Mmm, other things?" I asked. "I don't think I know what you mean. I'm so young and inexperienced. You should elaborate in great detail to help me understand."

"I'll tell you more when we complete our mission. Something for *you* to daydream about." He brushed his lips against mine. I sighed as he continued into the forest.

"I hope the plan works," I said while following him. "I just sort of blurted it out without thinking. I'm surprised everyone agreed so quickly."

"It's a good plan. The best we have, by far. You have an excellent mind for battle tactics, Aly."

"It seemed obvious once I saw the map."

Jax ducked under a branch, then held it back for me to pass. "Things hidden to most seem obvious to the gifted."

I laughed. "I'm certainly not gifted, though I appreciate the flattery."

"Why would you say that?"

The intensity in his voice gave me pause. "I don't know. I've always been mediocre at everything. Occasionally *average* at some things, but proficient in none. It's been that way for runetracing, or my physical appearance, or other skills like hunting with my uncle."

"Your physical appearance is anything but average," Jax said, eyes raking over my body.

"I wish you could go back in time and say that to a younger version of myself, who was jealous of the girls whose breasts blossomed quicker, and more fully."

"Massive breasts are not necessarily attractive," Jax pointed out. "Anything more than a handful is too much for me."

He reached over to try to get said handful, but I slapped his hand away with a laugh.

"But honestly, you should not focus so much on your current proficiencies," he continued. "You are young. Skill comes with experience and practice."

"Other Pyromancers at the Academy were far more skilled than I was. One of them would be better suited to this Quintelaide."

He shrugged. "There is more to a good Quintelaide than raw power alone. Melding personalities and teamwork are the most important qualities."

"Oh, good," I said. "Because I'm wonderfully average at that too, if Ryon and Harry's attitude toward me are any indication."

"Give them time. They will come around."

I waved a hand. "You're still being overly dismissive of my shortcomings. Half my traces fail. I cannot trace at all from horseback. That has already negatively impacted us in battle, and will certainly do so again."

"Arthur couldn't trace from horseback when he was your age," Jax said. "Took him a full year of lessons from Danni before he could." He stopped next to a tree and looked around. Then he twisted a dial in the side of one of the spider mine cubes and gently placed it on the ground. A tiny hiss of steam shot out the side, and then it went still.

As Maze had instructed, we backed away slowly until we were ten paces away. Only then did we exhale, and then move laterally across the forest to deploy the next two. With the three of them in a line, their explosions would warn us when the Silithik were nearing our position on the ridge.

"Do you think he's over her?" I asked.

"Who, Arthur and Danni?" Jax furrowed his brow in concentration. "Yes and no. He was like me in many ways: *fond* of Danni, but not nearly as attached to her as Ryon or Harry, or even Maze. He always kept his emotions deep down, as is common for a Mage."

"But...?"

"But even so, Danni was a terrible loss. For all of us, in many different manners. We lost a lover, a sister, a Quintmate. I have begun to move on, it is true. But I'm not sure any of us will ever *truly* be over Danni."

"Oh," I said.

He smiled at me. "But that does not mean we can't form new bonds with new people." He took my hand in his as if we were two lovers out for an afternoon stroll. "Why do you ask?"

I felt myself blush. "No reason."

"Aly..." He stroked my cheek with a thumb. "You forget that we are bonded, now. I can sense when you're hiding something."

"Arthur kissed me in the bath the other night," I said in a rush. "It was wonderful, at least I thought so, until he shoved me away and said he couldn't. He fled from me like I'd grown Silithik wings."

It was incredibly strange admitting this with Jax, another man who I was intimately involved with. But he only laughed.

"As I said, Arthur is less forthcoming with his emotions than most. Perhaps he needs more time to warm up to the idea. You felt something from the Dragon bond, I suspect. Let that guide your actions with Arthur."

I *did* feel his emotions through the bond: pain. He had definitely been agonizing over something. Danni's death, of course.

Jax stopped and placed the second spider mine. When we were a safe distance away he said, "So..."

225

"So?"

"So, who kisses better? The frigid Mage, or the dashing Warrior?"

I laughed. "Dashing?"

"Yes. Dashing."

"Good question." I made a show of waffling over the decision. "I may have to think on it."

"I would expect the answer to be obvious."

I grabbed his arm and spun myself into his embrace, then pressed my chest against his and batted my eyelashes up at him like a barmaid. "Why, perhaps I need a reminder from a *dashing* Warrior."

He kissed me there in the dark forest, long and sweet, and for several moments the impending danger was forgotten. I sighed when it was over, and rested my cheek against his chest. It felt good to just stand there in his arms.

"Well?" he said.

I grinned without taking my cheek from his chest. "Based on my research, I've determined you to be the better kisser."

"As I suspected."

I pulled away and looked up at him innocently. "Although my sample size is too small. I will need to collect more data."

The Warrior pretended to look disappointed. "If you must."

I smiled deeply, but Jax suddenly froze. He cocked his head. I heard the noise a moment later: a soft buzzing sound, growing louder. Like a cloud of flies.

"Are they here?" I whispered. "Did we wrongly gauge their speed?" I stared into the forest, expecting an army of beetles to descend upon us.

But Jax shook his head. "No. They are only scouts." He deployed the final spider mine, and then we jogged back to the edge of the forest where the hills sloped up to the ridge where the rest of our Quintmates were. Two Silithik wasps flew high above, straight toward the plateau where our horses were tied up. Suddenly, one of the wasps plummeted from the air like it had been swatted by an invisible hand. The second wasp curved around to flee, and I felt the familiar surge of runemagic being traced nearby. An *icebolt* raced upward from the ridge into the sky, striking the wasp on one of its wings. Then it was plummeting too, freezing into a block of ice as it fell. It hit the ground on the hill above us, shattering into a thousand icy pieces.

One shard of ice rolled down the hill and came to a rest by my feet. I picked it up. Inside the ice was what looked like a thin piece of wasp antenna. I tossed it back down in disgust.

"If they didn't know we were here already," Jax said, "then they do now."

29

Alyssa

Waiting for the approaching Silithik hives was the longest hour of my life.

We gathered on the plateau where we would make our defensive stand. Some of us ate. I chewed on a block of white cheese, but my stomach was too knotted to accept more than a few bites. Harry oiled his bowstring. Arthur went up the ridge to check the detonation wire, came back down and paced around our plateau, then went back up to check it again.

I knew that we needed to allow the hive armies to grow near before detonating Maze's explosives. It was the only way to destroy most, if not all, of the Silithik. But it still felt like standing in front of a charging bull and hoping we could step aside at the last moment.

Ryon passed around a flask of concentrated melon wine. Everyone drank deeply, so when it was my turn I did the same, but the liquid fire running down my throat was so strong it sent me into a coughing fit. Everyone laughed, but it was the good-natured sort. Nervous laughter before a battle.

Nobody spoke. I wanted desperately to carry on a conversation, to fill the silence with *something*, but I didn't want to disrupt the routine of my Quintmates. They'd done this more times than I had, so it was my duty to fall into their habits. Which was fine, because simply being near them was comforting in itself. Their presence through the Dragon bond was the warm camaraderie of a group that was about to go to battle together. It made me feel included. Part of something larger than myself.

The only exception was Arthur, who was a bundle of anxiety and grief. He kept his smooth face calm, but I could sense the torment he felt within. It was as if he expected the plan to fail. I wanted to take him aside and ask why he felt this way, why he was reacting so differently than the others, but I didn't want to embarrass him. Men could be touchy when it came to bravery and fear. *Best to leave him alone.*

It occurred to me that I'd never waited for a battle before. Every battle I'd fought in had been thrust upon me without warning. The first attack on the Academy. Finding my Quintmates in the Borderlands already backed into a corner. Stumbling upon the Silithik army in the tunnel, and practically running into the back of the Queen. In those situations, I'd never had *time* to be afraid. All I could do was react.

Waiting is far, far worse.

The cloud of dirt kicked up by the approaching army drifted across the valley, wide and menacing. We could pick out wasps floating above, spreading out beyond the beetles on the ground without advancing too far. No more scouting wasps ventured toward us. There was no need, I suspected. Two entire hives against a single Dragon Quintelaide? The battle would never be in doubt.

I glanced over at Maze's detonation device. *Hopefully that is true, but in a completely different way.*

Birds scattered from the forest below. Seconds later, the explosion of the first spider mine reached our ears, a hollow sound that echoed off the mountains along with the crackle of smaller explosions. Ryon was on his feet instantly.

"That's my cue," he said, covering his mouth with a kerchief and striding down the ridge.

Our plan involved Ryon meeting the Silithik in the forest, harassing them enough to lure them up to our position. I would throw some *fireballs* into the forest to create a little more chaos as well; the Silithik hated fire, and would take a path far around it— and hopefully toward our position. We could hold them off from the high ground for a while, biding our time while the rest of the hives drew closer to where the mining tunnels were dug.

And then we'd blow everything up and clean up what Silithik remained.

It was a sound plan on paper, but as I watched Ryon's shape glide down the slope, I felt a pang of fear for my Quintmate. One of the other spider mines finally detonated, and then a moment later so did the third. Ryon's shape disappeared into the forest, and the excitement and bloodlust that pulsed from his bond dimmed with it.

Jax picked up his helm, but held it under one arm as he waited.

"Should someone join him?" I wondered out loud. "Surely he would do better with you at his side..."

Jax shook his head. "The darkness gives him strength. Right now, Ryon is worth ten of me. I would only get in his way."

"Alyssa?" Harry asked.

I nodded and switched to my *imbue* runetablet. As we had rehearsed while waiting, Harry stuck arrows point-first into the ground in a line. I stopped in front of each one and traced my *imbue* spell, filling each shaft with runemagic as I had done in the courtyard with Ollie. Not enough to make the arrows unstable, but enough that they would pack some punch when they struck their targets. It was a relief to do *something* proactive while Ryon was fighting down in the forest. When I was done, a line of 12 arrows bristled with runemagic in front of Harry. The Ranger smiled in thanks as I returned to my position.

Unable to see anything through the trees, I focused on the Dragon bond. It was faint from this distance, but clear enough that I could almost imagine what was happening based on the emotion trickling through. Bloodlust as Ryon met the first Silithik in battle. Surprise as one slithered behind him, narrowly missing his head in a wide slash. A pang of urgency as he rolled away, then anger as he leaped back to his feet with daggers drawn, returning to bloodlust as he tore into the beetle's carapace with his twin daggers.

I wondered how much of it was accurate. Ultimately I was just happy to continue feeling *anything* from the bond. I hoped I wouldn't learn the pain of such a connection being severed today.

Jax touched me on the arm. "It's time."

I gave a start. "Are you certain? He's still fighting in the forest..."

"Stick to the plan," he replied with calm authority. "The odds of hitting him are incomprehensibly low. Ryon will be fine."

His fingers lingered on my arm a moment longer, and then he pulled on his steel-backed gauntlets. I readied my runetablets, but of course they were already clipped to my belt, one of the things I'd done while nervously waiting. I took a deep breath, let it out slowly, and touched the *fireball* rune. The runemagic practically leaped from the tablet and into my body with an ease that surprised me. I traced my finger along the grooves until I had enough runemagic, then aimed my hand at the sky. Like exhaling, I sent a medium-sized *fireball* shooting from my fingers. It arced down into the forest below, hitting the far end of the line of trees, exploding silently from this distance.

I traced another *fireball*, a third, a fourth. I sent them down into the forest in random areas and hoped none came near our Shadow, who was still a bundle of fury in the back of my head. I almost felt sad to see the peaceful forest go up in smoke, the flames spreading quickly from where my spells had struck. But it was the simplest way of keeping the Silithik from exiting the valley through the pass to the south, while ensuring they clumped together tightly.

So far, it appeared to be working.

Wasps began floating toward us, and were quickly dispatched by

Harry's arrows and Arthur's *frostbolts*. "Let Harry focus on the wasps," Jax told Arthur. "We need to save your energy for the larger spells."

Arthur didn't answer, but he ceased tracing. He was still a tight ball of anxiety and doubt in my mind. I couldn't blame him now; I was practically trembling as I watched the edge of the forest, desperate for Ryon to appear. His emotions felt hazy, as if the smoke in the forest were clouding our bond as well as our view. I imagined him surrounded by flames, his escape cut off as the Silithik bore down on him...

He burst into the open to the left of where I was watching, jogging lazily. In unison, the five of us on the ridge relaxed. A group of beetles emerged from the trees, slithering after Ryon like hounds on a hare. Abruptly he turned back and leaped at them, moving from one target to the next like water flowing down a stream, and everywhere he moved a beetle fell dead to the ground. Then he was running up the hill again, sprinting the final hundred paces up the ridge and somersaulted over a boulder, chest heaving as he took a knee at my side.

"Sad to see my *fireballs* didn't hit you," I joked. "It appears I need to work on my aim."

He pulled away the kerchief from his mouth and sneered. His skin and clothes were black from the smoke; only his eyes and teeth were white. "You came bloody close!" he said, then paused to cough a black wad of phlegm onto the ground.

"You're wounded," Arthur said, pointing to a thick gash in his upper arm. The Mage knelt to tend to Ryon, readying a healing rune from his pouch, but the Shadow waved him off while coughing.

"There are drillers among the army," he said. "I was nearly skewered by a volley of spikes."

For some reason, Arthur's face went deathly white, and he glanced at me before looking away.

"Drillers?" I asked. "I thought they were rare."

"They are," Harry said while nocking one of my *imbued* arrows.

"We'll pick them out," Jax said. "Look for darker grey Silithik among the brown." The others surely knew what a driller looked like; the instruction was certainly for my benefit.

"Any bruisers?" Harry asked.

Ryon was still panting. "Didn't... see any. But. This mutation of beetle... is different..." He paused to cough. "Shorter claws on each hand. Almost like fingers. And they're bloody *quick*."

"Good!" Maze said cheerfully. "I was beginning to think this would be too easy."

The forest fire was raging now, black smoke billowing from a dozen different places up into the sky, where the gryphon circled like a buzzard waiting for its prey to die. The anger I had for the supposed ally being only a spectator to the battle disappeared as I watched the Silithik army emerge from the forest in greater numbers. The beetles—and drillers, though I couldn't see any—slowly slithered up the hill toward our ridge. Within moments, they covered the mountain face below like a mass of maggots on a corpse. The line of them stretched far to the north, circling around above us.

I hope this plan works.

The first beetles reached the bottom of the ridge and began the slow trudge up the final, steeper incline. Jax held up a gauntleted fist, instructing us to wait. We had already tested the ideal range of our spells from the plateau, yet it was torture waiting with my hand on the runetablet, itching to trace. The enemy seemed to be *right there*, almost close enough to touch, even though I knew in actuality they were over a hundred paces away. Flames consume me, I could hear their chittering!

I checked the runetablets on my belt once more: *fireball, fireflow,* and *flame barrier*. The latter would be especially useful once the Silithik reached the top of the ridge; a final obstacle for them to pass through to reach our little plateau. Until then, it would be nothing but *fireballs* and *fireflows*. My hand rested at my side, the thumb scratching along the corner of the first tablet.

With a flourish, Jaxon lowered his fist.

Runemagic poured into my body as I began to trace. To my left, Arthur was a similar blossom of sudden runemagic. I drank deep from the well of power, savoring the simultaneous ecstasy and agony that tingled along my nerves, in my veins, even in my *mind*, heightening my senses at the edge of the plateau. The Silithik seemed to come into focus, every individual chittering sound as clear as if they were whispering directly into my ear. I could smell their awful musk, a scent like rotten flesh buried in sand. I could taste the remnants of the melon wine on the back of my throat.

This was what the world should feel like. Existence while not runetracing was dull by comparison.

I pulled the runemagic into me until I knew I was close to my limit, and then shot out my right hand. The *fireball* that materialized was as large as a horse, and heat buffeted my cheeks and hair. It arced through the air, falling downward far sooner than the smaller *fireballs* I'd sent into the forest. Jax's timing was perfect: the spell crashed into the third row of beetles, exploding in a bubble of fire that expanded outward with a blinding white flash. When it was gone, so were the Silithik, leaving a gap in the army where 50 beetles had been.

Arthur's spell was coalescing in the air to the left of where I aimed, a *blizzard* forming from a clear sky. The shards of ice that plummeted onto the Silithik were as long as spears, impaling them into the ground where they thrashed and screeched, the alien sounds of pain drifting up the ridge.

For a while, it wasn't so much of a battle as it was a slaughter. Runemagic traced from a position of height was impossible to withstand. The other four members of our Quint watched as Arthur and I rained doom down on the bugs, killing them in wide swaths. The dead Silithik husks soon piled up, encumbering the rest of the army in their death march up the incline. I was numb to the destruction, focusing solely on my finger as it moved along the rune, and the wonderful energy filling my chest again and again.

Eventually, wasps joined the battle and darted toward our

position. Harry picked them out of the air with normal arrows, and I sensed when he grabbed an *imbued* one from the ground and sent it soaring. Out of the corner of my eye, I saw the sorcerous shaft fly toward three wasps clustered tightly together, striking the center one and exploding in a ball of fire. The wasp it struck exploded into a hundred individual pieces, while its two companions plummeted from the sky on fire, leaving trails of smoke in the air.

Someone whooped at the sight, but I couldn't tell who because I was already focusing on my next spell.

Yet as easy as it was, I knew it was ultimately futile. The numbers were not on our side. The two Silithik hives continued streaming from the forest, advancing farther up the ridge with every second. I switched runes and sent a *fireflow* down the mountain, the expanding wave of fire igniting the beetles and knocking them back. But more beetles took their place, and before I could trace a second *fireflow,* they had advanced another few paces.

Slow and steady. That's what would give the Silithik victory.

If not for our special trick.

"A few minutes longer!" Jax announced. I was dimly aware of him checking the straps on his shield, and then unsheathing his sword from his scabbard.

Something hissed through the air over my right shoulder, then again above my head. "Drillers, right slope!" Ryon called.

"On it," Harry said. I felt another *imbued* arrow fly away from our position, exploding somewhere out of sight. "Got them," Harry said.

"Three more coming up the right," Maze said, holding a telescoping eyeglass up to one eye. "Still not within range."

"Let me know when they are," Harry said, turning his sights to another line of wasps and releasing three arrows in quick succession.

As I fell into a rhythm with my spells, I allowed myself to feel hope. We had a plan, and we were executing it. So far, it appeared to be working. And my feeling was mirrored back at me by my Quintmates, all of whom felt even more determined and hopeful.

It's going to work. All of us can feel it.

Except for Arthur, whose dread grew with every passing second.

30

Arthur

My dread grew with every passing second, yet I continued tracing spells against the Silithik army clamoring to get up the slopes to our location. None of this was familiar from my dream, yet. But it was close. Like hearing a few notes of a song before recognizing which one it was.

I traced my *blizzard* spell exclusively, pumping a steady flow of runemagic into the air above the battlefield. The ridge and hills below were covered with Silithik beetles that were skewered on the long spears of ice that fell from the sky. Like a field of blue wheat ready for harvest. These obstacles slowed the rest of the advancing army a measurable, if not consequential, degree. Still they came.

"On the left!" Jax called. "They're moving up the inclines there."

"On it," Alyssa said, turning her *fireballs* in that direction. Spheres of flame landed among the Silithik on the steep incline, killing beetles and knocking boulders free that rolled down the mountain, crushing dozens more.

With Alyssa's attention on the left, the Silithik in front of us advanced more quickly. Jax and Maze stepped up to the edge and met the first line of beetles to reach us with their weapons, swinging downward from the high ground. Ryon moved farther to the right to extend our line, slashing and kicking the beetles away from the plateau.

"A little longer!" Jax roared above the fray. "The back end of the hive is nearly in position!"

I continued tracing my *blizzard*, knowing it would not be enough.

The moment it happened was surreal. The beginning of my dream fell into place seamlessly, and I looked around at my surroundings with new eyes. The mountains, the high plateau looking down into the valley. The river which split the valley in two. The endless swarm of Silithik.

"Behind you!" Jax shouted.

This is it, I thought, stopping to watch the Tinker.

Maze whirled, swinging his sledgehammer in time to catch a beetle across the head, caving-in its carapace. Harry continued shooting arrows to the right, keeping most of the wasps at bay, but one finally got by. Ryon leaped into the air and removed its stingers with two rapid swipes of his daggers, landing with the agility of a cat.

It's happening.

"Maze, they're in position!" Jax roared, pointing at the mountain peak with a gauntleted fist. "Do it!"

Maze knocked away another beetle, then hobbled over to the object we guarded: a metal box no larger than a boot, with a slender plunger sticking out of the top. A coil of copper wire ran out of its base and up the mountain ridge toward the peak above. Toward the explosives we'd planted in the mine shaft.

He gripped the plunger with both hands, shouted, "Hold on!" and then slammed it into the box to trigger the explosion.

I felt powerless as the dream unfurled around me. It was the final confirmation that it was all true. Everything was happening exactly like in the dream, down to each individual Silithik dying at the edge of the plateau. I was a spectator to fate rather than an active participant.

Maze stared at the trigger box a moment, then pulled back the plunger to try again. There was a clicking sound from the box, but no more. He turned a crank on the side of the device, which made a high-pitched *whirring* noise.

"No!" Maze wailed. "Why isn't it working?"

I turned to face Alyssa. She would finish tracing this *fireflow* in a moment, then it would be her turn to speak. The last words she would say to the Quintelaide before she died.

"Maze," Jax grunted as he cut a beetle clean in half. "If this is a joke, you've chosen a poor time for it..."

"It's not a joke, damn it all! Something must have cut the cable." He tossed the device down with disgust. "I'll go check the line."

Alyssa's runemagic cut off. Here it was. She was about to mount her horse and try to be the hero.

I don't have to feel powerless.

A sudden burst of defiance blossomed inside me, as powerful as any runetraced spell. I raged against the idea of not being able to stop the dream from happening. I was a Frost Mage; I was thoughtful and analytical. There was no such thing as fate. And even if there was, I couldn't simply stand by while it killed Alyssa. My Pyromancer. A woman who I was beginning to care for.

I had to try. To do anything else was to surrender.

Without thinking, my fingers flew over the *frostbolt* rune at my belt. I traced the bare minimum required and launched it, striking the ground between Alyssa's feet. The *frostbolt* made a cracking noise as it burst, creating a jagged block of ice half a span wide. Freezing her in place.

Confusion and betrayal flashed in her round eyes. "What... Arthur!"

Ryon looked at the block of ice pinning Alyssa to the ground, then at me. "Have you lost your fucking mind?"

"I'll check the wire!" I announced while mounting my horse. "If I can't find anything wrong with it, I'll trigger the explosives myself."

Jax whirled, his face masked by the steel helm. "The explosion from that close may kill you."

A smile found its way to my face as I said the line from my dream: "It won't matter if we can't bring down that mountain!"

Ignoring the cries from Alyssa, I whirled my horse and galloped up the ridge, determined to make my own fate.

31

Alyssa

"No!" I screamed as I tried to pull my legs free.

It was surreal: Arthur accidentally hit me with a *frostbolt* spell in the middle of a flaming battle. Worse, he didn't seem to notice or care! He was riding up the ridge to fix the explosives like a mad man, and the emotion I felt from him through our bond was *satisfaction*.

"Arthur!" I yelled. If the trigger wire was not repairable, a *fireball* launched into the mine would do the trick. But Arthur had no such spells at his disposal. None of his ice runetablets would trigger the explosion. "What are you—"

I stopped and looked down at my feet. And something clicked in my head.

No. I don't believe it.

"Left!" Jaxon roared, spinning his shield to knock a charging beetle aside. He stabbed with his sword and the bug went still, and then Jax was stepping forward to the edge of the plateau to meet the next one in a bull rush.

One of Harry's *imbued* arrows exploded to my left, but I ignored it while pulling out the letter from Lady Anis. *Save it for a time of great struggle,* she had said. *When you feel paralyzed with indecision, as if your legs are stuck in blocks of ice.*

The blocks of ice weren't metaphorical. They were flaming *literal.*

I laughed. I actually laughed, with the beetles creeping in and my legs frozen to the ground. I laughed as I watched Arthur's shape disappear up the ridge, leaving only the emotion from his bond: satisfaction, and determination. And there, just below, and affection that bordered on love.

"We need fire support on the right incline," Ryon called.

I didn't pay any attention to him as I broke the wax between my thumbs. Numbly, I unfolded the paper, which held only a single line:

Follow him up the ridge, or you are both lost.

I felt myself smile. *Good. Because that's what I flaming wanted to do anyways.*

"Alyssa!" Jax turned and saw my situation. "How..."

I let the letter fall to the ground as I quickly traced the smallest *fireball* I could manage, enough to sear away half the ice. I ducked to avoid a diving Silithik wasp and then broke my legs free.

"I'm sorry," I shouted as I put a foot in Fireball's stirrup and leaped into the saddle. "I have to go!"

"What?" Jax said.

But I was already kicking Fireball into action, abandoning four allies in order to save one.

32

Arthur

Those few minutes riding up the ridge were the most carefree of my life.

I hadn't realized how paralyzing it was knowing the future. Being enslaved to my doom. Knowing my Quintmates would all perish, overrun by the two Silithik hives. Watching it unfold and being powerless to stop it. But I wasn't powerless. I'd changed my fate.

I'd changed Alyssa's, too.

Now, the dream wasn't a curse. It was a strength. Because I knew what was going to happen, and when. As best as I could tell, I was ahead of the dream by around 30 seconds. Plenty of time to fix the cable and get away before the drillers poured over the ridge and overwhelmed us.

From my view climbing the ridge, I had a tremendous—or terrible, depending on how you wanted to look at it—view of the valley to my right, swarming with Silithik in every direction. They flowed out of the forests and across the sloped land like ants whose hill had been kicked over. They were in the perfect location to be destroyed by our explosives. I just had to get there in time.

In spite of everything, a laugh escaped my lips.

I reached the place from the dream where the cable was severed. Sure enough, it ended next to a rock, cut as clean as if by a knife. I dismounted and bent down to grab the end, but I couldn't see the other half. I moved up the ridge on foot and found it: the rest of the cable had slid off the ridge a few paces, lying next to a larger boulder.

I slid down, grabbed the end of the wire, and scrambled up the ridge while counting down the seconds in my head. Maze said the connection would work if simply tied together, but I wasn't sure if it would detonate the moment the cables touched, or if I would need to go back down the ridge and have Maze trigger it again with his Tinker box. I should have asked for more details.

Eleven seconds. Ten. I bent down to the cable and tugged, pulling the two ends closer—

Something punched me in the chest. I was falling backward, the sky rolling across my vision as my shoulders hit the ground. My chest, just below the shoulder, stung from the blow. A rock thrown from an explosion? Or a shock passing through the cable? I wasn't sure if...

I stared down at the long chitinous spike sticking out of my chest. *Huh*, I thought. *Where did my plan go wrong?*

Noticing the wound made it real: pain raced through my body and forced me to roll onto my side. I moaned in agony, and my vision darkened at the edges from the pain. I gritted my teeth and tried to get up. *I need to get up. I still have time.*

The single driller appeared on the ridge above, silhouetted against the mountain peak.

I reached for my runebelt, fingers finding the same *frostbolt* tablet I'd used to freeze Alyssa in place. It was difficult maintaining the concentration to runetrace while my entire right side was on fire with pain; the runemagic kept drifting away, just out of reach of my grasping fingers.

Focus, damn you!

The single driller slithered down the ridge toward me. It could tell I was harmless; its split mandible flexed open and closed, but it never fired another spike. The alien jaw made the bug look like it was sneering in victory. My horse snorted as the Silithik neared, and then he finally abandoned me and galloped back down the ridge.

The driller slowed as it neared. Although similar in shape and size to a beetle, it looked less menacing: instead of four arms with razor sharp claws, it possessed only two short arms that hung uselessly in front of its thorax. Beetles had radial mouths with rows of teeth, but drillers had smaller mouths with fluted teeth that fired chitinous spikes like the one currently lodged in my chest. And instead of a cluster of asymmetrical eyes, the driller had two diagonal eyes on the side of its head that were as dark as night. Overall, it looked almost innocent.

Three wasps hissed overhead, ignoring me on their way to my Quintmates.

The driller cocked its head at me. The look in its two large eyes almost reminded me of curiosity. A decidedly human emotion. Like it was thinking about me specifically.

Runemagic finally swelled in my chest, and I raised my right arm just enough to guide the *frostbolt* into the driller's thorax. It exploded in a blast of ice, coating the beast and knocking it two paces to the right. Half-frozen in ice, it tumbled off the edge of the ridge and out of sight.

I leaned my head back against a boulder in exhaustion. Blood was flowing down my chest and soaking my robes. I wondered how long until I lost enough blood to pass out. Or enough to die. Dying came after passing out, I knew. A man needed blood. You couldn't just let it all flow away.

My thoughts were scattered. Another sign of blood loss. A cloudy mind. Obvious, on account of the spike in my chest. Since Frost Magi couldn't sorcerously heal themselves, I needed to resort to traditional methods. Put pressure on the wound. Apply a tourniquet. But the latter was impossible—I couldn't cut off blood circulation to my entire chest!—and the former was like sticking my hand into boiling water. Touching anywhere near my chest brought so much pain that I thought I might vomit.

The explosives. I had to get up. The end of the wire was *right over there*. I didn't need to go far to grab it, drag it back, and connect it to the other end. I could crawl there if needed. *After a moment. I'm tired.*

Motion at the top of the ridge distracted me. Three drillers slithered towards me, heads cocked in curiosity like the one I'd already dispatched. The academic part of my brain wondered if they possessed slightly more intelligence than beetles.

"Go away," I told them. "I have to save my Quintmates."

My words surprised them, and they slowed for a moment before continuing their advance. The sour smell of Silithik musk crowded into my nostrils. I resisted the urge to cough, because *that* motion would certainly cause me to pass out from pain.

Night began to fall. *No, that isn't right.* My vision was narrowing at the edges. Another sign of blood loss. It made me feel sad. Not for my own life, but for the naive thought that I could change the future. That I could save her.

Her.

My struggling thoughts focused on Alyssa. The young Pyromancer, completely average in skill but incredible in so many other ways. I wanted to learn more about her. I wanted to experience the world with her.

I wanted to *be* with her, intellectually and emotionally and in every other way.

That wouldn't happen, now. It was my fault. I should have told the others about my dream, about what the fortune teller had said. I shouldn't have been so embarrassed that I kept it to myself. It was all so obvious in retrospect. It always was.

I let my thoughts return to Alyssa, because that felt better than focusing on my mistakes. Thinking of her made me feel warm against the icy fingers spreading through my chest. Thinking of her made me feel safe, in spite of the three drillers standing only a few paces away, their short arms flexing as if they wanted to grab me. None of it mattered except Alyssa. Warm, pulsing Alyssa, who was like a ball of fire surging toward me...

I blinked as a streak of light shot across my vision, knocking the center driller away and igniting one of its comrades. Another *fireball* appeared, smaller, striking the remaining driller in the chest and splashing liquid flame across its body. The bug's scream was more high-pitched than a beetle's as it collapsed to the ground, writhing in its flames.

Alyssa came galloping up the ridge, red hair flowing behind while she leaned over the horse's neck. As she neared, she smoothly threw one leg over the horse and jumped off, landing at a stride while pointing at the screaming drillers. Her fingers were a flurry on her runetablet, and two more *fireballs* ensured that the drillers were truly dead.

She whirled to me, hair framing her face like the licks of flame she'd traced to save me. For a moment she stood triumphant, slender body so beautiful against the blue sky beyond.

"You know, those things aren't so scary if you kill them *before* they fill you with spikes." She knelt at me and her face twisted with worry. "I guess I don't need to tell you that."

"You did it," I blurted out. "You traced from horseback."

She examined my wound for a quick moment, wrapped an arm underneath me, then helped me to my feet. The agony made me scream so loudly that for a few moments I couldn't hear anything but my own voice.

"Not exactly," she said as she guided me to her horse. "I had to slow Fireball to a walk. Why did you come up here alone?"

"I had to," I groaned. The adrenaline of her arrival gave me a boost of energy. "It was the only way to succeed."

"Yes, I can see you were *quite* successful." She nodded at the spike sticking out of my chest.

I smiled. "Better me than you."

She helped me put one foot in the stirrup. "It could have been neither of us! What were you thinking freezing me in ice, you great flaming fool? And don't you dare tell me it was an accident."

I let her put a hand on my behind and push me up into the saddle. Somehow, I remained conscious through the pain. "Just trusting what someone else told me."

Her expression changed; she almost looked like she understood what I meant. "You're still a fool. Tell the others I said so." She took the reins and spun the horse around.

"The cable..." I protested.

"He's a fool, Fireball, but you only have to suffer him a moment."

I felt runetracing, and then a flash of heat on my cheek. Something fell from the sky a few paces away, landing on the slope of the ridge. A wasp, wrapped in flames.

"We have to... detonate the powder..." I managed to get out. The world was dimming around me again.

"No shit! That's what I'm going to do."

Before I could argue, she slapped the horse's rump, sending us galloping back down the ridge.

I twisted in the saddle in time to see Alyssa running toward the mine entrance.

33

Alyssa

Everything made sense in those moments while I sent Arthur away on my horse.

This was what Lady Anis had told him. Something about this battle—something he must do. That explained why he'd frozen me to the ground and tried to fix the copper wire himself. He knew something the rest of us didn't.

Better me than you. Was I supposed to get hit in the chest with a driller spike? The thought made me shiver. But there was no more time for retrospection now. Maze's copper wire had slid halfway down the ridge, out of reach. If I didn't blow the mine, my Quintmates would be overrun by the Silithik. What I needed to—

A Silithik wasp soared over the ridge to my left. It hesitated like it wasn't expecting to find me here, which gave me enough time to trace a quick *fireball.* It moved at the last minute, causing me to miss its body, but it hit one of its wings instead. The terrible monster screeched, spun, and crashed to the ground.

I darted around it, not bothering to finish it off. I needed to get close enough to the mine entrance to throw a *fireball* inside. I just hoped that would detonate Maze's powder. He said they placed the kegs inside, but not *too* deep inside. *Maybe the runestone dust in the air will ignite,* I hoped.

I rounded a boulder and stole a glance back down the ridge. I could barely see the plateau where my comrades still fought. Jax was a whirlwind of gleaming armor, and bright flashes in the air marked where Harry was firing the arrows I'd *imbued.* They were still alive. I didn't have much time, but at least I wasn't too late.

Everything was chaos as I sprinted up the ridge. Wasps soared high overhead, thankfully ignoring me while diving on my Quintmates. Individual Silithik beetles appeared on the ridge ahead of me, forcing me to pause long enough to knock them back with *fireballs.* Within minutes, the entire ridge would be overrun.

Above, the dark maw of the mine entrance came into view. Without hesitation, I traced a medium *fireball,* taking my time to line up my aim, accounting for the height and arc. I held my breath as the sickly-sweet runemagic raced through my veins, then formed at the tip of my outstretched finger. With a *WHOOSH* of air it flew away, over the boulders and down, falling into the frame of the entrance.

Relief overwhelmed me. *I didn't fail the trace. I succeeded when it mattered.*

I only felt the movement behind me because of my heightened senses from the runetracing. Moving by instinct rather than thought, I threw myself forward and felt claws slash through the air where my head had just been. I rolled onto my back and traced another *fireball,* throwing it into the space where I expected the beetle to be. The bug moved into it at the perfect moment, catching the spell right in its cluster of insect eyes, searing a hole clean through its head.

Not waiting to bask in my victory, I scrambled back to my feet and continued up the narrowing ridge. My spell hadn't detonated the powder. I needed to get closer. Dangerously close, though that wasn't a concern for me anymore. All of us would perish if I didn't detonate the powder. My focus narrowed toward that end.

Get to the mine entrance.

Blow the powder.

Destroy the Silithik in the valley.

I leaped over rocks and slid around boulders, deathly aware of the beetles and wasps closing in behind me and to my right. I doubted I would have time to slow and kill anyone who blocked my way. I prayed that I wouldn't find out.

Get to the mine entrance.

Blow the powder.

Destroy the Silithik in the valley.

A beetle lurched over the edge of the ridge ahead, finishing its climb. I swerved to the left and dove over a boulder, turning the motion into a roll and then continued my sprint, hoping the beetle would hesitate long enough for me to get a head start. I didn't need much time. Just a few seconds. A single trace.

Get to the mine entrance.

Blow the powder.

Destroy the Silithik in the valley.

I sucked in each breath and my legs pumped, climbing the last few paces of the ridge. My hand hovered above my runetablet, ready to trace one final time. I would only need one trace. Anything longer would mean death.

Get to the mine entrance...

I rounded a boulder, and there it was: the dark square of the shaft, with the tilted cross-beam. Four beetles came around the side of the entrance toward me, but I only had eyes for my target. I breathed deep of the runemagic, finger sliding along the grooves of the runetablet with deft precision.

Despite the distractions and the pressure of failure, I'd never traced anything so perfectly in my life. The runemagic leaped through the tablet and into my soul, swelling me with energy until I felt like a water skin, practically overflowing with it. With my senses heightened I could hear the flutter of wasp wings above and to my right, and more directly behind me. Driller spikes shot across my vision, punching into the rock to my left. I knew the next volley of spikes would not miss, just like they had not missed Arthur.

Arthur. The Frost Mage who'd saved my life in the battle outside the capitol. Who'd tried to teach me how to trace from horseback. Who genuinely wanted to help me become a better Pyromancer.

As I released the *fireball*, my last thought was of him, and the growing affection I felt through our bond.

34

Arthur

My only thought was of Alyssa and the growing affection I felt through our bond.

Her horse carried me down the ridge toward our Quintmates, urged on by the swarm slowly pressing in around us. Wasps flew overhead, but didn't seem to care about a horse and a dying Frost Mage. Driller spikes hissed through the air somewhere close, but probably not directed at me. I was dimly aware of it all as I clutched the reins and did my best to remain conscious in the saddle.

Alyssa saved me. She had cast aside her own safety to ensure I got away. It was heroic.

It reminded me of Danni.

Once I realized it, the thought remained firmly in place. Part of me never expected Alyssa to adequately replace our previous Pyromancer, but she was filling the shoes admirably. In some ways, she was better than Danni.

She is our Pyromancer, no matter what the others think.

I reached the edge of the plateau and found it swarming with bugs. The horse reared up and kicked one driller in the back of the head, caving in its skull-like carapace and then charging forward over its corpse. Somehow, I managed to remain in the saddle, although the jostling sent bolts of pain through my chest.

"Another bomb coming!" Maze yelled before hurling a metal object overhand. It soared over the ridge and landed somewhere unseen, but the explosion was a concussive force that I felt in my eardrums. Bits of Silithik began raining down on us.

"That started a rockslide on the mountain face," Jax yelled. "It bought us some time. Arthur!"

The huge Warrior jogged to me, shield-bashing a wounded beetle on the way. I groaned as he touched my chest next to the wound. "Steel save me, how are you still conscious?"

"Only with great effort," I admitted.

"Harry! We need a healing salve!"

The Ranger nocked an arrow, drew, and released with a soft twang. He jogged toward us without watching to see if he'd struck his target, and scowled when he saw my wound.

"Not as good as a Mage's healing, but this should stop the bleeding." He pulled a paper pouch from his pocket, then tore away the corner with his teeth. "It'll hurt like every arrow in the world is piercing you at once."

"Behind you!" Ryon cried.

Harry whirled in time to raise his arm protectively. The beetle's claws slashed across the Ranger's buckler and staggered him. The salve pouch went flying in the air. Then Maze was there, swinging his sledgehammer sideways above Harry's head to knock the beetle away. A second crushing swing finished it off.

"Bloody bugs," Harry hissed, holding his arm. Blood trickled through his fingers. "Ahh, that stings!"

"Where's Alyssa?" Maze asked. He was looking directly at me. "*Where is she?*"

"Saving us."

Maze opened his mouth to say something, but then an explosion made the ground tremble beneath us. It was distant, like the sound of approaching thunder. Then a second explosion shook the entire ridge and threw my brothers to their knees, and Alyssa's horse danced sideways to keep her balance. Up the ridge, the mountain peak that housed the mine entrance was a cloud of dust and smoke, expanding almost in slow motion. It reminded me of a volcanic explosion I had been fortunate enough to witness when I was a boy. Rocks flew into the air in every direction, pebbles and rocks and even boulders that were as large as cottages.

And then the world ended.

That second explosion was repeated again, and again, and again, a thousand times in the blink of an eye, cascading away from our plateau. The earth groaned and heaved with god-like force, an earthquake that was everywhere all at once. It was deafening. It was terrifying.

My Quintmates remained on the ground covering their heads, but from horseback I saw it with wonderful clarity. The underground explosions moved down the valley, an incomprehensibly large ripple that tore apart the hills and forests. Trees were catapulted into the air like blades of grass. Entire hills collapsed into nothing. The expanding ripples were like the waves of the ocean, an incredible energy that cascaded away from us throughout the valley.

And everywhere the wave traveled, Silithik perished. Their chittering turned to high-pitched screams of death, and silence followed everywhere the explosion went. A crack cut the middle of our plateau, and then the far side was swallowed down into the valley, carrying with it Harry's bow, Maze's trigger box, and dozens of Silithik corpses. Our horses tossed their heads in terror, unable to comprehend what was happening.

All across the valley, great fissures opened in the ground, swallowing scores of beetles in an eye blink. One pocket imploded so deeply that it devoured most of the forest fire, extinguishing it swiftly and leaving only smoke. In the distance, the tall mountain peaks of the eastern range trembled and then changed, entire ridges and peaks collapsing into the valley, a silent horror before the rolling thunder finally reached our ears. To the north, where our own mountain range curved into view, similar rock slides ravaged everything in their way down into the valley. Where once a thick mass of brown Silithik had been, now were only corpses along the slopes.

Jax finally stood, one hand held to his head. He looked around to ensure all of us were safe, eying the sudden drop-off of the plateau edge with surprise, and then wariness. A few hundred Silithik had survived in an area relatively undamaged by the explosions to the south. For now, they appeared frozen with confusion.

But my eyes were glued to the sky. To a small rock that had been launched in the air, soaring away from our position almost gracefully as it neared its apex. Because I knew, with supernatural understanding, that it was no rock. It was a person, a young Pyromancer who I could feel through our bond, launched into the sky from the explosion.

"Alyssa," Jax whispered when he realized, eyes locking onto her.

Helpless, the five of us watched her fly to her death, the woman who had managed to destroy the Silithik and save everyone but herself.

35

Alyssa

I was flying.

I'd had a dream like this last week, after the battle outside the capitol. I'd dreamed I was being carried above the battle by an angel, weightless and carefree. This felt just like that. Everything had been peaceful and calm. I got the sense that I didn't need to worry anymore.

Jax had been the one carrying me from the battlefield, then. *Who is carrying me now?*

I opened my eyes to a crystal blue sky that instantly reminded me of Arthur's eyes. Intense, but warm. Familiar. I'd grown to take them for granted these past few days. An ever-present comfort.

Then I realized that the wind was whipping my hair all around my face. Violently so, like one of the surge storms that rolled west out of the Sunrise Sea and blew half the shingles off the roof of the cottage where I grew up.

But this wasn't wind.

With calm realization, I saw that I was flying through the air. The valley was far below, the hills and forests that were being churned up by the explosions underground. The runestone in the mines detonating, a chain reaction of runemagic that I could almost feel in my chest.

It worked. Our plan flaming worked!

Maybe that's why I felt so calm as I soared higher and higher into the air. Either that, or because my brain had no mechanism for comprehending this kind of doom. In any case, I accepted it without thought. I'd saved my Quintmates. I'd destroyed the Silithik hives.

Surely all of that was worth the life of one mediocre Pyromancer.

I closed my eyes and tried to send as much love through the Dragon bonds as I could, though I doubted that's how the connection worked. I didn't care. It felt right to me. *I did this for all of you. So that you could survive.*

And I felt their love returned, five individual threads of varying strength. Jax's love, hot and intense. Arthur's affection, warm and new and wonderful. The others, Maze and Harry and even Ryon, were more gratitude than love. The mutual camaraderie that came from battle. That was good enough for me. It was better than the way they *used* to feel about me, when I had been thrown into their Quint against their will.

It doesn't matter what they think, now. It's all over. They would be assigned a new Pyromancer, one who would probably be stronger and more experienced. The kind of Quintmate they deserved. I was sad to think of it that way, but I was relieved, too.

I was accepting my fate when it was snatched from me.

There was a jerk, and I felt sharp pain in my back. Everything remained the same except my Dragon uniform fit more tightly around my body, squeezing my chest painfully. I twisted my head to look. Massive wings beat around me as the gryphon recovered from whatever maneuver had been required to snatch me from the air, grabbing my uniform in his talons. "Flames and fire!" I yelled over the wind, both a curse and a cheer. "You saved me!"

It was a dumb thing to say, but I wasn't exactly practiced in witty remarks during near-death experiences. In any case, the gryphon didn't seem to hear me, or was too focused on his flight. The land beneath us spun as he turned, flying back to the south. I could see my Quintmates there, on the ridge overlooking the valley. That area was relatively undamaged from the explosions, as we'd expected based on the position of the mine tunnels. There were hundreds of Silithik still milling around in the valley, some of them climbing the ridge to fight my Quintmates. But hundreds of beetles were better than hundreds of thousands, and I knew my comrades could handle them.

The feeling of victory changed: not only had we won, but everyone was going to be fine. My chest tightened with realization. *All of us are going to walk away from this.*

The gryphon screeched softly, which sounded like a curse to my ears. I quickly saw why. The mine explosions hadn't affected the Silithik wasps, dozens of which were converging on us. They spread out in every direction, growing in size.

I felt the gryphon tense right before he dove.

My stomach lurched queasily as the gryphon pulled to the right, folding his wings close to his body. The wind roared in my ears as we plummeted, almost reckless in our speed, so much so that I wanted to yell to the gryphon to slow down or pull up but the words were caught in my throat.

The gryphon extended his wings and leveled out suddenly, jostling me in his talons. The moment he did, two wasps shot across my vision, falling below us in their own dives. Before I could yelp, the gryphon lurched to the left and dove again, shorter this time, but again with the intent to avoid the wasps which narrowly missed skewering us with their curved stingers.

"Burn me," I cursed as the wasps fluttered past. "Flaming hell!"

The gryphon darted and dove, turned us around, then dove again. It was a valiant effort against overwhelming numbers, but the numbers *were* overwhelming, and when one wasp finally stabbed him in the wing, I felt his entire body shudder. He screeched in pain, falling sideways while flapping his other wing helplessly. We spun and tumbled toward the ground, his talons still gripping me as firmly as a predator holding onto its meal, and my view alternated between blue sky and brown earth. Blue-brown, blue-brown, blue-brown, with the brown growing wider and more detailed, and I realized we would hit the ground a split-second before we did.

The gryphon landed first, cushioning my fall with his body. I bounced and rolled, hair wrapping around my head with dirt and grass, and then everything was very still.

I stared up at the sky, blinking away the dizziness. Silithik wasps filled the sky high above me, growing larger as they neared. Movement next to me made me roll over: the gryphon was returning to his human form, wings evaporating into his back and feathers fading away into nothing. Seconds later, he was nothing but a nude human, his skin pink like a newborn child.

Get up, I urged myself. My thoughts were hazy, each one requiring conscious effort. *He's injured. I can trace. But I need to get up.*

I put my hands on the ground and pushed up to my knees. The dirt was loose, like a freshly turned field ready for planting. The smell of soil and sulfur hung in the air, with the deeper taint of Silithik musk. I coughed, which made me wince in pain and clutch my side. One of my ribs felt broken.

I realized there was motion around me. I froze, moving only my eyes.

Beetles were everywhere, slithering through the upturned trees without acknowledging us. In the confusion they must not have realized we had crashed, or that we had survived. They moved up the ridge, toward the plateau and my Quintmates. Their numbers were much thinner now, though still hundreds remained. From the plateau, my comrades would dispatch them easily.

But they were up there. And I was down here.

My heart pounded in my ears, and I felt myself panicking. I tried to force myself to calm down. Which, of course, was impossible. My breathing hastened, and there was a slight wheeze from my nose as I tried to remain perfectly motionless.

One beetle tossed its head as if shaking off a headache, then paused. It twisted to face the gryphon on the ground. I prayed that my rescuer would remain motionless, but then the beetle turned its dark gaze toward me. Its cluster of eyes reflected the sunlight, nine orbs of alien thought.

I slowly lowered my left hand to my runebelt. Miraculously, all three runetablets remained on their hooks. I traced as fast as I dared, the sweet trickle of energy flowing into my body like a fountain of pure life.

The *fireball* struck the beetle in the thorax, knocking it back two paces where it writhed in fire.

It was like a trance had been broken among the Silithik. The nearby beetles stopped their advance toward the plateau and considered their flaming brother, then chittered angrily. A dozen of them surrounded me. Too many to fight by myself.

But I had to try.

Gritting my teeth, I readied another *fireball* before the beetles closed in.

36

Arthur

Everyone screamed, with shock and joy and even disbelief, when the gryphon swooped down and snatched Alyssa from the air.

Everyone except me.

I winced as I touched the spike in my shoulder. My every instinct was focused on making myself recover. Alyssa wasn't safe yet, not in that gryphon's talons. Not with hundreds of Silithik wasps still patrolling the sky. I needed to recover so I could help *her*.

I retrieved my *healing* runetablet from my pouch and traced, folding my right arm up to touch my chest next to the spike. With nowhere to direct the energy, it dissipated into the air. Yet I continued to trace, trying to make it work by willpower alone. It was a losing effort.

It is impossible to heal oneself. Every Frost Mage was taught so at the first Academy, before ever putting finger to rune. But there was no logic to my actions now, only desperation. Exasperated and running out of strength, I focused on my bond with Alyssa. A pulsing warmth in the back of my head, stronger than those of my brothers. A pulsing beacon of love and joy.

And pain, too. I could sense the wounds she possessed, likely from the explosion.

It was something.

I focused on that pain and traced again, keeping her in the center of my mind's eye. Alyssa's wounds. And as I traced, I felt the energy coalescing the way it should. Clumping together like snow rolling down a hill. I knew it was dangerous holding so much energy with nowhere for it to go, but I didn't have the time to worry about that. I had to make this *work*. The runemagic swirled and shifted inside of me until it was nearly too much. And then, when I would have released it into the target of my healing, at the last moment I shifted my focus from Alyssa to myself. To the shard of Silithik chitin lodged in my chest.

The energy was like water hitting a dam. With nowhere else to go, it shook me to my core and spread out in all directions. It scoured my nerves and pulsed in my muscles. It vibrated inside my skull and blurred my vision. I could feel every speck of myself, every fiber and piece of me, pulling apart. I screamed, but my finger continued tracing, pulling more and more energy into my body. The runemagic raged against the dam, cracking the surface, and I knew I was going to die.

And then the dam opened.

I gasped as I felt a trickle of the runemagic escape the barrier, knitting the skin around my wound. It was a tiny fraction of the amount it should have healed, but it was *something*.

I spent a moment gathering my breath, then slapped at Maze to get his attention. He'd been rummaging through one of the bags, looking for bandages and ointment.

"Rip it out," I told him.

He lifted his welding goggles up to his forehead. "You want me to do what?"

"Rip it out!" I growled, gesturing at the spike.

There must have been a frantic edge to my voice, because he didn't argue. He took hold of the driller spike with both hands, looked deep in my eyes for confirmation, then yanked.

The force pulled me halfway out of the saddle before the spike came free, tearing away skin and muscle with it. I screamed and exhaled at the same time, my vision going white with pain for a moment, yet I somehow didn't pass out. Blood flowed out of my wound and ran down my chest.

"What did you do?" Jax demanded, rounding on me. "Maze, the wound!"

I was already putting them out of mind as I traced again, this time pulling as much runemagic from the tablet as I could. Every runetracer had a limit as to what they could comfortably trace, a self-imposed line in the dirt which they dared not cross. I lumbered past my own line as if it were never there, finger moving quickly over the rune, my entire body brimming with runemagic to the point that my nerves felt simultaneously burned and frozen. It was too much energy. Far too much. It threatened to incinerate me from the inside out, scouring my very soul away in a wave of runemagic. I was queasy with it, and ecstatic. It filled my stomach and eyes until all I saw was white.

And still I traced more, focused on the woman I could sense plummeting from the sky.

I did not consciously release it. Rather, I shifted my focus from Alyssa's pain to my own, and the runemagic poured out of my grasp like the bottom of a barrel breaking away. My senses were numb to it; I heard nothing but a rushing roar, drowning out the sound of my own scream. My vision stung like I was staring directly at the sun, and my tongue tingled with an acrid taste. My insides were broken down into tiny pieces, then blew away, and then somehow jerked back together again with a snap.

And slowly, the wound in my chest healed.

I didn't know how long it went on—seconds, or minutes, or days. I didn't remember stopping the trace. The next thing I knew, I was slumped over Alyssa's horse, my cheek against her red mane. Exhaustion pressed down on me like a weight, and I had to fight to keep my eyes open. I touched my chest; the skin was hot to the touch, but the wound was closed shut. *I did it? I healed myself?*

As miraculous as that was, it was a secondary thought.

My Quintmates spoke loudly to one another. I heard the distant rumble of thunder. When I sat up straight in the saddle, I found the others staring out into the valley. Alyssa and the gryphon plummeted from the sky like two rocks tied with string. My comrades felt helpless as they watched.

I refused to feel the same. Because I had an idea.

I hope Alyssa remembers. It will only work if she does.

I flicked the reins and dug my heels into the horse's flank. Ignoring the cries from my brothers, I galloped down the slope and into the valley.

37

Alyssa

I traced like I'd never traced before.

Fingers moving in a flurry, I threw up a *flame barrier* behind me to create partial cover against the five beetles converging from that direction. I barely had enough time after that to send a *fireball* at the beetle looming over my gryphon savior, then throwing another ball of flame at a wasp diving onto us. Before the wasp had hit the ground, I sensed a beetle charging through my *flame barrier*, sizzling as it disintegrated.

There was no time to pause: I traced the smallest *fireflow* I could to the right, igniting three beetles before they closed in, then turned to the left to dispatch the cluster advancing from that side. I switched back to *fireballs* to harass the wasps hovering above. All of them missed, but I hoped it would keep them at bay a little longer.

I strode toward the gryphon's body while tracing. He didn't move, but his chest still rose and fell with labored breath. He'd saved me, so I was going to do my best to return the favor.

As I traced, switching from wide-moving *fireflows* to individually-focused *fireballs*, I had the most intense flashback. I stood over another wounded man, more of a boy than a man, wearing the Academy uniform he'd always worn. Brennan lay dying on the balcony of the Academy great room while I desperately tried to keep the Silithik at bay. There were too many descending the stairs and falling through the ceiling, but I tried. I screamed, and raged against it, and in the end failed to save him.

In a valley far from that Academy, I stood over the gryphon and gritted my teeth. I couldn't let it happen again. This man was a stranger, but I would not fail him the way I had failed Brennan.

The thought added fervency to my fingers as I traced. The air was cloudy with smoke from the fires and dust kicked up from the explosions, so I only saw silhouettes charging at me before I loosed each spell. Two beetles to the right, both dispatched by a single medium *fireball* that exploded on contact. A wasp that dove and missed us by two paces, then took one of my *fireballs* to the side, igniting its thin wings like paper. I paused to set up a new *flame barrier* to guard my back, though it wasn't as strong as I wanted it to be before I had to turn my attention to the four Silithik to my left. One of them must have been the driller shooting spikes in my general direction, hissing in the air far too close to my head. Those I killed with a *fireflow*, the flames fanning out and hitting several more Silithik behind, and igniting the upturned trees that had been churned up from the mine explosions.

No matter how many I killed, I knew it was a losing battle. The enemies drew closer with each spell. Soon I was hitting them from only a pace away, the heat scouring my cheeks as I avoided being ripped open by their vicious claws. My fingers began moving slower on the runetablet as well. I was running out of strength. There were hundreds of more Silithik all around. It felt like a noose was tightening around my neck.

The new source of runemagic was like a beacon of light in the distance, brilliant and blue cutting through the haze of battle. I picked out Arthur charging down from the ridge on horseback; dimly, I wondered how he was still conscious. The thought disappeared as he continued tracing, pouring the runemagic into his body and then dispersing it in the sky. Forming a *blizzard* spell.

Directly above me.

I glanced up at the shards of ice beginning to fall from the sky. "I'm here!" I tried shouting, which only came out as a rasp. How could he not feel my own runetracing? Maybe he was delirious from the pain, unable to tell what he was doing. *He's going to kill me.*

Then it hit me. Arthur knew I was here. He knew the situation was desperate. A joke I'd told him days ago came back to me. One I'd made in jest.

I should start tracing a flame barrier *spell above me during battle,* I had told him. *As a shield against any stray* blizzards *you might trace.* I was teasing him for having poor aim.

But it wasn't a joke now.

I tossed another *fireball* at a wasp as I felt the *blizzard* strengthening above. A jagged spear of ice struck the ground two paces from me, as long and as thick as my leg. I switched to my *flame barrier* runetablet, using my free hand to swipe above me, creating a sorcerous shield to protect myself and the gryphon from the *blizzard*. One jagged spear of ice struck the half-formed *flame barrier* and continued through, smashing into the ground half a pace away. The *flame barrier* needed to be stronger to destroy one of those before—

Movement to the left drew my attention. Still tracing, I jumped backward as a beetle charged through the space I'd just occupied, its finger-like claws slashing harmlessly in the air. It stumbled from its momentum, then came back around, so I switched runes and sent a *fireball* through the middle of its thorax.

Something smashed into my shoulder from above, knocking me to my knees before coming to a stop on the ground. The shard of ice was only as thick as my wrist, but the end was flat and wet. Diminished from the barrier. Hissing with pain, I resumed tracing runemagic into the *flame barrier*, but a second bolt of ice crashed through and hit me in the head.

The world spun. My cheek was pressed to the cold dirt, and the gryphon's unmoving shape occupied most of my vision. I heard the high-pitched screeches of dying Silithik all around as the *blizzard* reached its full strength, a constant pounding in the ground with each knife-like length of ice. My *flame barrier* kept them from impaling us by burning away the pointed ends, but they came so constantly now that it was like being beaten with clubs rather than stabbed.

Covering my head with one hand, I tried to get to my knees and trace. I needed to pump a little more energy into the *flame barrier*. It wouldn't take long. The Silithik weren't even attacking anymore. A few paces to my right, a skewered beetle writhed in agony on a spear of ice, pus oozing from its insect-like body. Bolstering the *flame barrier* would only take a moment. But another length of ice clubbed me in the shoulder, followed quickly by one to the gut, knocking the wind from my lungs. I gasped for air. It was like trying to breathe through a thin straw. Another piece of ice hit me in the head, sending stars flashing across my vision. More pieces of ice hit the gryphon, who groaned loudly over the sound of dying Silithik.

I curled into a ball and prayed the bombardment would end. It was a useless prayer because I could feel the *blizzard* above, still incredibly potent with runemagic. Worse, I could feel my *flame barrier* diminishing rapidly. In a few more seconds it would burst, leaving us unprotected from the storm.

I was going to be killed by my Quintmate's spell. It was so ridiculous I might have laughed.

The power of the *flame barrier* dimmed until it was barely noticeable. It would happen any moment. I braced myself for the end.

The horse burst through the clouds of smoke and came to a stop next to me, whinnying loudly. For a confused moment I wanted to yell at the animal to get away while it could, that my *flame barrier* couldn't protect it for long.

"Don't move!" the rider yelled. A familiar voice.

Arthur.

Before I knew what was happening, he was tracing a new spell. The air on the ground coalesced into mist, then cracked together as it formed a wall of ice that climbed into the air. Arthur gestured with one robed arm and the ice grew upward, curving over us like the crest of an ocean wave, frozen in time. Arthur continued his sweeping gesture on the other side until a full arch of ice protected us. I felt my *flame barrier* finally pop, but it didn't matter anymore. The bolts falling from the *blizzard* bounced off the protective ice barrier, the shattered pieces cascading off the side like handfuls of diamonds.

"Arthur!" I cried, finally able to find my voice. "What are you doing here?"

He dismounted from his horse—*my* horse, Fireball, I realized— and knelt to me. "You were supposed to trace a *flame barrier* to protect yourself from my stray spell."

I chuckled, which quickly changed to a wince of pain. I definitely had a cracked rib. "I tried! You didn't give me enough time!"

"If I'd delayed any longer, I would have found a corpse waiting here. However, if you prefer it that way, I can ride back up the ridge and do it over."

Before I could point out how it was unlike him to make a joke in the middle of battle, he leaned in and kissed me. Unlike the ice he'd conjured, his lips were warm and wonderful. His affection poured through the bond like a sunrise, so brilliant that it dimmed everything else by comparison. I closed my eyes and leaned into his lips and wished we could stay there forever.

"You're not going to run away after this kiss, are you?" I breathed.

Arthur cupped my cheek tenderly and gazed at me with eyes that were as blue as the ice surrounding us. "Never, Alyssa. Never again."

"At the risk of sounding prudish," Maze said, "might I suggest you two save that for another time?"

We looked up and found the Tinker atop his horse, just outside the protective arch of ice and holding his mechanical shield above his head. The *blizzard* spell had diminished to the point that only flurries of snow fell, strangely peaceful after the violence that had left at least two dozen Silithik skewered on long rods of ice all around us. Jax appeared next, then Harry and Ryon, the latter of whom wasn't mounted and paused to slash at an impaled beetle he passed.

"There's still hundreds of bugs in the valley," the Shadow said, casually wiping both daggers on his thigh. He used one forearm to brush away his black-and-grey hair from his eyes. "But they're scattered in groups of two and three. Easy to clean up."

"Yeah, all right," I groaned, resting my head back on the ground. "Give me two minutes for a quick nap and I'll be fresh and ready to go. On an unrelated note: how long does a cracked rib take to heal?"

"Depends on the skill of the Frost Mage on hand," Maze said. "So in our particular case, your ribs might *never* be healed. You traced the *blizzard* on top of her, man! What were you thinking?"

I laughed in spite of my ribs, out of exasperation or relief or even genuine mirth at the situation. After a moment, the others laughed with me, a chorus of deep and rich voices still too stunned to truly understand the victory we'd earned.

38

Alyssa

Our trip back up the ridge was somber, like something out of a dream. Hundreds of Silithik were impaled on long spears of ice from Arthur's *blizzard.* Most of them were dead, but some still writhed and hissed as we passed. It was like walking through a wintery graveyard. Jax carried the nude gryphon in his arms as we returned to the remains of our plateau.

At first, I declined Arthur's offer of healing. He looked so weary, as if someone had come along and stripped the energy out of his body. But any movement I attempted made me cry out in pain, so once Arthur was done healing the gryphon's many wounds, he insisted on tending to me.

The boys had suffered a variety of other wounds during the battle. Harry had three slashes across his back like someone had taken a whip to him, and Ryon was walking with a limp thanks to a rock landing on his foot after the powder detonation. He tried to hide it, and then pretended it was wounded from a beetle, although we instantly saw through the lie. Jax had a vicious gash on the inside of his shield elbow exacerbated by carrying the gryphon, but when Arthur tried to heal it, he threatened to disembowel the Mage if he didn't get some rest first. It proved to be a good decision: Arthur practically collapsed onto his bedroll, and was silent the rest of the evening.

Harry used a pouch of healing salve on the rest of us, just enough to keep the wounds from turning foul before we could get real healing. Ryon passed around his flask of strong liquor. This time, I didn't cough as the fire ran down my throat. Twilight came early as the sun fell below the mountains up above our ridge. Jax helped me down next to my own bedroll, next to Arthur. "Are you going to get jealous, me sleeping next to Arthur?" I teased. "I might kiss him." I made a few smooching noises to illustrate what I meant.

Jax only smiled. "I'll steal you away when I come to bed, after the first watch."

I pouted. I *hated* girls who pouted, but I was feeling silly from exhaustion and Ryon's liquor, and this was the perfect time for a good pout. "Why does the big strong Warrior always have to be the one defending everyone else?"

"Because this big strong Warrior is the least wounded of the group. Or at least, the most awake." I wanted to point out that Maze was relatively undamaged, but Jax was covering me with a blanket and it felt nice. "Enjoy Arthur's warmth. It will be a chilly night with the wind on the ridge."

I wanted to insist that I take the first watch, but the next thing I knew I was dreaming of flying, and this time I was the one with wings soaring through the sky, and there were no Silithik wasps to stop me.

*

I woke groggy and with a pounding ache in my temple.

Arthur's bedroll was empty, but when I tried to roll over, I found something stopping me. Jax's massive body was curled around mine. I closed my eyes and nuzzled against him, savoring the warmth and peacefulness of morning.

But once I'd woken, it was difficult to get back to sleep, and my bladder was full to bursting. I slid out from the blanket and tip-toed my way across the ridge to the seclusion of an especially large boulder.

Sighing with relief, I returned to our camp. Smoke drifted from the remnants of the fire, where a kettle was suspended on a tripod. Jax hadn't stirred, and on the other side of him were Maze and Ryon sharing the same blanket, the Tinker's head resting on the Shadow's arm. I stored the image away in my mind for later teasing. Beyond them, near the horses, was a pile of blankets and the gryphon's human head sticking out. He'd survived, judging by the rising and falling of the blankets. That hadn't been a certainty before the healing.

I stepped around my Quintmates to get to the edge of the plateau. Harry crouched on a rock, his short sword held downward in both hands. He nodded at me, then to the steaming cup on the rock next to him.

"Where's your bow?" I asked, taking the cup in both hands. It was pleasantly warm.

"Lost it during the battle," he said, as forlorn as a boy who'd had his heart broken for the first time. "Went over the edge when *this* half of the plateau collapsed. Found it broken in half."

"I'm sorry." I took a sip of the liquid, which was bitter and rich. I smacked my lips. "What is this?"

"Bitterbean juice. Mashed and steeped in boiling water. The taste grows on you, I promise. It's better brewed than chewed, in my opinion."

He eyed me as I took a second sip. "Not bad," I lied. It was even more bitter and foul taken this way! "Where's Arthur?" I asked to change the subject.

I felt a pang of curiosity from Harry. It was *almost* jealousy. The barest hint of it. Maybe it was my imagination. Or maybe I was slowly winning him and my other Quintmates over after all.

"He went down to the river to refill our water skins," Harry said, a little too casually.

"Is it safe?" I asked.

"Aye, it is. The valley is quiet. Maze figures the surviving bugs all fled through the north pass, back toward the Borderlands. I didn't see a single one during my watch. Not even in the distance."

"So it actually worked?" I said in disbelief. "The plan?"

He grinned. "Like a well-fletched arrow flying true. You are surprised?"

I shook my head. "I'm not sure I actually expected it to work."

"I don't think any of us did," Harry admitted. He scanned the horizon, careful not to look in my direction. "It was a brave thing, riding up the ridge to detonate the powder."

"It's not brave when it *has* to be done," I said.

"On the contrary. That's when it's bravest." He glanced at me. "Bravery doesn't matter when there's nothing on the line, does it?"

I smiled. I appreciated his kind words, but my actions were guided by a letter from a particularly cunning fortune teller. I wondered where the letter had ended up in all the carnage of the battle. Probably buried under a ton of rocks.

I sat on the rock next to him, looking out over the remnants of the valley while pretending to enjoy the bitterbean sludge. For several minutes we said nothing, simply enjoying each other's company. When the cup was cold, I put it down and stretched. "I'm going to go find Arthur. Maybe take a bath in the river."

I felt that pang of curiosity return as I looked for the easiest way down the ridge.

"Alyssa?"

I turned toward the Ranger. "Yeah?"

"Nice work." He nodded once. "With, you know. Everything."

I quickly picked a route down the ridge so he couldn't see the huge smile on my face.

*

It felt good to go for a walk. My body was stiff, and moving around helped my muscles loosen up. I prodded my ribs, which were only faintly sore. *Thank goodness for runemagic healing.*

The terrain of the valley was unnatural to the eye. Most of the rolling hills had collapsed in the cascading explosions, and what few remained intact seemed to rise higher than they should. The dirt was loose and compacted under my boots with every step, almost like snow. The forests were in the worst shape, with trees launched in all directions and in various states of collapse. Upturned roots created a labyrinth of obstacles to climb and duck under. I passed one tree with its foliage planted in the ground and the roots sticking in the air, a complete inverse of what it should be. Many more trees were nothing but chunks of splintered wood. Although Silithik corpses were scattered everywhere, they weren't as numerous as I expected. For every dead beetle on the surface, there must have been 20 swallowed by the earth.

The sun was still hidden behind the remains of the mountain ridge to the east, but the valley wildlife was awake. I saw rabbits and squirrels wandering around, lost in this new place. Farther along was a doe idly picking at a patch of grass that had somehow survived, a perfect green circle untouched by the destruction. I felt bad for the animals whose homes had been destroyed. At least the ones I saw had survived. How many more had perished along with so many Silithik?

It made me deeply sad in spite of our victory. This had been a beautiful place just yesterday, when Jax and I had walked through the forest and listened to the chirping of birds and the soft call of forest crickets. It was a harsh reminder that war was terrible, regardless of who won. Even great victories caused unimaginable wounds. For a fleeting moment, I wished we could communicate with the Silithik. Show them all the death and pain, and come to some sort of peace. More than just a temporary ceasefire. It was a silly thought, but I wished it nonetheless.

The river was as chewed up as the land, though less so in the bottom of the valley. The water continued to flow, finding new paths to travel in dozens of smaller rivulets that would eventually combine to form a single river again. Until then, it was a murky mess of a swamp. Arthur wouldn't fill our water skins here, so I followed the river north.

I discovered him in a clear section of the river next to two fallen trees, which created a small pool of still water. He ducked under the surface and splashed back out, tossing his yellow hair behind him in a spray of liquid. He used one hand to slough water over his other arm, scrubbing at the skin.

He looked so handsome, even just the upper half I could see. I realized part of it was because of the emotions I felt through the bond: happiness and peace. Instead of anxious and resigned, he was warm and calm in a way I'd never sensed. He seemed like a new man.

No, that wasn't right. It was more like this was the real Arthur all along. The one I'd seen in the past few days had been unusually burdened, and now that weight was lifted. He was finally the best version of himself.

He was facing away from me, unaware that I was watching. A naughty idea popped into my head.

I smiled.

39

Arthur

It was a new day.

Although the water was frigid, and I would have preferred the hot baths of the capitol, it felt *wonderful* to get clean after a battle. Like erasing the terrible memories of what had happened. The carnage and the fear. The water washed it all away, leaving only clean skin and a clean mind.

I hadn't realized how much my dream had affected my life. Knowing I would die had tormented me for years. Knowing Alyssa was the Pyro in the dream had made things worse these past few days. Only now that the burden was removed did I recognize it. The freedom left me feeling light, and happy. I wanted to smile at everything. I felt silly, and for once I *liked* feeling silly.

I'd survived my dream. The dream I'd been having for years, never knowing that it was the future until that damned woman had told me. I would need to visit her when we returned to the capitol to let her know the future could be changed. That we weren't merely prisoners of fate. No matter what loomed on the horizon, we always had the power to change it. So long as we had the courage to *try.*

The whole experience made me stronger, I could tell. I had agency over my life. If I could change my future, I could do anything.

SPLASH.

Something landed in the water behind me. I whirled and reached for my side, which was stupid since I wasn't wearing my runebelt. But it wasn't a Silithik that had ambushed me, but a grinning woman with full lips and red hair hanging wetly down her shoulders.

"Good morning!" Alyssa said with a huge grin on her face.

I laughed. Laughing was easy, now. "It's not a good idea to sneak up on a Frost Mage like that, especially so soon after a battle."

She arched an eyebrow. "Oh? Are you wearing your runebelt under the water?"

I squeezed the water out of my hair, then tied it back in a tail to let it dry. "I might have been. You couldn't have known."

"Oh, I think I did." She splashed water at me. "Besides, I've already been the accidental target of your runemagic in the past day, and I managed to survive. I'm not scared of you, Frosty."

"Accidental?" I sputtered. "I intentionally aimed that *blizzard* over your location. That was the point!"

"I guess we'll never know," she said, ducking her head all the way under the water. She came back up and ran her hand along her scalp, brushing the wet hair back. "This isn't as relaxing as a hot bath in the capitol, but it's close."

"I was just thinking the same thing." The tops of her breasts floated underneath the surface, barely visible. I felt my cock stir and my cheeks redden.

Alyssa ran her fingers over her neck and shoulders, cleaning away the grime. "So Lady Anis told you to freeze my legs to the ground? That's why you visited her?"

I gave a start. "Not quite."

"Oh, so that was your genius plan all along, then?" she demanded, face full of anger. A moment later she ruined the mask by grinning.

"Lady Anis confirmed what the future held," I explained. "It was a dream I've had for years. The battle on the ridge. I knew the powder would not detonate. I knew you would ride up the ridge, and get hit in the shoulder by a driller spike. And then..." I trailed off, unable to say the words: *and then we would both die.*

Alyssa seemed to understand. "It looks like she told us what we needed to hear."

"It appears so."

She stepped through the water toward me, then pressed her cheek against my chest in a hug. "I'm happy you tried to save my life." Her voice was hot smoke.

"I'm happy I succeeded."

She draped her arms around my neck, pressing her bare breasts against my chest. "Show me how happy you are."

So I did.

40

Alyssa

Pressed up against Arthur's body, I could feel him tremble. Even without the Dragon bond to tell me what was in his heart, I knew that if I pulled away I would see tears in his eyes. I clung to him tighter. When he finally tried to pull away, I kept my arms around him and looked up into his eyes. "So is that why you broke off our kiss in the bath?"

He coughed in surprise, then turned it into a grimace. "I knew you would die. It was all I could think about. Being around you with such knowledge was torture."

"And yet you still spent time helping me practice runetracing?"

"I did."

My chest felt tight. I couldn't imagine the pain he must have felt knowing I would die. I wouldn't have been able to function with that knowledge. Yet he had, and still helped me.

Oh, my sweet Frost Mage.

I had to kiss him. It was a need, not a thought, my wet lips locking onto his. His surprise turned into hunger too as he kissed me back, as desperate for me as I was for him but neither of us knowing until right then.

His tongue slid into my mouth and I moaned deep within my chest. His hands spread along my back, fingers bumping up the ridges of my spine, feeling me all over as if it were the first time and he wanted to memorize my topography. Like I was a runetablet I wanted to trace. I mirrored his touch, feeling the wide muscles of his back, leaner than Jax but still strong and firm in his own way.

As our kiss intensified, his hands slid down to cup one of my ass cheeks, then the other, squeezing them between his fingers under the water. I sighed into his mouth as I reached behind and did the same to him. He was tight and firm like a chiseled boulder; I could barely get two handfuls, it was so solid! And then his fingers slid in between my cheeks, down and behind until he reached my sex, sliding along the slit which made me moan, while his other hand came around the front and rubbed me from that side, gripping me from two angles at once, sliding along my lips without entering.

I've needed this, I thought, wondering if he could understand through the bond. *I've needed you so badly, Arthur.*

His member was stiff and slick against my belly now, so I slid one hand away from his tight rump and around his hip, dragging my fingers along the underside of his hard staff. He sharply inhaled at my touch which made me grin into his kiss, and I moved my fingernails up the tip and then along the other side, teasing and feeling. As if he *could* read my mind, he slid one finger inside of me, just the tip, and then it was his turn to grin as he teased me.

Finally I grabbed the base of his member, wrapping my fingers tightly around it and pulling on it like it were the reins to a horse. He groaned loudly, a wonderful sound I had never heard him make, and then responded by inserting his finger deeper into me. Back and forth we went, me stroking faster and him pushing past one knuckle and then the second, escalating ecstasy in our seclusion of the river.

"Ohh," he moaned, fingers shuddering inside me. His crystal

blue eyes were filled with pleasure. "Oh, Alyssa!"

His member trembled along with his fingers as he roared his climax for all the valley to hear. I stared deeply into his face, savoring every second of pleasure he felt through the bond, loving that I could make him feel this way, and then I was clamping down my own sex around his fingers and gasping with my own small climax.

"That was fast," I said innocently when he'd come down.

He looked horrified by my comment, then burst into a fit of giggles. His sharp cheekbones rose in a smile. "It's been a while."

"It would certainly appear so!" I said.

I realized his last time was probably with Danni, and instantly felt embarrassed that I'd said anything. But Arthur didn't seem to notice, and even looked sheepish for a moment.

"It was actually a few days ago," he admitted.

"What!"

"After our incident in the bath..." he began.

I shoved him away. "You went somewhere after that?"

"No!"

"To a brothel?" I demanded. "Or someone else you know?"

"No! Stop!" He braced both of my forearms with his long fingers. "After the bath, I went back to my room and tossed and turned. When I finally fell asleep I had... An arousing dream."

I blinked. "Oh?"

"Yes. An arousing dream involving you."

"Oh. Well then." I tilted my head back so I could look down my nose at him. "What sort of arousing things was I doing?"

"Maybe I'll tell you another time," he said, touching his finger to the tip of my nose. "But in any case, when I woke up I... *Traced my own rune*, as it were."

"What do you mean?" I crossed my arms and pretended to look

confused. "What rune did you trace, Arthur? I don't understand."

Rather than answer, he plunged his arms down into the water. I yelped with surprise as he scooped up my legs and pulled me to his chest, then carried me to the shore next to our little pool.

"I'm chilly," I said.

"Then I'll have to warm you up."

"How?" I said, playing innocent again. "I'm the Pyromancer. What methods of warming do you know, Frosty?"

"I like it when you call me that." He deposited me on his Dragon robe, which was laid out flat like a blanket. I bent one knee, and he leaned in with his beautiful face. "I like it a lot."

He kissed me again, but only for a quick peck. Then he leaned back and rolled me over until I was flat on my belly, ass in the air.

"I don't see how this is warming me up..."

Arthur planted a fist on either side of me, then lowered himself to kiss the back of my neck. His legs surrounded mine, and his cock rubbed against my ass, still stiff even after his watery climax. Slowly, for the next few minutes, Arthur kissed all over my body: neck, shoulders, up one arm and then down the other. He kissed each individual bone of my spine. He never used his hands; only his lips caressed my body, sensual and intimate.

"Still cold?" he asked, kissing my lower back.

"If I say yes, will you keep going?"

"I'll continue no matter what you say."

His lips moved down the meat of one cheek, pressing his lips firmly into the skin, feeling my depth. Down my thigh he went, nuzzling the back of my knee, then the calf, and feet. He paused to raise my leg in the air, hands massaging into my feet wonderfully while he kissed each toe, one at a time. Back up my leg he went, and I tensed as he neared the back of my sex, but he slid over it and down the other thigh, repeating the caresses on that leg. Soon I was breathing slow and deep, almost in a trance from his sensual touch.

As he went back up my thigh, his hands moved along the inner part of my legs, wedging them apart ever so slightly. My skin was perfectly dry now except for my sex; I could feel the cool air on it as he spread me wider, and I knew I was drenched with desire. I tensed as his lips climbed, sliding toward the inner part of my thigh. I could feel his breath on my wetness.

"You're torturing me," I said, my voice throaty with need.

Finally, I sighed as he brushed against my pussy. He kissed the left side, then the right, then planted one right in the middle of my slit. I trembled and buried my face in his robe that was our blanket, inhaling the smell of him, letting it surround me. Arthur's hands slid up my hips as he kissed my sex, fingers sliding to my ribs. He gripped my waist tight.

The moment he did, his tongue shot forward into me. I groaned at the sudden pleasure, a lightning bolt traveling through my torso. Farther his tongue pushed, as deep into my sex as he could go until his entire face was buried between my cheeks, nose pressing into my behind. Only then did his tongue slide back out, slower than he had entered, and I exhaled as if I'd been holding my breath for ages.

Back and forth he went, making love to me with his tongue while gripping my waist like a vice to hold me in position. I surrendered to him with my mind, my soul, and my body. He increased speed with each thrust, just a *little bit* faster each time, his tongue writhing up and down like he wanted to taste all of me. Soon he was crashing his entire face into me, rocking my body with the force.

"Harder," I begged.

He answered with a rumbling moan that vibrated into my sex.

"Harder," I whispered. My words came out against my will. "Harder, oh please, more, *more...*"

My Frost Mage moaned with me as the waves began to crash, like the surges of power that came from a runetablet but deeper, more intense. This was nothing like the small climax I had felt in the river from his fingers. I felt my toes curling, and I drove my hips into his face, desperate for more. Finally I reached my limit, the line that I knew would destroy me from the inside out from tracing too much, and I screamed and clenched my eyes shut and for a long while there was nothing in the world but Arthur's tongue and hands and voice.

I was panting when my vision returned, his dark robe pressed against my cheek on the ground. His grip lessened on my waist and his mouth left my sex, and I shivered as the cool air rushed in.

But Arthur was climbing back over me to kiss the back of my neck. "How was that?" he asked in a heady voice.

"Like the ecstasy from tracing runemagic," I said, reaching back to touch his skin. He was hot like an ember. "It burned me alive from the inside-out. But, you know, in a good way."

He put his mouth close to my ear. "I like pleasing you."

I could feel his member against my thigh, rock hard again. The fact that my pleasure brought him to stiffness turned me on even more. With his body pressing me down, I reached back and touched his sex, guiding it lower.

"You know what would please me now?" I said, feeling the need stir inside me again. His desire mirrored back into mine through our bond.

"What's that?" he whispered.

"This." I guided the tip of his cock against my lips. They were so wet, inside and out, that his head slid inside with wonderful ease. Just the tip. I tightened my lips around it, clutching it like I was afraid he would leave.

"I don't know if I can go again so quickly..." he said.

"You may not know," I said, pushing my hips up. His tip slid a fraction deeper. "But I do."

He planted his arms on either side of me, pillars of lean muscle that held up his gorgeous body over me. Slowly, I rocked my ass up and down, pushing his hard length deeper and deeper inside of me. He wasn't as wide as Jax, but he was shockingly *long*, and soon he'd filled every part of me.

"Slowly," I purred, twisting so I could look into his eyes. He was beautiful above me, yellow hair pulled tight in a tail. "It's intense. In a good way."

He grinned and leaned down to kiss me, slow and soft. I closed my eyes and melted underneath him, his cock moving in and out steadily while his lips nibbled at mine. There was nobody else in the world then—no Archons or Field Marshals or terrible Silithik hordes. It was just the two of us, and we had all the time in the world.

"I think you were right," he said, breaking our kiss and hanging his head in concentration. Up and down he pumped now, long and deep with every stroke.

"Is that so?" I purred. "Tell me more."

"You feel amazing," he whispered. "Better than I ever imagined."

"So do you." I pushed up against him to meet him halfway down his stroke, pulled away, and pushed back again.

"I thought you wanted me to go slowly."

"I did, then." I was thrusting backwards now, my cheeks slapping gently against his thighs. "Now I want *this*."

It was like unleashing an animal. He bent down to kiss my neck, then leaned back off of me until he was on his knees, still inside of me. He grabbed my behind with both hands, squeezing it together as he thrust deeper, filling every speck of me.

"Oh yes," I gasped as he struck a sensitive place, sending new tingles of pleasure through my body. "There. Right there."

"You like this?"

"Yes, more!"

Arthur's grip tightened around my waist like it had when it was his tongue inside of me, and he thrust harder, and harder. He was so strong, so much stronger than he looked while wearing his robe, handling my entire body as he had his way with me. Through the Dragon bond he was a pulsing river of ecstasy, focused entirely on me. That excited me as much as the cock that was driving into me— the fact that he wanted *me* more than anything in the world.

I began moaning, feeling another climax just on the horizon. Arthur must have known because he let go with his left hand and let it curl underneath my hip, pressing his fingers up against the hood of my sex. I shuddered at his touch, then surrendered to the wonderful feeling as he rubbed it in a circle, pressing it down into the skin with his calloused runetracing finger.

"Burn me to *ash*," I cursed.

"Is that fine?" he asked.

"Fine?" My entire body quivered. "Don't you dare stop! Ohh!"

My breathing became rapid as he simultaneously thrust with his cock and rubbed with his fingers, dual trickles of ecstasy altogether similar to runemagic entering my body. Like before, I felt it begin to fill me, wave after wave of it, more than I could handle, it would *kill* me if I didn't release it...

"Alyssa," Arthur gritted out, making my name a curse and a prayer all at once. "Oh *Alyssa*..."

His grip on my hip tightened, holding me possessively, and that's what threw me over the edge. I gasped and screamed with pleasure, exhaling every bit of air from my lungs. But that wasn't enough, because Arthur was hitting his climax too, and that extended mine, thrashes of light and deafening sound. Arthur was everywhere: his smell in my nose, his presence in the back of my head, and physically inside of me. I felt his cock shudder and gush inside of me while I tightened around him.

His roar was deep and long, like the explosions that had ravaged the valley, except now I was the one being ravaged and turned inside out, and I loved every intense moment until we both fell to the ground, sweaty and sated.

41

Alyssa

We walked back out of the valley hand-in-hand, not saying anything and not needing to. The sun had crept above the mountains by then, and the rest of our party was awake.

Harry arched an eyebrow at us. "Feeling cleaner, now?"

"Aye, it felt good to get the sweat of battle off me," I said.

"Are you sure you got it all off?" Harry insisted. "You didn't come back dirtier than you left?"

I frowned as I stepped onto the plateau. "What do you mean?"

Maze, who was stirring eggs in a cook pan over the fire, barked a laugh. "You know we can feel *everything* through the Dragon bond, right?" He winked at me. "And I mean *everything*."

I realized then that everyone else was casually trying not to look in our direction. Jax wore a sly grin while he fiddled with his pack, and Ryon was sharpening his daggers. Harry pretended to remain on watch, scanning the sky for threats.

They know. Of course they do. I must have blushed so strongly that my face matched my hair.

"So what happens now?" I said, hoping to change the subject.

"Well," Maze said slowly, "after breakfast I'm going to use my *runemessage* device to inform Tyronix that we've completed the mission by destroying the entire bloody valley and its network of mining tunnels. Then, once the Archon gets word that we managed to survive, he'll probably send us to another impossible valley to fight *three* full Silithik hives by ourselves."

"Either that, or he'll command us to return to the capitol to answer for destroying half the runestone mines in the Archenon," Arthur added.

"Or that!" Maze agreed cheerfully.

I joined Jax over by his pack. "About what just happened..."

He turned and embraced me. For a few moments I savored the solidity of his body, the comfort of his strength. "I am happy, Aly."

"Are you sure?" I asked. "I know you said you would be fine with such a thing, but..."

"I want us to be a Quint again," he said, and I could feel the joy and relief through our bond. "However that shakes out, as long as we are all one, then I am truly happy."

Another shape in a black Dragon uniform came around the side of a boulder. I did a double-take as I realized it wasn't one of the members of our Quint. He was tall and fair, with eyes that were slanted ever so slightly.

"Gryphon!" I blurted out.

"His name is Halonyx," Jax said.

"We gave him your spare robe," Maze said. "On account of him being nude and all. Hope you don't mind."

Arthur smiled and said, "Pleased to make your acquaintance, Halonyx. I am overjoyed to see you in good health."

Halonyx approached us. He was strangely familiar in a way I couldn't place. "I am only in good health because of you, healer," he said in a crisp, clipping accent. "I owe you my life."

"And I owe you mine," I said. "Thank you for saving me from plummeting to my death."

He smiled, which tightened his fair, narrow face. "Of course. That is my sole reason for being here, after all."

"It is?" I said. *Flames, why is he so familiar?*

"You weren't spying on us for the Archon?" Maze asked.

Halonyx frowned. "The Archon? Why would I spy for that man?"

Then it hit me. I opened my mouth, but Arthur blurted it out before I could.

"I saw you at the fortune teller."

"Yes!" I said. "I saw him too!"

"What were *you* doing at a fortune teller?" Ryon asked Arthur, but none of us paid him any mind.

"The story is long," Halonyx told us. He crossed his arms over his slender chest and smiled. "I have always been interested in occult craft. It is a matter of curiosity. My comrades stationed in your capitol have always ridiculed me for it, until they finally purchased a session with Lady Anis for me as a joke. But I took them up on it and went gladly."

His smile faded.

"Suffice to say, Lady Anis knew more about me than I knew about myself. She told me... *things.*" He stared off in the distance, and was quiet for several heartbeats. "She told me to follow the Ninety-First Quintelaide when they ventured east. To observe without interfering, until I was truly needed. She said I would know when that was."

Ryon slowly stood, and pointed with one of his daggers. "You came all this way because of something a fucking fortune teller told you?"

Halonyx nodded. "Unfortunately, I've abandoned my own duties to follow you here. I will be reprimanded when I return."

I winced. "Maybe we can put in a good word with your commander? Explain how you saved us?"

Halonyx blinked placidly. "I am not sure that will help, if it is true that your Archon intends for your Quintelaide to perish."

"Good point."

"I will happily receive whatever punishment is given to me. It was worth saving your life. I will go to my grave believing it to be so." He sighed heavily. "But I will be departing now. It is a long flight back to the Archenon capitol, and I would like to be there before the sun climbs too high."

Jax clapped him on the back, and Maze shook his hand. I watched him from a short distance away, still trying to wrap my head around the entire thing. He nodded politely to me, his gaze lingering, before turning away.

"I'll leave the robe on a boulder over there," he said. "Won't need it once I shapeshift into my winged form."

He began to walk away.

"Wait," I said, darting around the campfire. "Let me see you off."

"Haven't seen enough nude men today?" Ryon said with a sneer.

Maze slapped his mechanical knee. "Don't take it personally, Arthur! I'm sure you'll satisfy Alyssa next time." Arthur responded by tossing a pebble at the Tinker.

I ignored them as I followed Halonyx up the ridge and around a massive boulder. There was something bothering me about this entire situation. Something I had to know.

When we reached a flat section of the ridge, Halonyx turned and faced me. "If you intend to apologize for the trouble I am in, please do not. It was my decision to come here, and mine alone."

"What did she tell you?"

His face was an unreadable mask. "I already told you why–"

"No," I interrupted. "You told us the *why*, but not the *what*. What did she say? The exact words."

Halonyx was quiet. He considered me, as if trying to decide what to do. His fair face was devoid of emotion. A blank page I couldn't read.

"Lady Anis told me an average girl was destined for *extraordinary* things," he finally said. His words were thick with meaning. "She told me if this girl perished, the war with the Silithik was doomed."

In one swift motion, he unclasped the robe and shrugged out of it, allowing it to slide to the ground. I was so shocked by his words that his sudden nudity didn't even register.

"I'm destined for extraordinary things? What does that mean?"

"Goodbye, average girl," he said, turning around. His back swelled grotesquely, spine lengthening and then disappearing under a blanket of white feathers. Wings sprouted and spread, and he let out a sound that was close to a sigh. With the legs of a lion he leaped into the air, beating his wings to gain altitude.

"What does that mean?" I shouted as he flew west, sun gleaming off his ivory feathers. "Tell me. *What does that mean?*"

Epilogue

Alyssa

I walked back to my Quintmates in a daze, the borrowed Dragon robe folded over one arm. *If this girl perishes,* Halonyx had said, *then the war with the Silithik is doomed.* How could that possibly be true? I was but one Pyromancer among thousands fighting in this war. Our Quintelaide was one among hundreds. How could we possibly be important enough to determine the fate of the war?

We did something incredible here, I thought while gazing out at the ruined valley. *What more does the future hold for us?*

My Quintmates were breaking down the camp and packing up their things when I returned. Arthur came over to take the spare robe, then gave my hand a tender squeeze.

"Are you well, Alyssa?"

"Call me Aly." I nodded. "And yes. Of course. Why would I not be well?"

He looked skeptical, and I knew he could sense the confusion in my mind, but he didn't probe any further.

"You sent the message?" Jax asked Maze, who was crouched over the *runemessage* box.

"Aye."

"Have they replied?" Jax asked.

"No."

Jax picked up his helm and held it in one fist. "Then why do you have that stupid grin on your face?"

"Because," Maze said, using his mechanical sledgehammer as a cane to rise to his feet, "I've informed them our *runemessage* device was damaged, and that we will be unable to receive new orders until we come to a stronghold that possesses a replacement."

I stared down at the device, which looked every bit as shiny and proper as if it had just come out of the workshop. "So you lied to them?"

With a whirl, Maze raised the sledgehammer with both hands and brought it down on the *runemessage* box. Brass gears and pieces of metal scattered in all directions, and the remains of the box looked like a loaf of bread that had been stomped on.

"See? Damaged!" Maze said cheerfully. "Not a lie at all."

"That's unfortunate," Harry said, deadpan. "Now the Archon can't send us straight to another death march."

Jax nodded. "A shame, indeed. At the very least, we will have a peaceful return to the capitol."

Maze kicked the remains of the device over the edge of the plateau. The six of us watched the pieces roll down the ridge, bouncing off rocks and scattering in all directions.

"I never got a chance to thank *you*," I whispered to Fireball, stroking her mane. "You did as much work during the battle as the rest of us."

Her nostrils flared as she snorted, unimpressed.

We took one final look at the valley, then rode single-file down the ridge and back through the south-west pass. Most of the route remained unchanged after the explosions within the valley, but three sections had been overrun with rock slides, and required us to dismount and lead our horses carefully. Despite the damage, it was easier to descend out of the Dragonspine Mountains than it had been to climb up the pass, and we were down in the foothills and turning west long before mid-day. The wind blew down from the mountains, carrying with it the smell of pine and dirt and faint Silithik musk. It blew at our backs, hastening our pace. Pushing us toward home.

Arthur was chatting with Maze about the details of the battle, so I urged Fireball up alongside Jax at the front of the group. He looked over at me with his blood eye and smiled.

"So," he said. "Are you ready to answer that question?"

"What question?" I asked.

"Who is the better kisser? The frigid Mage, or the dashing Warrior?"

After the seriousness of the past day, the plans and the fighting and all the death and destruction, the pettiness of the question was downright refreshing. I swayed back and forth in my saddle, considering the question.

I bit my lip. "As I told you before. The sample size is too small."

"More information is required," Jax nodded. "Arthur and I will help you gather the data on the way home."

"That would be ideal," I agreed.

"Together, if need be."

I gave a start. "Together?" Jax continued staring straight ahead. "You mean, *together*, together? Or is this some figure of speech I am not familiar with?"

"Perhaps you will find out on the journey," he said. "Tonight, if we can make camp away from the others..."

"Tonight!" I sputtered.

Jax rumbled with laughter in his saddle. My mind raced as I

considered Jax and Arthur, and the wonderful, erotic combinations we could make together.

"All joking aside..." Jax said.

"Joking? So you *weren't* serious?"

"...I'm pleased Arthur is as fond of you as you are of him," the big Warrior said. "He is a good man, in every possible way. You are a fine intellectual pair."

"We are," I agreed, glancing over my shoulder at the Frost Mage who smiled at me, then resumed his conversation with Maze regarding powder explosions.

"Being the only woman in a Dragon Quint is never easy," Jax continued. "Especially when you're replacing someone we've lost. You're handling all of it admirably. The responsibility, and the stress. And all the other complications."

I beamed at the compliment. I could sense how genuine it was.

"And the others?" I asked softly. "Maze, and Harry? And *Ryon?*"

"They are as impressed with you as I am," Jax said. His mouth pulled into a thin line. "And if they aren't, they will be eventually. I am certain of it. With everything I've seen in the past week, with what we've already been through, I know with all my heart you can handle them." He nodded. "You belong with us, Aly."

As we rode west and then north around the mountains, with our mission mostly successful and joy bursting from every bond, I was beginning to believe him.

Cassie Cole is a Reverse Harem Romance writer living in Norfolk, Virginia. A sappy lover at heart, she thinks romance is best with a kick-butt plot!

Books by Cassie Cole

Pyromancer's Path

Warrior's Wrath

Mage's Mercy

Tinker's Trial

Ranger's Risk

Shadow's Savior

Standalone Novels

Broken In

Drilled

Five Alarm Christmas

All In

Triple Team

Shared by her Bodyguards

Mage's Mercy

Saved by the SEALs

The Proposition

Full Contact

Sealed With A Kiss

Smolder

The Naughty List

Christmas Package

Trained At The Gym

Undercover Action

The Study Group

Tiger Queen

Triple Play

Nanny With Benefits

Extra Credit

Hail Mary

Snowbound

Frostbitten

Unwrapped

Naughty Resolution

Her Lucky Charm

Nanny for the Billionaire

Shared by the Cowboys

Nanny for the SEALs

Nanny for the Firemen

Nanny for the Santas

Shared by the Billionaires

Lightning Source UK Ltd.
Milton Keynes UK
UKHW012209220922
409306UK00008B/150/J